P9-DCR-659

THE MESSENGER OF ATHENS

THE MESSENGER OF ATHENS

A NOVEL

ANNE ZOUROUDI

A REAGAN ARTHUR BOOK
LITTLE, BROWN AND COMPANY
NEW YORK BOSTON LONDON

Reagan Arthur Books/Little, Brown and Company
Hachette Book Group
237 Park Avenue, New York, NY 10017
www.hachettebookgroup.com

First American Edition: July 2010
Originally published in Great Britain by Bloomsbury Publishing, 2007

Reagan Arthur Books is an imprint of Little, Brown and Company, a division of Hachette Book Group, Inc. The Reagan Arthur Books name and logo are trademarks of Hachette Book Group, Inc.

The characters and events in this book are fictitious. Any similarity to real persons, living or dead, is coincidental and not intended by the author.

Library of Congress Cataloging-in-Publication Data
Zouroudi, Anne.
The messenger of Athens : a novel / Anne Zouroudi.—1st North American ed.
p. cm.
"A Reagan Arthur Book."
Originally published : London : Bloomsbury Publishing, 2007.
ISBN 978-0-316-07542-8
1. Police—Greece—Fiction. 2. Islands—Greece—Fiction. I. Title.
PR6126.O97M47 2010
823.92—dc22 2009043617

10 9 8 7 6 5 4 3 2 1

RRD-IN

Printed in the United States of America

For Will

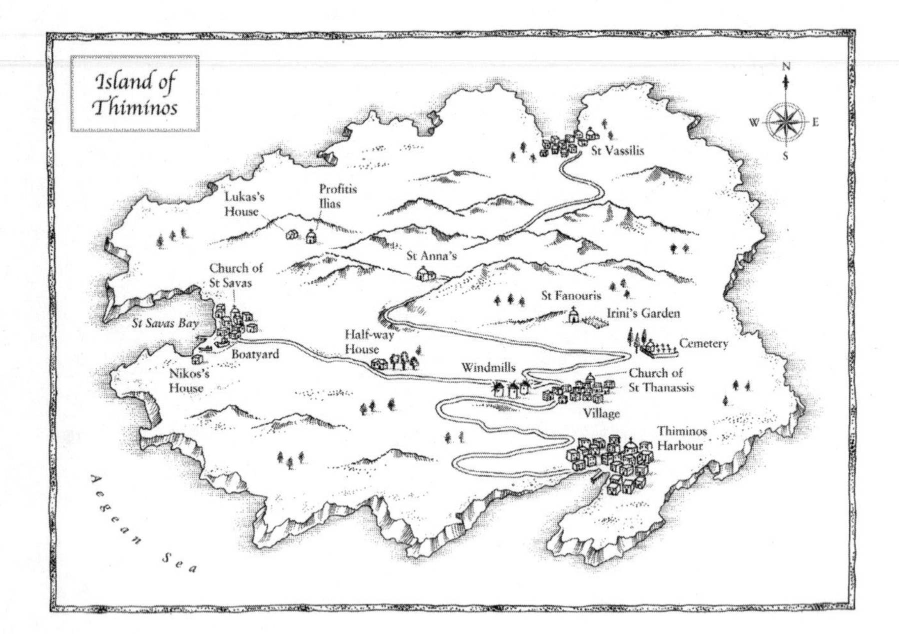
Island of Thiminos
N
W
E
S
St Vassilis
Lukas's House
Profitis Ilias
St Anna's
Church of St Savas
St Savas Bay
St Fanouris
Irini's Garden
Half-way House
Boatyard
Cemetery
Windmills
Church of St Thanassis
Nikos's House
Village
Thiminos Harbour
Aegean Sea

No words were lost on Hermes the Wayfinder who bent to tie his beautiful sandals on, ambrosial, golden, that carry him over water or over endless land in a swich of the wind . . . A gull patrolling between the wave crests of the desolate sea will dip to catch a fish, and douse his wings; no higher above the whitecaps Hermes flew until the distant island lay ahead . . .

Homer, *The Odyssey*

THE MESSENGER OF ATHENS

Prologue

It was the spring of the year; the air was light and bright, the alpines were in bloom. It was a fine day to be out.

She had been out there for two days.

They had found her, at last, but they were not treating her with reverence, or due respect. How could they? Beneath the rising helicopter, she dangled between a soldier's khaki-trousered legs, arms flung wide like a welcome, her own legs spread, open to them all. The deafening beat of the rotors, amplified and echoing off the canyon walls, killed all talk; but the men of the search party had already fallen into silence, now they were bringing her up. Along the unfenced roadside, in small, somber groups they waited—soldiers, policemen, civilians—looking across the scree of landslips, down towards the dry, rock-strewn riverbed where she had lain.

Dropping low over the dirt road, the helicopter hurled out debris: dust, stones, vegetation ripped from its roots. Behind the windscreen of an old, black Toyota, the driver draped his arm around the shoulders of a man with tear-red eyes, who, flinching, turned away his face.

Shielding his own eyes from the debris, an army officer screamed orders at a group of young soldiers—*Line up, four-a-side, line up!*—but his words, lost in the roar of the rotating blades, failed to reach them. Running forward, mad with impatience, he seized one of the boys by the arm and dragged him into place, pushing and shoving the boy's comrades into the two rows he had planned.

Catch her as she comes down, he shouted. *And don't screw up!*

They didn't hear him. They pulled faces and made obscene gestures at his back. New National Service conscripts, hair shorn gray and muscles still soft, they stood in two shambolic rows, hearts racing and self-conscious, arms outstretched to receive her.

Due respect, they had been told. Due reverence.

The other men looked on.

She began her descent. The wide canvas sling beneath her underarms set her at an angle, so her spread legs came first. At once, the boy soldiers were confounded: how to look up to receive her and not look up her skirt? Due respect, after all. But as she descended, the storm of whirling dust grew worse, more distracting. Snorting dirt from their nostrils, spitting grit into the road, when her legs came within their reach, none of them noticed. Above them, the winch man was yelling: *Get hold of her, you cretins!* They didn't hear him. Then her legs were before their faces, changing their dilemma—no longer how not to look up her skirt, but how ever again to think of a woman's legs without seeing these: the glistening of protruding, splintered bone, the foot angled bafflingly to the shin, the livid bruising spread over the yellow-tainted skin, the heaviness of purple at the backs of thighs and calves where her blood had pooled.

Steeling themselves to touch dead flesh, they took the weight. Her naked arms were cold, no worse than that. Preparing to remove the sling, they were coping, and confident that they had borne the worst. Then, the two boys at her head saw their mistake: her eyes were not closed as they had thought, but gone, eaten. Shrieking, they pulled their hands from under her. Her head snapped back. The officer, who had placed himself at a suitable distance, moved his mouth in curses they couldn't hear; running forward, he bullied the gagging boys back into place, putting her head in their hands as the others struggled to free her from the sling.

It was done. The officer signaled to the helicopter crew, who winched up their man and slewed away, upwards and to the south, out towards open sea.

The silence in the helicopter's wake seemed profound. Unprepared for the sudden quiet, the men coughed, ground out cigarettes, looked around. Some action was expected of them. She was here; now what? The boy soldiers held her at their waists, faces averted and grimacing.

Stepping up to the army officer, the Chief of Police brushed dust from the sleeves of his jacket and smoothed his hair. Now the air was clearing, the nauseating smell of her began to drift over them. Flies came from nowhere to settle on her face.

"Who'll take her down?" asked the army officer. He knew their superstitions and beliefs, and the local taboos.

"I'll ask Lakis."

Lakis, the Cretan, an outsider. Any job for cash. The Chief of Police beckoned to the tall, balding man standing beside a white pick-up and gestured—towards the corpse, towards the vehicle, a twist of the hand to ask the question in the silent language of the Greeks. Lakis bowed his head. *Yes.*

The army officer signaled to the boy soldiers. Staggering to the tailgate, they slid her into the truck, face-up on its dirty floor.

The Chief of Police called out to a black-robed priest—a young man, heavily bearded—who sat on a rock, smoking a thin, untidily rolled cigarette. The priest stood, flicking ash from the skirt of his robe. Approaching the pick-up, he looked in at her, and reached over the side to fold her arms across her breast. He raised his hand and made, slowly, the triple cross of the Orthodox church. Lowering their heads, the men all signed the same symbol, over their hearts.

Lakis took his seat behind the wheel. Hitching up his robes, the priest climbed in beside him, followed by the Chief of Police. Slowly, they moved away down the mountainside; one by one, the trucks, cars and jeeps of the search party followed.

It was no time for humor, but as he put the truck in gear Lakis could not resist a crude remark about the smell she brought with her; before they had reached the first bend in the road, the Cretan, the priest and the Chief of Police were all laughing.

One

Early morning, and a somber sky. The sea, stirred to sand slurry by a bitter wind, had turned opaque. The tires of the slow-moving garbage truck spread wide the pools of overnight rain; water ran through rusted guttering onto the steps of the National Bank and dripped onto the tables of the deserted fish market. On the café terrace, a stooping woman swept at wet leaves falling from a plane tree; in the church tower, a solitary bell tolled for mass. The small boats at their moorings rocked and tipped, pulling at their ropes. Beyond the headland, the horn-blast of the approaching ferry was lost in the rain-heavy squall.

On the upper deck, leaning on the railing which overlooked the stern, was a stranger, a fat man. He had stood there since the dim dawn had given enough light to show the dark sea passing beneath them, watching the foaming wake rise and fall away, waiting for the first view of their destination. From time to time, he took a pack of cigarettes from the pocket of the raincoat which flapped around his thighs, and smoked, the cigarettes burning down fast in the gusting wind; to every vessel he sighted he raised a friendly hand, as if acquainted.

As the boat docked, he did not join the small, impatient crowd waiting below for the ramp to drop, but waited, watching, as the passengers pushed onto the quayside.

A crewman, probing with a screwdriver into the workings of an anchor winch, called out to him.

"End of the line, friend."

The fat man smiled.

"Good day to you, then," he said, and, picking up the holdall at his feet, made his way down the iron staircase and onto the quay below.

He stood apart, sheltering from the rain under the portico of a butcher's shop. He smelt blood, and chlorine bleach. The crowed thinned, shouting greetings and goodbyes, carrying away its strapped-up suitcases, its bags of groceries, its badly behaved children, its crates of fruit. Then the crowd was gone, and he was alone.

He stepped out from the shelter of the portico into the rain.

He had, at first, no clear idea of where he would find them; but they gave themselves away. At the harbor's end, in the lee of the high sea wall, a dozen vehicles were haphazardly parked; amongst them, almost hidden, was a car in their distinctive livery. As he drew close, the car's white signage became clear: *Astinomia*. Police.

The stone face of the building to his left was alive with flourishing, pale-trumpeted convolvulus; and there, wrapped around with tendrils, obscured by greenery, he found their sign—POLICE—and an arrow angled upwards, following the long line of a slender stone staircase.

The fat man ran, quite lightly, to the top of the steps, where he faced a heavy, unmarked door. He pulled it open and walked through.

Their office, grand in its proportions, was austere. The plaster coving beneath the lofty ceiling was ornate; but the unvarnished boards of the floor were bare, and dotted with hammer-bent tacks, as if some covering, carpeting or linoleum had been ripped out and not replaced. They might have moved in only yesterday, or be leaving tomorrow; or they might have been there for years, without caring or noticing that there were no blinds to cover the cracked panes in the high, narrow windows which looked out across the sea, no lampshade on the naked light-bulb swinging from its long length of cord in the draft from the door, no filing cabinets, no procedural manuals, no posters or notices pinned to the pale walls, no chairs for visitors to sit on as they made their complaints.

He stood at the center of the room and placed his holdall carefully at his feet, as if it might contain something fragile. The three policemen watched him, silent and unwelcoming, as if he had intruded at a crucial moment on some private conversation. The undersized man at the utilitarian, steel-topped desk behind the door (whose uniform, too large, diminished him further) tapped the lead of a blunt, chewed pencil on the desktop, setting a slow rhythm for the lengthening silence. His eyes moved from the fat man to the door, as if he planned to leave the moment an opportunity arose; the contents of his desk—a stapler, an ink-pad, a rubber stamp, nothing more—did not suggest there was anything to detain him here. Across from him, a broad-set man, bull-headed, heavy-jowled, with thick, white hair and comical, dark eyebrows, leaned his elbows on a similar desk, similarly empty: three ball-point pens, all neatly capped, two opened letters in their envelopes, and an ancient Bakelite phone, whose plaited cord ran down between his feet and out through a hole drilled through the skirting at his back. His wet, red lips were slack, implying a bovine slowness and plodding wits. When the fat man entered, he shifted so his jacket's upper arm—embroidered in silver with a sergeant's chevrons—was forward, towards the fat man, ensuring that his rank would not be missed.

And at the back of the room, so far from the windows that the light was weak and the room was left in shadow, sat the third. He stretched his slender legs, crossed at the ankles, through the knee-hole of a capacious antique desk, between two ranks of small, brass-handled drawers with tiny locks. To left and right the desk held stacks of paperwork—cardboard files, blank forms, forms filled out and signed in duplicate and triplicate, applications for licenses, parking tickets, violation-of-permit notices, summonses, dockets, memos, letters, business cards, candy-striped computer printouts—and on the floorboards all around his feet were piled more files, their spines bearing dates, or numbers, or names. At the center of the desk, lying on the worn, gold-tooled leather, one file, closed, with a name handwritten in dense, black capitals:

ASIMAKOPOULOS. And from between the stacks of paperwork, like a rat peering out from a hole, he watched the fat man, the skin of his face eerily pale in the shadows, the deep black of his narrowed eyes and clipped moustache stark as ink drawn on white paper.

The dark eyes looked the fat man up and down, taking in his bulk, admiring his suit—both the cut of it, which flattered his bulk, and the cloth, a fine, gray mohair of such quality that, as the fat man moved, it shimmered with a lavender sheen. The eyes approved of the sports shirt the fat man wore beneath the suit—rich purple, with a small, green crocodile over the left breast. They noted that the waistband of his trousers was belted with Italian leather. But the gray curls of the fat man's hair were too long, and the prominent frames of his glasses were unfashionable, and dated. And his shoes, his shoes were baffling. For who but an eccentric, with such a marvelously tailored suit, would wear tennis shoes—old-fashioned, white canvas tennis shoes?

The fat man looked around at them all, and smiled.

The sergeant sat up straight in his chair, and shook the sleeve of his jacket so that the stripes lay flat on his arm.

"May I help you, sir?" he asked.

"I'm here to see the Chief of Police." The fat man's accent was clear, and well-bred. All his words were beautifully enunciated, like newscaster's Greek; such clarity of speech told them he was not from these islands, nor from anywhere within two hundred miles of their boundaries.

"I am the Chief of Police." The man in the shadows

spoke quietly, but with arrogance. He pulled his legs in beneath his chair, and he too sat up straight.

The fat man stepped over his holdall and crossed the room to stand before the overladen desk. He held out his hand. His manicured fingernails were filed square, whitened at the tips and buffed almost opaque.

"My name," he said, "is Hermes Diaktoros. I have been sent from Athens to help you in your investigations into the death of Irini Asimakopoulos."

The constable behind the door dropped his pencil. It rattled on the floorboards, then rolled, as if making its escape, towards the door.

The Chief of Police, leaning forward to take the fat man's hand, hesitated. The undersized constable jumped up from his chair to pick up his pencil, and the Chief of Police glared at him. Then he took the fat man's hand, and shook it, firmly, and pursed his lips as if about to speak. But he said nothing.

So the fat man went on. "I expect you're surprised at my name: Hermes Messenger. My father's idea of humor. He was a classical scholar."

The Chief of Police still didn't speak. He had no idea what the fat man was talking about. The constable, back in his chair, tapped his pencil on his desk.

"I call these my winged sandals." The fat man pointed to his tennis shoes, beaming at the joke. There was silence.

"I'm sorry," said the fat man to the Chief of Police. "I didn't catch your name."

"Panayiotis Zafiridis," said the Chief of Police. He

indicated the bovine sergeant: "Harris Chadiarakis"—and the undersized constable—"Dmitris Xanthos."

"A pleasure," said the fat man.

The Chief of Police leaned forward across his desk.

"Why are the Metropolitan Police interested in Mrs. Asimakopoulos's death?" he asked. "It was in no way suspicious. I'm afraid you have wasted your time coming all this way. Perhaps if you had telephoned first I could have saved you the journey." He shrugged, and put on an expression of regret. "Your problem, now, is there's no ferry out till tomorrow." He hesitated as if thinking, then pointed to the phone on the sergeant's desk. "Maybe we could requisition the coastguard launch to take you to Kos this evening. There is someone in their office who owes me a favor. You'll get a flight to Athens from there with no problem at all. Harris, get me the Port Police Office."

The sergeant's hand went to the phone's receiver, but the fat man turned to stop him.

"Just a moment, please," he said. He looked back at the Chief of Police. "Where is the body?" he asked, in a low voice.

The pencil tapping became faster.

The Chief of Police reached, frowning, for a notepad and a plastic ballpoint pen.

"Who has informed the Metropolitan Police of this death?" he asked, scribbling with the pen until the ink began to flow. He sounded concerned. "I believe we should take action in this matter. Wasting police time is a serious offense."

The fat man stepped forward and, placing the fingertips

of both hands on the Chief of Police's desk, leaned towards him.

"We were talking about the body," said the fat man. "I'd like to see it as soon as possible. Then I can get on with my investigation."

The pencil tapping ceased. The Chief of Police considered for a moment, then spread his hands.

"She was buried yesterday," he said. "There was no reason to delay. As I've said, the death was in no way suspicious."

"It matters not," said the fat man, easily. "I'll make do with the autopsy report."

Simultaneously, the sergeant and the constable opened drawers in their desks, found pieces of paper there and began to read.

"May I sit down?" asked the fat man, politely.

Sighing, the Chief of Police stood, and from the darkness of the corner behind him, lifted out a cane-bottomed chair.

"Thank you," said the fat man, placing it at an angle to the policeman's desk and sitting down. "I wonder if you might have an ashtray I could use?"

Opening one of the brass-handled drawers, the Chief of Police produced a heavy, cut-glass ashtray already half-full of gray ash and butts stained brown with filtered smoke.

The fat man reached into his pocket and took out a pack of cigarettes incongruous with these late years of the twentieth century—an old-fashioned box whose lift-up lid bore the head and naked shoulders of a 1940s starlet, her softly permed platinum hair curling around a coy smile. Beneath the maker's name (*Surely,* thought the Chief of Police, *they went out of business years ago?*) ran a slogan in an antique hand: *The cigarette for the man who knows a real smoke.* Taking out a matchbox and shaking it, the fat man frowned when there was no answering rattle from within. He placed the matchbox on the desk and searched again in his jacket pocket. Producing a slim, gold lighter, he knocked the tip of a cigarette on the desk, lit it, and replaced the lighter in his pocket.

"The autopsy report," said the fat man, exhaling smoke as he spoke. "I'd like to have my own copy, for reference."

The Chief of Police smiled and leaned back in his chair.

"You know," he said, "here in the islands, we do things a little differently from the way things are done in the city. We like to take a more personal approach. Being that much closer to the community we serve."

"And where are you from originally, Chief of Police?"

"Patmos," said the Chief of Police. "I come from Patmos."

"And you've served here how long?"

"Over a year."

"And you feel you have got to know the people here well, in that short time?"

The Chief of Police ignored the question. Instead, he went on: "In cases like this, part of our job is to avoid scandal for the family concerned. A good name is very important to these people."

"Where is the autopsy report, Chief of Police?" The fat man was beginning to sound impatient.

"Well," said the Chief of Police, "I decided it was unnecessary. No autopsy was performed."

The fat man's expression began to change, from genial to dangerous.

"How is that possible?" he asked. "Mrs. Asimakopoulos was a young woman in good health, was she not?"

The Chief of Police gave a sideways nod of assent.

"It was your duty to have an autopsy performed. You know full well it was. So explain to me why there was no autopsy."

The Chief of Police, believing he held all the aces, smiled triumphantly.

"Because," he said, acidly, "the cause of death was clear. Though not what was written on the death certificate. It was a delicate matter."

"So what was written on the death certificate?"

"Accidental death."

"And what, in your opinion, was the true cause of death?"

"Suicide."

"Suicide?"

"She jumped off a cliff." He shrugged. "Absolutely no doubt. Cut and dried."

"Even if it were suicide," said the fat man, playing with the ash in the ashtray with the burning end of his cigarette, "what could possibly be 'cut and dried' about a woman in a small, *close* community like this one committing suicide? What possible motive could she have had?"

"It was a copycat suicide. She had the idea from the postman."

"What postman?"

"The old postman who committed suicide."

"And what was his motive?"

"Who knows? Wife unfaithful, money troubles..."

"So was Mrs. Asimakopoulos's husband unfaithful? Did she have money troubles?"

The Chief of Police sat forward again.

"Mrs. Asimakopoulos was herself an unfaithful wife," he said.

"Really? With whom was she unfaithful?"

"I'm afraid I'm not at liberty to say."

The fat man looked at him for a long moment. "Do all supposedly unfaithful wives here jump off cliffs?"

The Chief of Police laughed. "If they did, there'd be only us men left."

The fat man did not smile. "So why this one?"

"She married a local man. She had relatives here who introduced her to her husband. But she wasn't from here. She came from the mainland."

"And you think that was sufficient reason for her to kill herself?"

"Possibly. Maybe she felt isolated. Homesick."

"How long had she lived here?"

"I've no idea. One year or ten, what's the difference? Harris!"

The ponderous sergeant, interrupted as he clipped one of his cheap ballpoint pens into the breast pocket of his shirt, flinched.

"I've no doubt you can enlighten us," said the Chief of Police to the sergeant. "How long had Mrs. Asimakopoulos lived here?"

The sergeant looked from the Chief of Police to the fat man, pushing out his lower lip as he considered.

"Two years," he said, at last. "I don't believe it's more."

"It's three, at least," interrupted the undersized constable. "My mother-in-law's brother lived in that house before Asimakopoulos rented it, and he's been dead a while now. Three years at least. Maybe even four."

The sergeant opened his slack, wet mouth to object, but the Chief of Police raised a hand to silence him and turned back to the fat man.

"In answer to your question, she hadn't been here long," he said.

"But certainly long enough to settle down and start a family?" suggested the fat man. "Did she have children?"

"I don't believe so." He looked back to the sergeant, who slowly shook his head.

"That's quite unusual for this part of the world, wouldn't you say—a young woman, quite recently married, and no offspring? If she was barren, that might be an important causal factor in depression. But you'll have spoken to her doctor about her mental health, I'm sure; if there were physical problems, I'm sure he would have mentioned them, would he not?"

The sergeant returned all his attention to his ballpoint pens, while the constable bent below his desk to retie his shoelaces.

"Our doctor is a very busy man, as I'm sure you'll appreciate," said the Chief of Police, smoothly. "But Mr. Asimakopoulos was his wife's senior by some years. Some would say he was a lucky man, to have a younger woman to keep him warm at night. But who knows? Perhaps he was lacking the . . . *potency* . . . of someone younger. A younger man might well have succeeded where he failed, the right man for the job . . ."

His expression brightened with lascivious speculation, but when the fat man frowned he averted his eyes, and rubbed at an invented itch behind his ear.

"How old was Mrs. Asimakopoulos," asked the fat man, "exactly?"

"Twenty-five, twenty-six, thereabouts. Maybe a little more, maybe a little less." The Chief of Police smiled. "I don't know *exactly*. In my experience, you can't force corpses to answer questions about themselves just because there are forms to be filled in."

"You didn't ask the family?"

"No."

"What did you ask the family?"

"I thought it better to let them get on with their lives in peace."

"Your consideration does you credit, Chief of Police, but it makes you look a poor policeman. And perhaps you would be good enough to tell us all"—he turned and gestured at the two men apparently absorbed in paperwork—"if we don't all know already, how much you charged for your consideration?"

Color flooded into the Chief of Police's cheeks, but the fat man, clearly expecting no answer to his question, stood and stubbed out his cigarette.

"As a man worthy to wear your badge, perhaps you should be asking yourself the question you seem to have neglected, Chief of Police. Perhaps you should be asking yourself, did she jump, or was she pushed?"

The Chief of Police forced a laugh of derision. "Such drama, Mr. Diaktoros! Murder, and bribery! These are the sleepy Greek islands! I'm afraid you have been too long on the mean streets of Athens."

The fat man picked up his holdall and addressed the undersized constable.

"I wonder," he said, "if you could recommend a hotel with a decent room?"

But the Chief of Police interrupted his reply.

"As I suggested, the Port Police launch..."

The fat man went to place a hand on the constable's shoulder.

"Walk with me," he said. "Show me the way."

As the door closed behind the fat man and the constable, the Chief of Police pulled his ashtray towards him, and, taking a cigarette from a crumpled pack, bent it to straighten the curve it had acquired. He picked up the matchbox the fat man had left on his desk and slid it open.

Sleek, with long feelers flailing, a huge cockroach darted forward out of the matchbox and scuttled at speed across the back of the policeman's hand, onto the file which lay on his desk.

"Jesus Christ!"

In revulsion, he swiped the vile creature to the floor, where it ran for cover amongst the candy-striped computer printouts.

As the bewildered sergeant looked on, the enraged policeman pursued it, stamping here, there, here, until the cockroach at last evaded him and disappeared amongst the stacks of official files.

The undersized constable took the fat man to the Seagull Hotel, an open-all-year rooming house owned by the policeman's second cousin. They walked side by side around the harbor, the constable full of questions he dared not ask, his anxious eyes scanning doorways and balconies, alleys and stairways, to see who observed them. The fat man strode with confidence, nimbly sidestepping the rain-filled potholes, and genially greeting everyone they met.

At the hotel door, the fat man thanked the constable and dismissed him, then watched as the man in uniform made his way slowly back to the police station, stopping here and there to speak: to the stallholder selling fruit and vegetables, to the proprietor of the electrical shop, to the patrons at the tables of the outdoor café. As he spoke, he pointed towards the hotel, and heads turned in the fat man's direction, so the fat man knew he had chosen well: the constable would be an excellent emissary in spreading word of his arrival.

The lobby of the hotel was dark, and unheated, and

the dour woman behind the reception desk was buttoned into heavy, home-knitted woolens. The desk was covered in yellowing newspaper, on which stood four squat candlesticks and an uncapped tin of Brasso. The woman looked him up and down over stern, half-moon glasses and smiled a lupine, hand-rubbing smile. Beyond her canines there were no teeth in her upper jaw; when she spoke, the fat man caught the fetid whiff of halitosis.

"Good day, sir, good day," she said, laying down a cleaning rag. "Are you looking for a room? I have one nice room free on the first floor, very clean, lovely view. No finer view in Greece."

She lifted the edge of the newspaper and pulled towards her a leather-bound register. With Brasso-blackened fingers she flicked week by week through its pages, from January towards this day's date. All the pages were empty.

"Will you be staying long?"

He glanced around the lobby, at the rows of unused glasses on the shelves behind the little bar, at the bowls of dusty, artificial flowers in the window recess, at the icon of the suffering Christ above the entrance to the WC.

"A few days, perhaps," he said. "Not longer than a week, certainly."

"If you're staying more than two nights, I can give you a special rate. It's the cost of doing laundry that's expensive, on short stays." She named a price. It was extortionate. "Much cheaper than hotels in Athens, I'm sure."

"I wouldn't know," he said. "In Athens, I don't frequent hotels. I'll pay you half that, if you're including breakfast and a daily change of linen."

He had expected argument, but none came. Instead she smiled at him, and he knew he had been fleeced.

"I'll get my husband," she said. "He'll show you to your room."

His room was cold, with no comforts: the floor was bare-tiled with no rug to warm the feet; the faucets in the poky bathroom dripped onto stained porcelain; the bed was hard and narrow and, beneath its starched white pillow-case, the single pillow was discolored with the secretions of many strangers' heads. The doors out to the balcony were swollen with winter rain, and needed a sharp kick to open them. Outside, leaning on the rust-spotted, cast-iron railing, he lit himself a cigarette and let his eyes travel beyond the harbor across the open sea, towards the outlines of the snow-capped Turkish mountains. But the beauty of the view was diminished by the lack of sunlight, and the low, cobweb-gray clouds hid the far horizons. He shivered and, stepping back into the room, stubbed out his cigarette in the ashtray at his bedside; then, picking up his holdall, he made his way out of the hotel and along the harborside.

The windows of the tourist emporiums were shuttered closed; the unswept backstreets were spoiled with wind-blown litter. Too early in the year for Easter's rejuvenations, in places the flaking whitewash had dropped like scurf from the walls of houses, exposing raw stone and brick beneath.

He came to the café where the undersized policeman had spoken with the patrons. It was a small *kafenion* of the old Greek style; a sign over the door gave the proprietor's name: JAKOS KYPRIOTIS. The wooden tables, outside and in, were covered in sheets of gingham-patterned plastic, held down against the wind by elastic knotted under the table rim. Between the glass-fronted fridges of imported beer and Fanta orange soda, a once-handsome man with Brylcreemed hair and an Errol Flynn moustache leaned on a stone sink; he gazed through the open doorway and across the sea, as if his heart and thoughts were very far away.

One of the terrace tables was occupied by three old men. A half-liter bottle of cheap retsina, almost empty, stood between them; before each of them was a tumbler well-filled with the yellow wine. The fat man pulled out a chair at a neighboring table and sat down, and as he sat, the old men fell silent. The fat man glanced behind him for the proprietor.

Then one of the old men turned in his chair.

"Pleased to meet you," he said, and he smiled a broad simpleton's smile, raising his hand in a cheery wave. The fat man inclined his head, politely, and glanced again into the café, where the proprietor was still absent in the distance.

The old man stood, and, holding out his hand, took an unsteady step towards the fat man. The two remaining at the table shook their heads.

"Sit down, you old fool!" said one. "Leave the man

alone!" But the simpleton, grinning, still proffered his hand to the fat man.

"Pleased to meet you," said the simpleton.

The fat man took his hand and shook it.

"Pleased to meet you," he said. Beaming, the simpleton stumbled back to his seat. The fat man looked again over his shoulder to where the proprietor had not moved.

The man who had not yet spoken raised his glass with a trembling hand and sipped at the wine. He leaned towards the fat man.

"You'll have to shout," he slurred. "He'll stand all day, pretending he doesn't know you're there. Jakos! Customer!"

The proprietor withdrew his reluctant eyes from the horizon and came to the doorway. He looked resentfully at the fat man, and raised his eyebrows in question.

"Greek coffee, please, no sugar," said the fat man. "And a bottle for the gentlemen." He indicated the old men, and the proprietor tutted his disapproval as he turned to go inside. The simpleton jumped up, and grasped the proprietor's arm.

"Jakos, pleased to meet you, pleased to meet you!" The simpleton held out his hand, but the proprietor ignored it and, wrenching his arm from the old man's grasp, went scowling to the stove.

The simpleton, dejected, sat down.

The third man drank again from his glass and, squinting, viewed the fat man. His eyes were deeply lined, as if the squint were habitual to him—perhaps through myopia, perhaps from the irritation of cigarette smoke: one cigarette, freshly lit, burned between his nicotine-stained fingers, while a forgotten second was a still-smoking, ashy remnant in the foil ashtray before him—or perhaps he was trying to pick the fat man's true image from two or three which split and swam before him. His rail-thin body was wasted from long-term abuse; the hand holding the cigarette shook.

"You've a friend for life, now you've shaken his hand," he said, clapping the simpleton hard on the back. "But you'll struggle to get much out of him except, 'Pleased to meet you.' He's an old fool. I say that as one who's known him man and boy. When he was young, he was a young fool. Now he's old, he's an old fool, and a pain in the arse. Still. We're all what God made us."

"Indeed," said the fat man.

"You'll be from Athens." The old man spoke triumphantly, as if he expected to impress the fat man with his perception. So the fat man put on a look of surprise, which made the old man smile. "I went to Athens once," he said.

But his companion contradicted him.

"You've never been to Athens, you lying bastard. You've never been further than St. Vassilis." He named the monastery and its hamlet five miles away, at the far side of the island. This man had a curious disability, a fusing of the vertebrae at the top of his spine. Unable to turn his head, when he spoke, his eyes swiveled towards the target of his remarks, but his torso remained rigidly facing forward. It made him both comical and grotesque, yet he might once have been an attractive man.

"I might've been to Athens," protested the smoker. But, anxious not to pursue the matter, he decided the moment was right for introductions.

"Thassis is the name," he said to the fat man. "Thassis Four-Fingers." He held up his left hand to show the stump where the index finger should have been. "This is my friend Adonis"—the fat man's eyes widened at the irony of the deformed man's name—"Adonis Spendthrift they call him. Tight as a nun's cunt on Good Friday. And this," he gestured towards the simpleton, "is Stavros Pleased-to-Meet-You."

Stavros, beaming, jumped up.

"Pleased to meet you," he said, and the fat man shook his hand.

The proprietor placed a glass of water and a small, white china cup before the fat man; the tarry coffee had the caramel scent of burned sugar. He nicked the cap off a bottle of retsina beaded with condensation and stood it at the center of the old men's table, then leaned his shoulder against the doorframe and looked out to sea.

Thassis Four-Fingers seized the cold wine and held up the bottle to the fat man.

"Thank *you,* sir," said Thassis, "and good health to you, sir." He splashed cold wine into their glasses; all three raised their glasses to the fat man, and drank.

The fat man sipped at his coffee.

"You'll have business here, I expect," said Adonis, twisting his eyes towards him.

The fat man bent down to his holdall, unzipped it and fumbled inside. He pulled out a bottle of shoe-whitener.

Like a dancer, he pointed his left foot, then his right, inspecting his tennis shoes. Removing the plastic cap, he dabbed the sponge applicator carefully on a scuff mark on the toe of the right shoe, and on a small splat of mud on the left. He twisted his feet, first the left, then the right, examining the shoes for further blemishes. Finding none, he replaced the cap, placed the shoe-whitener inside the holdall and zipped it up.

In fascination, the old men watched him. They had forgotten Adonis's question when the fat man sat back in his chair and answered it.

"I'm here to investigate the death of Irini Asimakopoulos."

The proprietor brought his eyes back from the far horizon.

"What's to investigate?" he asked. "Fell off a cliff, didn't she? Could happen to anyone."

Laughing, Thassis spluttered into his drink, but the fat man said nothing.

So the proprietor asked him, "What's your idea, then?"

Adonis, a shrewd man, smiled.

"He thinks somebody pushed her," he said.

"Who'd push her?" said the proprietor, derisively, and immediately from his uninhibited drunkenness Thassis provided an answer.

"Theo Hatzistratis's wife would!" he said. And he laughed again.

No one joined him in his laughter. Digging him with his elbow, Adonis turned his eyes towards the vegetable stall, where a woman was complaining at the number of caterpillars in the cauliflowers.

"What'd I say?" asked Thassis.

Silently, the proprietor disappeared into the back of the café.

"Why would Theo Hatzistratis's wife want to push Mrs. Asimakopoulos off a cliff, Thassis?" asked the fat man.

"Why'd you think?" asked Thassis. He dropped his head, suddenly maudlin. "Women. All the same. I'd sooner put my hand in a bag of snakes than trust a woman."

"Are you saying that Mrs. Asimakopoulos was having a relationship with Theo Hatzistratis?" the fat man asked Adonis.

"I'm saying bugger all," said Adonis. He emptied his glass and banged it down on the table.

There was silence for a while. Thassis began to hum a tune, a morbid song of a man's doomed love for a faithless girl; his humming grew louder until he broke into song, then shouted the lyrics at the top of his cracked old voice.

The fat man walked inside and paid what he owed. When he wished the old men goodbye, he received no reply.

Two

From the sea, the island of Thiminos showed exactly what it was: rock, one huge rock, so undercut by the salt water of the southern Aegean it seemed to float free, rising and falling in the swell. Mostly, the cliff faces of its coasts were sheer; where the slopes were gentler, they were all thin dirt and stone. There was little else: a few black pines rooted into the mountainsides at improbable angles; thorny, run-down shrubs between the boulders. And yet, here and there, it held a colorful surprise—on an empty beach, a tiny, white chapel in a garden of fresh, fuchsia-blossomed evergreens.

It was an island with no beauty of its own, but around its shores, where the sea ran the gamut of all blues—turquoise and lapis lazuli, sapphire, ultramarine and cobalt—the water and sunlight changed it. Gray rocks on the beach shone silver; there was gold in the dull soil on the mountain slopes. Fool's gold. Tricks of the light.

There was one way in and one way out: by sea. Five nautical miles adrift from any shipping lane, from the island's shores even the great tankers heading for the oil-rich nations of the Arabs were only micro-silhouettes. At night, their distant lights were strings of diamonds, slipping slowly away over the edge of the world.

One year before the fat man came to Thiminos, Andreas Asimakopoulos prepared for sea.

"For certain," he said, untying the oily rope that moored the boat to the jetty, "I'll be back with you by Wednesday."

Irini caught hold of his arm, and he brushed her cheek with dry lips; the odor of fish was about him already, even before he cast off.

"Take care," she said. "Good fishing."

She watched until the boat was out of sight, around the headland; in the moment when he disappeared from view, she waved once more, for luck. Whenever he left, she wished he would stay; his absence rubbed salt into her loneliness.

Then Tuesday night brought storms. She lay alone in bed, listening as the wind tore through the branches of the eucalyptus trees along the road and the rain pounded at the windows. She wasn't worried for his safety; he took care of his safety very well. She worried they would lose some roof tiles, and there was no one to replace them; she worried that a tree would come down on the house, and she would die alone. At midnight, she warmed a glass of milk and sweetened it with honey; propped up amongst the pillows (his and hers), she sipped, and drifted into dreams.

❖

When the night was over, she went walking, away down the empty road to the sea. The wind was still high; as she passed beneath the shimmying branches of the pale-barked eucalyptus, their limbs groaned, like souls racked.

And the wind was cold. It passed straight through her jacket, and through all the layers of her clothing. It gnawed her fingers, and drew the blood of her face to the tip of her nose, leaving her cheeks drained and pale. When she reached the seafront, even within the arms of the crescent bay the waves were whipped up and frosted with foam. To the right, where the shingle beach was narrowest and the road surface low, each seventh wave flowed smooth as cream across the road, up to the church wall, and the wall's base had become the terminus for the sea's flotsam: driftwood and plastic, shells, skeins of weed, bottles and rusting cans. Where the bus should stop, a deep pool had formed, and at its edge lay a tangle of yellow fishing-net, matted with sand and the white blade-bones of squid. With the toe of her boot she turned the net, releasing a small green-backed crab, which, frightened by the light, scuttled towards the in-running sea.

The church clock struck nine. Overhead, rain threatened.

She had known he wouldn't come. At the jetty, there were no boats. Beyond the bay's shallows, the mast of a solitary yacht dipped towards the water's surface, to port, to starboard, like the blade of a metronome, a corner of its furled sailcloth flapping loose.

She walked the road around the curve of St. Savas's Bay, watching the headland at the bay's mouth, just in case he still might come; he still might, and she still might have company tonight. The few white-painted houses were shuttered, their doors—head-on to the sea, a rope's length to the moorings—were closed. On the terrace of the small hotel, a woman swept languidly at wet leaves blowing from an overhanging almond tree; in the shelter of a ramshackle chicken coop, a rooster crowed over a run of shivering hens.

By the boatyard, the beach was crowded with boats, veterans hauled from the sea to pass the winter. Out of their element, the curves of their flanks seemed flat, the flow of their forms rigid; their paint was salt-bleached and cracked, their varnish lifting and peeling like dry, callused skin. Between their hulks, the shingle was stained with spent oil and diesel.

Last Easter, they had argued here. The root of their argument was the same as always: the promises he'd made before they married, he now chose to forget. He'd said they'd go away, and see the world; now, all the plans she talked about he ridiculed. It was his laughter that had made her angry.

Outside the boatyard workshop, she stroked the red-leaded ribs of a half-built *caique*. Shut away from the cold, the men were working, within; there were heavy blows, from a hammer, and the whine of a circular saw, slicing hull planks.

The men were working, so there would be fire. And behind the workshop, the brazier was stoked high with offcuts of fresh pinewood; its sap-sweet smoke billowed blue in the lee of the wind. She offered her palms to the flames, closing her eyes against the smoke, sniffing at the clean fumes of hot tar rising from a black, battered bucket at the brazier's feet.

The whine of the saw became silent; the latch of the workshop door rattled.

She didn't want to talk to them. They'd know Andreas was away. The older one, the one with rotten teeth, had a peculiar sense of humor; and the short one, the one with the missing fingers, would proposition her.

Me and you, he'd murmur. *No one will know; I'm not the kind to talk. We'll have a good time. Just tell me when to come.*

She lowered her hands from the brazier, and went on.

The house at the road's end was tall and once grand. Jutting out into the water, its broad terrace was worked from stones taken from the sea. On the lintel was fixed a painted sign: CAFÉ NIKOS. To the back of the terrace, as far as possible from the water, stood a single table, and four chairs; at the table, wrapped warm in heavy clothing, face hidden by the peak of a sheepskin cap, sat an elderly man.

She approached him carefully; he might be sleeping. She stood at his side, and watched the slow rise of his breathing. She waited, then placed a hand on his shoulder.

He pushed up the peak of his cap, like the slow opening of an eye.

"Uncle Nikos," she said. "*Kali mera.*"

The old man sniffed, and wiped rheum from his nose.

"I thought you were asleep," she said. "If you want to sleep, I'll leave you."

"Don't be ridiculous," he said. "Only a fool would sleep out here, in this cold. Bloody wind. It gets right in my bones. Sit, sit, Irinaki. I've been watching you. I watched you all along the road."

"What have you done with all the tables?"

"I stacked them around the back, out of the storm's way. I'll fetch them out again." He placed his hands on the arms of his chair, as if he might get up. A muscle tensed in his face, a wince. His hands relaxed. "By and by," he said. "It's still blowing. I'm too old to be hooking furniture out of the sea."

"I was looking for Andreas. He hasn't come."

The old man cast his gaze across the far sweep of the sea like a wise old salt, like a weather-hardened seadog or a time-served seaman. He was none of these, but he liked to play the part.

"No," he said, "not today. The weather's set now. Three, four days. He'll not be back before Saturday."

Unhappily, she sighed.

"All winter, the sea keeps us prisoner," she said. "No way in, no way out."

He patted her knee. "Sit a while. I'll make us some coffee. I'll put something in it to keep out the cold."

"Not for me," she said. "Andreas doesn't like me to drink."

"Well," he said, smiling, "who will tell him? When the cat's away, my dear, the mouse can do exactly as it pleases."

He hauled himself from his chair and walked heavily, with the carefulness of the suffering old, into the flagstoned kitchen.

He was not in business for the money, but for the company. He called his house a café, put chairs and tables on his terrace, and served drinks to anyone who sat down with him; but on days when he had no appetite for gossip or brewing coffee, and on days when he thought the calamari fishing might be good, the café was closed.

He blamed the *calamari* more and more, when customers found the kitchen door locked and the house silent. But in his heart, he knew his time was growing short. At night, the pains in his stomach too often wrecked his sleep, sabotaging his ability to battle through the day. These too were days when he "went fishing," shut away in the bedroom at the back of the house, blinds drawn, with a jug of water to drink and a pot to piss in, dozing, dreaming, remembering. Some days, he believed he'd never again leave that bed. On better days, he swigged chalky antacids directly from the bottle, and thanked God for some relief. But there was blood in his stools, and his appetite was all but gone. He was a frightened man: afraid to see a doctor, afraid of dying alone in the night, more afraid to show need, and fear.

He spooned coffee from the jar, and took the brandy bottle from the shelf. But the brandy was not his vice; it was from the medicinal-blue bottle of Milk of Magnesia that he surreptitiously unscrewed the cap, and, turning his back to the terrace, drank like a man addicted.

She put her hands around the coffee cup to warm them, but the coffee, cooled by milk and brandy, had no heat. He had added too much alcohol; it flamed her cheeks red, and set her stomach on fire. It worked its magic quickly. Soon, the bleakness of the outlook mattered less.

He took a cigarette from the packet and struck a light from a box of matches, cupping it against the wind. His hands shook, and the swelling of his joints made him clumsy, but he had had many years of practice. He drew in smoke.

"So," he said, wiping his nose with a finger. "Have you spoken to your mother?"

"The phone's still out of order. I went to the company office to tell them. Twice. They said they'd come. But they haven't been."

"Because they're idle." He flicked ash onto the wet stone terrace. "Go again. Make a nuisance of yourself."

"It won't make any difference. They won't come for me. They won't work for foreigners. Andreas can go, when he comes home." She looked towards the headland and the cloudbanks which hid the mainland. "If the weather were clear, we might see our village from here. I can see it, sometimes."

He dropped his cigarette butt into a puddle by his chair, watching the paper change from white to gray as it absorbed water. Her eyes were wet. He believed it was the wind, stinging them.

"You're deluded," he said. "Our village is fifteen miles up the coast." She crushed his cigarette butt with her foot. "You should phone your mother. She'll worry, if you don't. Use a public phone. If they're working."

"She worries less, now I'm off her hands."

"She misses you. Like you miss Andreas."

"With him gone, there's nothing for me to do."

"Some women," he said, "would be glad to have the freedom of an absent husband. No meals to cook. No shirts to wash. Time to walk, and talk to me."

"When you came here, Uncle, why did you stay?"

"Plain and simple. I fell in love with your aunt. And with this place. Look at that." He swept his arm across the breadth of the bay. "All this beauty. And listen." The waves were breaking on the jetty; across the bay, the canvas of the yacht's loosened sail snapped in the wind. "Silence. No traffic. No crowds. Peace, and quiet. The secret of a happy life. What more could you want?"

"Life," she said. "Excitement."

"Excitement is vastly overrated," he said. "Take it from me."

"A change of scene, then. Athens. Australia."

With a gesture, he dismissed both.

"Forget all that," he said. "Put it out of your mind. He married someone else. Your life is here, now. Andreas isn't the travelling kind."

"He told me he was. He told me he'd take me anywhere I wanted to go."

"Men say all kinds of things, when they're in love. Your life is here now."

"That's easy for you to say. You travelled everywhere. Saw the world."

"I travelled for my work." Venezuela, Costa Rica, Brazil. "It was hard being away."

The women, all those beautiful, willing women. It was hard to come back.

He took another cigarette from the pack. She stood, and took their coffee cups inside the house while he recalled. At night, he had played poker in smoky, run-down bars where the rum was cheap and red-lipped whores played salsa on the jukebox. And whether the cards were with him or against him, whether he was lucky or not, he always kept enough bills in his shirt pocket to take a girl back to his room. They'd go all night, those Latin girls, they'd lick and suck and ride until the sun was rising and all he wanted was to sleep. They didn't fake it, like all Greek whores who were only in it for the money. Greek girls were too inhibited; they had too much religion. Those Latinas just loved to fuck. One, he'd stuck with for a while—Flora, with that tiny waist and those massive hips, just begging for it. And the night he had to leave her, she brought her sister too, to make it memorable. Memorable! They'd tied him to the bed and made him watch the two of them together, unbuttoning each other's blouse, kissing each other's tits, playing with each other's fannies—sisters, for the love of Christ!—until he was begging them to come to him. And they left him tied up and rode him all night, taking turns to slide onto him, taking their time to get what they wanted, until he was so sore he begged for them to stop. Next morning, his parts were so swollen he could hardly walk; he had to take a taxi to the train station. And the driver had known the girls he was talking about, had slapped him on the back, laughing commiserations at his discomfort, and told him it was good he was leaving town, that no man alive could take two nights with those two.

He could feel a pleasant swelling in his trousers; if she hadn't been here, he might have gone to bed, given it a pull and tried to make something of it. But she was here, and sitting next to him again. The memory could be conjured back, when she had gone.

"It was hard to be away," he said. "It's the sacrifice some men make, to feed their families."

"Maybe marriage isn't for everyone," she said. "Maybe not everyone's made to stay in one place. I know what you think, Uncle. You think I carry a torch for Thomas. Mother thinks the same. But it wasn't him; I wasn't in love with him. He was gone too long. But all those postcards—the cities, and the beaches, and the outback—all those places he's seen, all the things he's done, I want to go there too. Maybe not for a lifetime, but I want to see it all for myself. You think no one should have dreams. Andreas is the same. Sometimes I wonder what my life would have been, if I hadn't married Andreas."

"What's the point in wondering that?" he asked. "You shouldn't think that way. We take the road we take. Then we make the best of it. There's no gain in wondering where the path not taken would have led. Anyway. All women marry. When that first baby comes along, you'll see I was right. A woman's joy in life is in her family."

"Babies tie you to the house forever," she said.

"You'll be surprised," he said. "You'll find there's nowhere else you want to be."

She nibbled at the tip of a fingernail. There seemed nothing else to say: the price of oranges, the prime minister's mistress, the postman's sudden death had been exhausted between them, days ago. But she, having nowhere to go, was not inclined to leave; and he, having no other company, wanted her to stay.

And so she said, "Shall I tell you what I dreamed last night? You can tell me what it means."

In anticipation, he leaned forward in his chair and steepled the tips of his fingers. He had invented himself a reputation as a student of dreams, as an interpreter of their meanings and warnings. It was, he claimed, a skill he had learned on his travels. But his talent was not in the reading of dreams; it was in persuading the credulous of his ability to do so. He possessed no special knowledge, outside the reading of popular texts of psychology and the handed-down interpretations of old women: a dream of fish was bad luck, a dream of crabs meant a difficult courtship, a dream of lizards meant an enemy's knife in the back. His self-promotion as seer fed his voyeurism, and his appetite for gossip; by this means, his harvest of all the island's troubles was always fresh. But over time his vicarious habit, his close attention to the nocturnal adventures of his neighbors, his long experience of life and his knowledge of what became of his dreamers had given him a certain insight. Twice, he had understood that the dreamers had foretold their own approaching deaths. He had kept silence; time had proved him right. And he knew the symbols of betrayal and infidelity: kisses and thieves, abandonment and foreboding. His observations were rarely direct. Not everyone wants to hear the truth. But he might, sometimes, pour a little poison in an ear as he refilled a glass of ouzo, or drop a dark hint as he removed an ashtray. A word to the wise is sufficient. The willfully blind could choose to remain so.

"I dreamed," she began, "that I was sitting in a wonderfully comfortable armchair. It was the most comfortable chair I've ever sat in. It was as if it was made for me; I felt happy sitting there." She shifted on her wooden, cane-bottomed chair. "You know, Uncle, these chairs are not very comfortable. They're too hard to sit on for long. You should buy some new ones."

"But that," he cried, pointing a triumphant finger towards the sky, "is my masterstroke! Over the years, I have given this a lot of thought, a *lot* of thought." He banged a fist on the rain-spattered table. "Think! Consider, my dear, the people who live here, the people who visit my makeshift café. They are, by nature, amongst the laziest people in the world. They are not like other people, not even like other Greeks, and certainly not like other nationalities, Germans, say, or Japanese. Here, they sit for hours and hours over a single cup of coffee, telling you how hard they've been working and how tired they are. When it rains, they won't go to work; even the children don't go to school if it's raining. To do a job which would occupy a German for ten minutes would take one of these people a day and a half.

"Now, I want you to imagine what would happen if the chair you're sitting on were comfortable. You have nothing else to do today. You would settle into your chair—and perhaps never leave! I would be bringing you coffee all day long! Later on, you would ask me for blankets and a pillow, and sleep where you sit! When George the bus driver came in to drink his beer, he would sit down, make himself comfortable—and decide not to drive the bus anymore today! Beyond all doubt, Athimos the plumber would do the same! There would be no more public transport on this island: our drains would remain forever blocked! So I, in a moment of genius, had this idea. I sought out and installed in my café the most uncomfortable chairs I could find. It was not difficult; we Greeks are very good at producing uncomfortable chairs. And you'll find none of these hand-picked chairs has four legs the same length. They throw you slightly off balance, so you can never quite relax. Always, within half an hour, your backside is numb. You stand up to relieve it, and while you're standing up, you might as well go about your business. It is a carefully thought-out strategy which has so far never failed me. It is perfect for ousting both bores and drunks alike. It is a strategy so brilliant that I wrote to the government suggesting a national ban on comfortable chairs in any form. Imagine the improvements in productivity! Greek manufacturing would lead the world! But I must be honest: they haven't yet replied. Probably some ambitious politician has stolen my idea and is furthering his career by selling it as his own."

There was a short silence.

She smiled at him. "And who could blame him?"

He grinned, and lit another cigarette.

"Anyway," she said. "I was sitting in my comfortable chair, somewhere I knew, perhaps our kitchen. But it was without any other furniture. Then I looked up, and there was a woman sitting opposite me. She was sitting on a wooden chair, the kind that never has four legs the same length. And uncomfortable."

"Exactly like these," he put in.

"Exactly like these. And she, she was the most beautiful woman you could ever imagine. She wasn't young, though she had no lines in her face, not even when she smiled. Her skin was porcelain smooth, and bright with health, touched with gold, as if she had been kissed by the sun. Her hair was the blonde of a Scandinavian, all beautifully woven with flowers. And her face—her lips were full like a young girl's, and her eyes were captivating, mesmerizing...such a beautiful, beautiful face. On her forearm, she wore a coiled bracelet, a silver snake with jeweled eyes, and she was so lovely I gazed and gazed at her. I wanted her hair, and her bracelet. I wanted to be like her. No, more than that. I wanted to *be* her.

"And I knew she was in the wrong chair. She didn't speak to me but I knew we should change places. I didn't want to, not at all. I wanted to stay in my lovely chair, but I knew I must give it to her. So I got out of my soft armchair and she went and sat in it, and I sat on her uncomfortable one. Then she smiled at me and pointed towards my feet. There was a parcel there I hadn't noticed, some kind of gift in a box, gorgeously wrapped in cellophane and ribbons, and I knew it was for me."

She was silent, remembering.

Nikos said, "Did you open the parcel?"

"No."

He leaned forward to press his point. "Take an old man's advice, Irinaki. Don't."

They sat on for a while, in silence, growing colder.

"Dreams of Aphrodite are always dangerous," he said. "Especially to married women."

"Aphrodite?"

"Who else could she possibly be? Listen to me, Irini. I'm quite serious. You must avoid the gift of Love she brought you at all costs. It will end in heartbreak. Love your husband. He's a good man."

"Yes, he's a good man," she agreed. But love? She looked past him, considering: was affection an adequate substitute, or just a pale form of an emotion valuable only in its deeper state?

"Anyway," she said, "old age is making you superstitious. There are no gods."

"Why so certain? Look." He gestured towards the hillsides, and at the open sea. "This is their terrain. They're not far away. Some say when the people stopped believing in them, they ceased to exist. But this view's still what it was when Jason built the *Argo* and the Minotaur was eating virgins in the labyrinth. Two thousand years, and nothing's changed; and don't think they've gone!

Orthodoxy is just a façade, a veneer. If you look around, *really* look"—he pointed to the center of his forehead—"using *this* eye, then you start to see. They're here. They're watching. And interfering."

Far inside his stomach came a shot of pain, as if a spiteful finger had found and poked at the heart of its disease.

"They play with us still," he said. "And they still don't play fair. Christianity demands a life of good behavior, but there's a straightforward payoff at the end. That's why it was so easy to persuade the ancients that they should dump Zeus and his whole rotten family in favor of the Israelite. The old gods are self-serving, and vindictive. Except on rare occasions. Sometimes, when the mischief had been bad, old Zeus would make amends. Sometimes, he'd do the right thing. He had it in him."

"You shouldn't talk this way," she interrupted. "Mama would think you're leading me into paganism. We're Christians now."

"Yes, but why?" he persisted. "Why did we change allegiance? I'll tell you why. Reliability. You know where you are with Christ. Live a good, clean life, and buy your passage into paradise. With the old ones, virtue made them jealous. And happiness was worse. They didn't like to see mere mortals happy. If you were too happy, they'd rape your wife or kill your herds or sink your ships. No wonder they were ousted. Only they didn't go far."

"But if they're here," she said, "why don't we see them? There were so many of them. People used to run across them all the time, in ancient times. I've never met anyone who's met a god."

"Perhaps you met one," he said, "in your dream last night. And if you met one in the street, I suppose they'd look ordinary enough. They wouldn't go in for bright lights and halos and crowds of angels, would they? They leave that to the opposition. They're more underhand. Discreet. Sly."

The church clock struck ten. She closed her eyes and, flexing the cold-rusted joints of her fingers, turned her face to the sky as if the sun would warm it. Outside the hotel, two men were talking to the woman there, and as they spoke, the woman continued to sweep, her hands moving the broom forwards and back, compelled by habit. When the taller man threw back his head, it was a moment before the wind brought his laughter to their table, so that man, and laughter, seemed disconnected; and, though dismissive of her uncle's odd advocacy for deities long dead, it seemed possible, at least, that someone other than the man she could see might have laughed—someone who stood, invisible, beside her chair.

She shivered. The two men were on the road, heading towards them.

"We have company," he said, squinting his eyes into clearer focus. "Our respected constabulary, hard at work."

"I must go," she said, rising.

"Irini." He grasped her hand and held it between his own. His skin was pale between the bones, and molded over every vein. "A favor, my dear. Go for me to the cemetery, and take your aunt some flowers. I can't go myself. My old legs won't walk that far." He released her hand,

and delved into his trouser pockets. "Yellow. Yellow was her favorite color."

"Last time, you said pink."

"Did I? Well. As you say, we all like a change." He offered her a banknote of low value.

"You should go yourself, sometimes," she said. She looked at the banknote. Her mother said he kept a fortune hidden in the chimney. "You could take a taxi."

"Pah." He pinched at his tongue as if pulling at a swallowed hair, then turned in his chair and spat. "Waste of hard-earned money. The walk will do you good. And call your mother. Don't forget. Say hello from me."

"Why don't you call her?" She pushed her chair beneath the table, and pocketed the banknote. "She'd like to hear from you, too."

"I would if I could," he said. "You know I would, but I've been waiting a month for them to come and repair the phone."

Panayiotis Zafiridis, recently installed as Chief of Police, believed in the power of first impressions. He was keen to impress the ladies; the new leather jacket, the sharp creases in his trousers, his close-cut, slicked-down hair all said so. Stellios Lizardis, his constable, believed in the power of advertising. He belted his trousers high on his waist, to lift and plump his genitalia. As they passed close by Irini on the road, they spoke respectfully—*Yassas*—but, a few paces on, the Chief of Police stopped and turned to make a full assessment.

The comb which held her hair in place had slipped, and lustrous, black hair coquettishly hid one dark eye. He scanned the slow switch of her wide hips, and ran his tongue across his thin lips.

"Look at that," he said. "Couldn't you just—"

Lizardis held up his hand.

"Don't say that here. She's the old man's niece." He inclined his head towards Nikos's house, where, with a carrying wind and the amplifying power of water, Nikos might catch their words.

They had reached the boatyard. Inside the workshop, all was silent.

"He might make an introduction," said the Chief of Police.

"She's married."

"I like them married. They demand less time."

Lizardis was ambitious. He was keen to impress the new man with his local knowledge.

"I can tell you about her," he said. "When she was still on the mainland, my brother's friend's brother knew her. He knew the family very well."

The Chief of Police took Lizardis by the arm, and pulled him behind the wooden flanks of a beached boat.

"No one will overhear, here," he said. "How *well* did this guy know her?"

Lizardis shrugged.

"He was posted close by her village for his National Service. There was some family connection, so he went visiting from time to time. He made a move on her, once. He didn't get anywhere."

"No finesse, then," said the Chief of Police. "A woman like that wants careful handling."

Lizardis shook his head.

"It wasn't that. She was engaged to someone else. At least, there was an understanding. Whether they'd exchanged rings or not, I don't know. But the family wasn't happy: the fiancé had gypsy blood, on his mother's side. He went away, to make his fortune in Australia. The way I heard it, her family paid his ticket to get him out of the way. He was gone a long time—years—with her sitting at home, waiting for the call to go and join him. But when the call came, it was from his sister, saying he was marrying someone else. Well, they didn't let her know it, of course, but the family was over the moon, because all this time they'd had someone suitable lined up, someone she wouldn't even look at. So when they knew the gypsy was out of the running, straight away they went paying their respects to their groom-in-waiting. They were all ready to go to the priest and get the banns read. Happy ever after."

"Groom-in-waiting? You mean the guy she's married to now?"

Lizardis shook his head.

"It got complicated. True or not, rumors went about that she and the gypsy had been more than friends before he left."

"You mean he'd been screwing her?"

"That's what people said. So then the family's choice pulled out. Soiled goods. She was high and dry and not getting any younger. There was a big family conference, and they settled on Asimakopoulos. He was in the market for a wife. Old man Nikos here introduced him to the family."

"Not exactly made in heaven, then, this marriage?" The Chief of Police's voice was hopeful.

"He's a decent guy."

"But she's been around, hasn't she? And if she likes those gypsies, maybe there's some hot blood there, just waiting for the right hot-blooded man..."

Lizardis's face showed doubt.

"He wasn't a full-blooded gypsy," he said. "The gypsy blood was generations back. And my brother's friend's brother didn't get anything from her except a slapped face."

"Even so," the Chief of Police clapped Lizardis on the back, "we have to start somewhere, do we not?"

They crossed the beach and made their way to the café, where Nikos sat, waiting, at his table.

"Chief of Police," said Nikos, "good morning to you. And Stellios, how are you?"

Nikos's smile was broad. The Chief of Police was always welcome, at Nikos's café; Nikos had a particular interest in him. He had observed about Zafiridis a tenseness, and a watchfulness, which his newness to the job, and to the place, could not explain. The Chief of Police, suspected Nikos, was not quite what he seemed: he was a man with something to hide, some secret he would not want to see revealed. There was a challenge there, which could be met; if played carefully, if lulled and wooed, the Chief might make a slip. A man with secrets—a man who lied—was always vulnerable to error; a man with secrets who held high office was a pigeon ripe for plucking.

Nikos offered them the best of his dubious chairs. Zafiridis, sitting back from the table, crossed one foot over his knee. Above his short, beige sock, the flesh of his calf was pallid, and sparsely covered with feeble, dark hairs; amongst them ran the tail-end of a knotty vein, swollen and varicose.

The wind scattered powdery ash from Nikos's cigarette; like flaking skin, it settled on Zafiridis's thighs.

"Who was that lovely young lady we passed on our way here, Nikos?" asked the Chief of Police, stroking away the ash.

Beneath the table, his companion prodded at his foot.

"You mean my niece, Irini," said Nikos, unconcerned. "She's a lovely girl, isn't she? She's married to my good friend, Andreas Asimakopoulos, a fisherman. They have a house, away up the road." He pointed with his thumb. "But what about your family, Chief? You said last time we met that your wife would be joining you, soon. Has she still not arrived?"

He glanced at Zafiridis's right hand, and confirmed what he had noticed before: the third finger bore no gold ring.

"She doesn't like to travel, when the weather's bad," said Zafiridis.

"You'll be missing her," said Nikos. "And tell me, have you sampled any of our local delicacies yet?"

There was a note of mischief in his voice. The policeman looked at him with frosted eyes.

"You'll find our oysters very good," said Nikos. "I'll tell Andreas to bring you some, when he returns."

"In that profession, he'll be away a good deal of the time, your friend," said Zafiridis. "Your niece must get quite lonely."

"She has me. We keep each other company."

"Forgive me, Nikos, but an uncle is not the same as a husband."

"Your concern for my niece's well-being is touching, Chief. Are you afraid she may be molested on the way home? Or perhaps your interest is more . . . *personal?*"

Lizardis cleared his throat, loudly. The Chief's thin mouth bent, like a rod, into a smile with no warmth.

"Just doing my job, Nikos," he said. "It's my job to protect people."

"Well," said Nikos, baring his teeth in his own cold smile, "don't plan on offering your kind of protection to my niece. You would insult me. In any case, she's a respectable girl, and not corruptible by you."

The Chief of Police laughed. "What a low opinion you have of me, Nikos. And what a high opinion of women. You and I both know that in here"—he tapped himself with a finger where his heart should be—"in here, they're all whores. All open to the right offer. And now, how about making us some coffee?"

At the house, Irini was alone. The day slipped slowly by, and into early decline. The lark which Andreas kept for the sweetness of its song seemed listless in its tiny, bamboo cage. Irini filled the pot from which it fed with fine seed, and waggled her fingers through the bars to stir the bird to eat; but the lark turned its head away, and remained unmoving on its perch.

She sat down at the window and watched a spider weave its web beneath the sill, then watched the struggling of a moth that blundered into it. She knocked moss from the outhouse roof, and swept the scattered geranium leaves from the courtyard steps. She picked and tied a bunch of sage, and brewed hot tea from some of it; but the tea swam with drowned mites, and she threw the sage away. She thought of Andreas, and whether he was keeping dry; she thought about Nikos, and whether he was staying warm.

As evening fell, beneath the small domestic sounds—the chink of a cup cleared away, the bright applause of a TV game show, the drip of water in the sink—the silence gathered strength. The silence, day by day, was growing louder, and the day was almost here when she would understand the paradox: that this silence was not silence, but the swelling sound of emptiness.

Three

Each time she leaves, my wife calls out to me—"I'm going now, Theo"—as if I want to know. She'll take her time, but still forget my cigarettes, or something, so later on she'll have to go again, and she'll complain, and ask me to drive her down in the truck. And I'll say, The walk will do you good, and she will want to say, Well, you go then, but won't quite dare. And I'll watch her from the window as she descends the path, and she'll slyly pull that put-on face to let me know she's suffering, for me.

She finds it hard, she says, living here. It's hard for everyone, I say.

But you won't see it.

Like memory, rose-pink and dangerous, imagination distorts truth—so you, the traveler, conjure what you dreamed you'd see. Here's your village: a cluster of white-washed houses, all alight with dazzling geraniums, nestling together on the majestic hillside, looking down on a blue, shimmering sea.

No. Live here, and learn. Truth, and consequences. Here's my village, high on the hill, exposed to the elements, whatever they bring. To thwart the marauders of centuries ago, its siting was perfect—but time's moved on, and the road's still so difficult, each coming and going is a journey. Its warren of pretty, cobbled streets that draws you to explore—Where does this go? This way, or that?—makes weary walking for old legs and women weighed down by heavy bags of shopping. And quaint, close-packed houses put your neighbors in your face—better keep your nose clean—and the cracks and crannies of old, stone walls make homes for every kind of vermin. At night, we fall asleep to the scuttlings of beetles and the scrabblings of rats.

Thodoris Hatzistratis—Theo—had been born on this island, and here he was likely to die. His father, and his father's father, and his father's father's father—all had been born here, and, with the instinct of small-time farmers, all married island girls and bred their blood line pure, like livestock. All would be buried, one after the other, in the same cemetery plot; all would occupy it for the Orthodox-prescribed time—seven years, or ten—and then their bones, picked clean by the creatures who manage our decay, would be disinterred, and laid in the crowded ossuary, stacked tibia on fibula with their fathers, and mothers, and sisters, and wives: as close in death as in life.

To know the place of his grave from early childhood has an effect on a man. To place flowers on the ground where he himself will one day lie makes him fatalistic, pessimistic. Ambition and ideas for life atrophy—after all, what is the point? Life's point, on this island, was always clearly visible, up there on the hillside. Eyes raised from chores or play took in the high, white cemetery walls, where for every one of them the family tomb was waiting for their corpse. All knew exactly where life was leading them; all the eating, drinking, fornicating, worrying, working, wishing it were different, wishing there were more, were only steps on that narrow road. They were all travelling together, towards the cemetery gates.

Some years had passed since great-grandfather had been disinterred. Today, Grandpa was to take his place.

Grandpa lay, rigid and cold, in his pine coffin on the parlor table. The coffin, one of the undertaker's standard sizes, was too long for him; it overran the table ends, and the mourners, coming and going, cracked the door on its foot. Every chair in the house had been carried into the parlor, backed up to the walls beneath the gilded icons; red-eyed from crying and from lack of sleep, the women sat where they had sat all night, lighting long, brown candles, snuffing them as they burned low, watching that the Devil didn't come to steal Grandpa's soul.

To see him lying there made Theo's heart ache.

He bent to kiss the old man's forehead. The skin to which he touched his lips was dry, and jaundiced like the skin of corn-fed chickens. The lines of Grandpa's face had dissolved, and his wrinkles—deep enough, in life, to hold a matchstick—had all gone: his complexion had reverted to a youth's. The women had made him respectable, much more so than he ever was in his late years; they had shaved him, and scrubbed and clipped his nails, and put him in his suit, his wedding suit (he owned no other, but age had shrunk his frame, and his arthritic hands were covered by the jacket sleeves almost to the fingertips). He wore a white shirt, bought this morning for this occasion; they had pressed out its pinned-in creases—the sweet smell of ironing starch mingled with the candle smoke—and its collar, buttoned tight, hung loose around his neck.

Around his nostrils, a fat fly crawled.

The women—his mother and Aunt Maria, Aunt Anna and poor Aunt Sofia—watched him in silence. Elpida, Theo's wife, yawned. He'd asked her not to wear that skirt; it didn't cover her knees. Theo pushed by her to where his grandmother sat at Grandpa's side. He squeezed his grandmother's hands, touched his face lightly to hers, left and right; the wetness of her tears was cold on his cheeks.

"Theo," she whispered. *"Theo mou, agapi mou."* He was unsure whether she meant him, or Grandpa. He had been baptized with his grandfather's name; he was the living memorial now to Grandpa's time on earth.

"May his memory be eternal," he said. "He's with the saints now, Grandma."

There were voices from the street. Aunt Sofia lifted the curtain of hand-crocheted net and peered through the window at her back.

"The priest's here," she said.

The women began to wail.

In the kitchen, Pappa Philippas was preparing the tools of his trade. He was a tall, stooping man, gaunt-faced with pale eyes set in hollow, shadowed sockets. The children were afraid of him; if he caught them in misdemeanors, he pinched them with his bony fingers. He had never married; he had been disappointed in love. As he had aged, his disappointment had overgrown him, like ivy.

"Condolences to you, Theo," said the priest. His voice was slow, and morbid. "Your grandfather was a good man."

He laid an ornate incense burner on the stove-top, and beside it matches, a cylinder of charcoal and a tiny box of incense. Theo unscrewed the top from a bottle of Scotch and held up the bottle to the priest.

"Drink, Father?"

"Just a small one, Theo. I don't like to drink while I'm on duty."

On a tin tray covered in an embroidered cloth, the women had laid out rows of mismatched glass tumblers, brought from other homes, borrowed from the neighbors. Theo poured a finger of liquor for them both. Pappa Philippas struck a match and put the flame to the charcoal until it fizzed bright sparks, then placed the charcoal in the burner. Choosing a piece of opaque, ivory-colored incense from the tiny box, he laid it carefully on the hot charcoal and lowered the lid of the burner. Heavy, rose-scented smoke billowed through filigree holes.

Pappa Philippas drank down his whiskey, and, gathering up the jangling chains of the burner, gave a practice swing. He closed his eyes for a moment, whispering a few words in rehearsal—*Holy God, Holy Strength, Holy Immortal, have mercy on us*—then, opening the door into the parlor, he began the mournful chant of the Service for All the Dead.

✥

The men had gathered outside. They smoked, sipped whisky, found nothing to say. Theo's father, Michaelis, leaned with Uncle Janis against the house wall, arms around each other's shoulders, the stubble of mourning already on their faces. Uncle Janis was weeping; his father's eyes were bloodshot. Theo's brother, Takis, stood with Cousin Lukas. Out of respect, Lukas had washed his hands; the grime still on his forearms formed a sleeve above his wrists. Takis had slicked his hair back like a pimp. He swigged on a bottle of German lager and winked at Theo. *O God of spirits and all flesh, who trampled down death and crushed the Devil, giving life to your world; O Lord, give rest to the soul of your servant Thodoris, who has fallen asleep, in a place of light, a place of green pasture, a place of refreshment, whence pain, grief and sighing have fled away.* The wind was from the north, and bitter, and the sky threatened rain; through the closed, curtained window of the parlor, the priest's voice droned on.

On a plastic chair beneath the oak tree, Grandpa's great friend Nikolas sat alone. He clutched a small bouquet of flowers picked from the orchards—white-petaled marguerites, wild orchids, yellow poppies—their stems wrapped around with a crumpled paper bag. The poppies had lost their freshness and were wilting. Theo went to shake Nikolas's hand, but the old man in his loss seemed not to know him.

From the doorway, Aunt Sofia beckoned, pale in widow's black faded with too many launderings. Below the uneven hem of her home-sewn skirt, the pale-green lace of her nylon slip showed bright against the once-black serge. They had given her a tray to collect the glasses the whisky-drinkers were done with. As he approached her, she grasped his forearm.

"Theo," she said, urgently, "they're nearly finished. They're nearly ready."

As she spoke, they heard the final words—*Eternal be thy memory, dear brother*—and a chorus of light coughing as the women, released from head-bowed prayer and pious attitudes, cleared their throats of candle smoke and incense.

"Collect the glasses quickly, then, Aunt," he said. He turned his back on her and, making his way amongst the men, he placed his hand on the shoulders of the four who were to help bear the coffin.

"Time," he murmured. "It's time."

Smiling, always smiling, Aunt Sofia moved amongst the men, offering them the service of her tin tray, until the tray was heavy with empty glasses; and, because the slack, under-used muscles of her thin, aged arms complained, she, afraid of the mess, the rumpus there'd be if she let it fall, balanced it on a chair where no one sat.

The women filed out into the street. Aunt Maria's eyes fell on Aunt Sofia, pink-cheeked, hand on her delicate heart, resting. Aunt Maria's fat jowls wobbled. She marched across to where Aunt Sofia stood, and snatched up the tray. A glass fell; as it shattered, all the mourners turned to stare at Maria, at the shards strewn across the lane.

Aunt Maria's face turned red.

"I was afraid that would happen," said Aunt Sofia, timorously. "That tray's very heavy, isn't it, Maria?"

"Look what you've done!" hissed Maria. "Look at the mess! Go and get a broom and get this cleaned up!"

Aunt Maria laid the tray down on its chair. The pallbearers ground out their cigarettes and went into the house; the undertaker, carrying a hammer and a small Nescafé tin rattling with nails, followed them.

Uncle Janis brushed the tears from his cheeks. Michaelis was flushed with whisky, and the sting of the bitter wind. The focus of his eyes drifted, to Theo, to the men and women gathered at the doorway.

"Are they ready for us?" asked Uncle Janis.

"Yes, Uncle. It's time."

His uncle clapped him on the back.

"You're a good boy, Theo," he said. "Your grandpa's favorite."

"He's everyone's favorite," said Takis. At the foot of the orchard wall, the thistles were high, and dense; he pitched his empty bottle there, and it fell silently amongst them, unbroken and hidden. "Our own Saint Thodoris."

Michaelis moved to cuff his ear, but the alcohol made him slow, and Takis bent out of range.

"How dare you?" Michaelis's words were slurred; their endings ran into their beginnings so none of them were clear. "How dare you take that name in vain on such a day?"

"Leave him, Mikey," said Uncle Janis. "He doesn't mean it."

Cousin Lukas had a reputation: he always spoke the truth.

"He means it," he said. "He's jealous."

"Jealous!" scoffed Takis. "Why should I be jealous of him?"

They gave him no answer. Heads lowered, they walked together to the house.

In the parlor, the first nail in the coffin lid was hammered home.

The church of St. Thanassis glowed with the light of candles; the flames drew long shadows from the unlit corners, and made skulls of the carved faces of the long-dead saints. They laid the coffin on the cloth-draped trestle table, and at the lectern, Pappa Philippas turned the page of the calf-bound book. *Truly all things are vanity, life is but a shadow and a dream, and vainly do humans trouble themselves, as the Scripture says: when we have gained the world, then we shall dwell in the grave, where kings and beggars are the same; therefore, O Christ God, give rest to those who have passed over, as you love mankind.*

Six years ago, Theo had been married in this church. He remembered his wedding day as if it had happened to someone else, someone he had known well but had lost touch with and could picture only vaguely. He could replay pieces of the day like a home movie, cutting from scene to scene without continuity. A good day, his best day, a glorious warm day of early summer. He remembered his brother stumbling into the bedroom they had shared in the small hours before the wedding, Takis stinking of cigarettes and beer, giving Theo sex tips before falling asleep in his clothes. He remembered sitting with his mother at the kitchen table, very early in the morning; he had watched the sun rise. She had made his coffee exactly how he liked it, not too sweet, and had placed his cigarettes and lighter in a clean ashtray before him. He remembered the hiss of the gas in the little stove his mother used only for coffee, and the dropping note of the coffee's singing in the pot as it came to a boil. He remembered an emotion he was unable to put a name to—regret, perhaps—and had held her hand, and said his thanks, and his mother had begun to weep. He remembered the dish of sea urchins Uncle Janis had brought him at lunch to bring power to his loins, and how all his relatives had crowded around to watch him eat them, ensuring the male prowess of the family would not be compromised. He remembered how loud the bouzoukis had sounded in the small house as they picked out the old songs, the old men's favorites, and how the old men had sung along, raunchy songs of lust, sad songs of love gone wrong, romantic songs of port-bound sailors far from home longing for the smile of mother. He remembered his first sight of Elpida in her wedding dress, what a princess she was, so beautiful, wonderful in white, smiling shyly on her father's arm. At that moment he had fallen in love with her, for that day at least, so when the time came to make their vows, he had been able to believe in the words he was saying. He remembered that after the ceremony, when he and Elpida were two minutes married, tied together forever by the silk ribbons of their orange-blossom crowns, as the congregation pelted them with sugared almonds, a nut caught him right in the eye; it had hurt so much he had wanted to cry, but knew that to do so, to cry on one's wedding day, could bring only the worst of bad luck. He remembered dancing for his bride in his shirt sleeves, hot from cheap Metaxa and red wine, with his friends crouched in a circle at his feet, clapping the rhythm for him. He had danced with her; he had danced with every woman in the place. He remembered the plates of food put before him—soft-boiled octopus, grilled lamb, roast chicken, olives marinated in herbs and salted fish, fried courgettes with garlic sauce, a rich stew of aubergines, tiny sea snails in their shells—and how he had eaten nothing, because he had felt his life was beginning at last; he had no time to waste eating.

And he remembered being, finally, alone and naked with Elpida. She had wanted to please him, but had no clear idea of what was expected of her. When she had seen the size of his member, she had been afraid, and penetration had been difficult, and very painful for her. She had cried, afraid that she had failed him and that he would send her back to her mother's house in disgrace; embarrassed and unhappy, they had fallen asleep, two strangers left alone to make the best of it.

She was standing here, next to him, and when he glanced at her she gave him a little smile. But his face remained somber. He had seen his brother smile at her, from across the nave, and he had seen the way she dropped her eyes, and lifted them, and returned his smile, with a warmth she did not seem to feel for him.

When the service was over and Grandpa had been carried up to the cemetery and laid in the ground, the men left the women to it. The women fussed and cried, worriting about oil for the candle glass, bickering about whose flowers would be shown to best advantage where. Grandma, hysterical, lay down in the dirt and declared she would never leave the graveside, never.

The neighbors wandered home. Theo walked slowly with his father and Uncle Janis down to the *kafenion* in the village, old Nikolas and a few others with them. Not Takis: no one had seen Takis since they had left the church. They said little; they were all miserable. Michaelis called for whisky; the waiter brought a bottle.

They drank in silence for a while, but when the whisky began to blur the edges of their sadness, they started to tell stories about Grandpa, of the way he had been, and the things he had done.

"The old fool and his teeth," said Uncle Janis. "I'll never forget that day. When his teeth got so bad they just had to come out, he let that idiot Thassis persuade him he knew how to fix them. Down he went to the beach, made a driftwood fire and gathered all the sea snails he could find. He heated the snail shells in the fire until they were hot and then he bit down on the shells with the bad parts of his teeth to burn the rottenness out."

In chorus, they laughed the refrain, "The old fool!"

"Aye, the old fool! His mouth was ruined! Sore and blistered for days. But he was too proud, or too scared, to go to Kos to see a dentist, so that was that. Pained him ever after, didn't they? Spent his last years eating wet bread and paps. Bit of fish, sometimes. What did he used to say, Mikey? 'Nothing that a bit of clove oil won't cure.' The old fool."

There was silence. Above the bar, a caged canary sang. Michaelis picked up the whiskey bottle and splashed spirit into all their glasses.

"A toast to him! A toast to the old fool, wherever he is!"

On into the evening they drank, until they had drunk themselves through cheerfulness and maudlin again. Theo's head began to ache, and he wanted to leave; and yet, reluctant to go home, he stayed. Through the open doorway, he watched a woman make her way down the street. Her hair was long, and full; he watched her until she turned the corner, out of sight. On and on they sat, keeping company, sharing memories, until they heard the roll of thunder overhead, and it began to rain.

It's still raining; it's pissing down. We're sitting in the house. We've been sitting in the house for three days.

Nothing changes. The years all start the same and end the same. This one limped around to another winter just like last winter. Next winter will be no different. These old stone houses are cold as death. The cold gets inside you, under your skin, chills your bones until they ache with it. We wrap ourselves in our coats, wear them all day, inside and out. We can't change our clothes; it's too cold to undress, and our clean clothes are damp, stinking and rotten with the mildew. There's nowhere dry enough to air them. Where the bedroom walls back onto the water cistern they're crawling with fusty gray mold. We all cough from damp-filled lungs. The rain runs in like it owns the place. It comes under the doors; it comes around the window-frames. The carpets are all rolled up in the middle of the room. There are wet towels everywhere, soaking up the water, adding to the damp. Every hour or so, Elpida fetches a bucket and wrings out the towels. Her hands are red from the work, chapped and cracked, split between the fingers. Without the carpets, the wind whistles up through the cracks in the floorboards, rattling the glass in the china cabinet.

In the mornings we put up with the cold; I lie on the sofa with the blankets from the bed piled on top of me, watch TV, smoke. Elpida cooks, winter food. Boiled cauliflower. Lentils. Chick-peas. Fried eggs. Stuffed cabbage. Oranges. I dream of meat, a thick beef stew, maybe roast lamb. But when it rains, we don't work; when we don't work regularly, there's no money for meat. When she's not cooking, Elpida makes work for herself, cleaning everything she can think of: the light fittings, the chair legs and, between cloudbursts, the street outside. She runs to the baker's for bread. Me, where can I run to?

In the afternoons, when Panayitsa comes home from school, we go to Elpida's mother's. The TV's always on but no one ever watches it because someone's always babbling on about nothing: how the woman next door let her kids go out in the rain and how she never sweeps the street in front of their house; whether the women are going to the festival at St. Katerina's tomorrow; will the ferry bring fresh vegetables. I smoke a lot, drink a lot of sage tea. Sometimes, Elpida switches on the electric fire (but only one of the two bars) and we all pull up a chair and huddle around it — me, Elpida, mother- and father-in-law, Panayitsa and Elpida's grandmother, the mad, miserable old crone. My mother-in-law doesn't understand anything about electricity except that it's expensive. She unplugs the fridge at night to save money. If there's a break in the rain, her father goes out in the yard, burns some sticks in a brazier and brings in the hot ashes, so before long we can't see each other for smoke. Eventually, if we wait patiently, night comes. We go home, Elpida and Panayitsa go to bed, together, for warmth. I lie on the sofa under my blankets, freezing in the dark, smoking, and I wait.

If I went out, where would I go? The boredom makes me die inside; nothing to do, nothing, nothing to do.

Yesterday my mate Short George was passing, so I chewed the fat with him for a while. He and Tall George are going to Kos for a few days for a change of scene. I used to go with them, before I was married. We used to have some good times: go to a nightclub, drink in the bars, ride all over the island on our motorbikes. Have a change from home-cooking. Go to the cinema, look at the shops, maybe buy some new clothes. Find some girls, sometimes.

I'm a married man now, a serious man with a family. That life is over for me. What could I do?

I just wished him a good journey.

Four

Because the house was neither here nor there—not at the quieter port, where the smallest boats came and went, nor at the village heart, where the streets were lively with wives and rowdy children—it was called the Half-way House. Along the lane a few souls passed: old men, bound to routine, ambling to valley allotments, to water gardens already soaked by overnight rain; occasionally a car, truck, taxi or lorry; on weekdays, at eleven, the postman, precarious on his scooter. And, once an hour, bald-tired and rattling, the twelve-seater bus.

In summer, when the heat was overwhelming and no cooling wind blew off the mountains until the late hours of siesta, it was a good house, shaded by the overhanging eucalyptus on the road, the back yard given shelter by the olive grove and one vigorous vine which gave no grapes. But in winter, it was a trial. Wind drove the rain under the badly fitted door and around the unsealed window-frames; water pooled on the marble floor and on the tiled sills. She piled the sills with towels, which must be wrung out and then dried, somehow; she mopped the floor, repeatedly. But the water, once in the house, carried damp into the walls, where it couldn't be mopped, or soaked up by towels; soaked up instead by stone and plaster, it festered there, revealing itself eventually as foul, black mold. It climbed the walls, and crept across the ceilings; the spores spread like infection into their clothes, the laundered bed linen, the carpets and the rugs she'd made by hand. And the damp made it always cold, and dank; on sunny days, they sat outside for warmth. No house—no home—should be like that. But their landlord was in Athens, and never came here; more importantly, the rent was very low. It would have to do, he said, for now. If they were thrifty, before too long they'd build a dream house of their own.

Andreas hawked the cream of his catch on the mainland: the spiny-backed German fish, two good-sized snapper, peachy pink, the slender, silver bream and the ugly John Dory, the clawless local lobsters which had crawled into his traps, the urchins and the oysters he had gathered. Some of what he made, he spent on necessities—fresh stocks of ice, loaves of fresh-baked bread. He prepared his nets and lines to make his final casts, and, when all was in order, he set sail in the direction of home.

The ocean was his element almost as it was the fishes'. Under power, he steered the boat to rock over the gentle swell, or head-on to meet the rising giants, the wakes of ships and ferries. Where there was land—islands or islets, he knew them all—he ran her in close, to take advantage of their shelter; where there was no land, without reference to his compass his course was straight, as if the ruts between the waves were roads that he knew well. When it was time to halt, he remembered where the rocks would hold his anchor, and where it would drag useless across the sand, and let him drift; he remembered where he'd had success, the tiny coves and inlets where the catches had been good, and there he set his nets.

And he knew his quarry. He knew the habits of each species: the times they liked to feed, the weather that they favored, the depth that they would swim. He knew which bait would be their downfall: a sugar-coated slice of shrimp, a luminous, squid-shaped lure, a crumb of bread or ham. It was, to him, a contest, which the smartest of them won. When the fish stole the bait, and got away with it, he cursed them. But, often enough, there was that weight on the line, that vibrating and tugging which told him he might win, if he was fast enough, and hauled in the fish thrashing and frantic, before it shook itself free.

He pulled them in and held the jerking, slippery, panting creatures to force the hooks back through their bony lips. His callused hands absorbed their slimy oils; the big fish bled, and spattered him with blood through gasping gills. This sharing of their fluids was, he believed, crucial to his skill. And every day he fished, he ate of them—raw urchins from the shell, sardines grilled on a fire, a tin of mackerel—and the acids of his stomach broke down their bones and skin and melded them with his. This way, he said, he shared their essence, and made their secrets his.

His life was with those sea-bred creatures. He shared

their spirit, and their gift of silence. In another life, he'd choose to be a merman.

On Saturday, early in the morning, while she still lay in the warmth of the bed, Andreas came home. A key rattled in the lock, the door opened and quietly closed (she left the bed; the room was cold; she pulled on socks and slippers). A chair scraped across the kitchen floor, his striking lighter rasped, he coughed (she found her robe; bobbing before the mirror, she smoothed her bed-wrecked hair). As the smoke of his cigarette reached the ceiling, she was at his side, holding his hand, smiling at his smile.

He kissed her lightly, with salt-dried lips; his long-unshaven whiskers scratched her cheek. He looked a wild man, windswept, sunburned, filthy. His eyes, so swollen and pouched from broken sleep they were only slits, were sore and red. And body, breath, clothes, he stank: sweat, oil, onions, piss. And fish.

"Hello, wife," he said, still smiling.

"Welcome home," she smiled back. "I'm glad you're here."

She made him tea, and fried him eggs, and as he ate, he told in brief the tale of his travels—where he had sailed, what he had caught, the ones that got away—and as he spoke, the stink rose off him like a miasma.

When he had eaten, he fetched the wooden barrow from beneath the vine. They walked together, companionably, in silence, down towards the sea, passing the verges where he used to gather her posies of shy, mauve cyclamen and bright, white marguerites. But he didn't think of posies, not today.

At the jetty, he tied the boat in close, and loaded up the barrow. The polystyrene boxes dribbled clouded, scale-filled meltwater; within the boxes, the last of his catch—whitebait, bony sardines, petrol-blue garfish, long and thin as tubes, and gray mullet (which would go cheap; the people didn't like it)—lay blank-eyed on chips of ice, discolored and matte from their dissolving.

In the tiny cabin, she gathered up the blankets and the pillow from the plastic-covered mattress where he slept, and spread them on the wooden engine-casing to dry. The boat rocked gently with the movement of the sea; it swilled the bilge water beneath the deck like claret in a goblet, releasing its bouquet: spilt diesel, fish guts. She picked up his one plate—its rim held a clear imprint of his dirty thumb—his cup and bowl, the knives and fork and spoon, the empty water bottles and the beer cans, the tin of corned beef he hadn't eaten, the remnants of a stale loaf, the peel of an apple.

She used to ask him, sometimes, to take her with him; she viewed his life romantically, as one of exploration.

But he, knowing the truth, objected.

"It's man's work," he said. "You'd find it too uncomfortable." (And women at sea were bad luck. They talked too much, and felt the cold. They were nervous when the sea was rough, and prone to sickness.)

Now she understood the facts, and straightened out the mess and never asked. His life away from her was squalor, and survival.

"I'll be home for lunch," he said, and he trundled the barrow off along the seafront, calling to the women as he went, "Fish! Fresh fish!"

Irini watched him go. The women appeared in the doorways, brandishing their purses, flirting with him for first pick and extra weight. She saw him smiling, shyly, pleased. He pulled off his woolen cap and ran his hand over his baldness; but when one of the women, laughing, reached out and touched the smoothness of his head, the jealousy she sometimes used to feel just wasn't there.

Around the bay, on the terrace of the café, the four chairs at Nikos's table stood forlornly empty.

Irini headed home alone.

She was pleased to have an occupation. She made him *pasticcio,* fat, hollow pasta baked with rich meat sauce and cheese. He spooned in his food like a man starving, ripping lumps of bread from the loaf, wiping clean the plate. Beneath the table, one of his gifts to her—an octopus—slithered in a bucket, waiting to be beaten to a soapy pulp on the courtyard stones. His second gift—a leopard-spotted moray eel—lay on a platter, stiffly coiled, in the refrigerator, the hook still through its upper lip, a length of bright-blue nylon line attached.

"I had to cut the bastard loose," he said, "before it took a finger." He feared these snake-like fish: a year before, when one had sunk its teeth into his palm it had not let go until he smashed its skull with a spanner. Turning septic, the painful wound had stopped him working for ten days.

On the back of his hand, the scars remained, small dents in a jaw-shaped, curving ridge.

His gifts were meant to please her, and she tried to be pleased, but there was gutting, and beheading, and skinning, and beating, and boiling, and frying to be done, before she could enjoy them. Money for new shoes, she would have kissed him for.

He pushed his empty plate away, and pulled a roll of banknotes from his pocket. He counted them onto the table. He had done well.

"Pass me the tin, wife," he said.

She took down the biscuit tin from its place upon the shelf. Giving her ten thousand drachma, he forced the roll into the tin, already stuffed with notes.

"You haven't taken any while I've been gone?" he asked, and she lied. No.

"Because," he said, "it won't be long before we've enough to buy the land. And then we're halfway there."

He hadn't given her enough. He never did. He didn't know the price of meat, or milk, or oranges. It didn't matter. The tin was always there, when more was needed.

Andreas pulled the crust from a small piece of bread and, lifting the birdcage from its hook, carried it outside. He hung it beneath the vine where the sun was warmest, and, taking a crumb between thumb and finger, offered it through the bars to the silent lark.

"Come on, Milo," he coaxed. "A treat for you, a song for me."

Cautiously, the bird watched him; then, hopping along the perch, it picked the bread from his fingers.

"Good lad," he said. "That's my boy." The bird took another crumb, and another. As Andreas walked back inside the house, the bird lifted its head and began to sing.

Neither pleasure, nor distaste, but disinclination: she felt the inconvenience of undressing, at this time of day, and anticipated the discomfort of nakedness, in the damp chill of their bedroom. But the duty was hers, as much as preparing his food or ironing his clothes; it was a common enough bargain, her compliance for his money.

He did his best; he tried to make himself a temptation, lying ready but casual on the bed, his erection pushing up, ridiculous, beneath the towel around his waist. The bathroom had restored him to domestic humanity: his beard was gone, his nails were scrubbed, his hair was slick and flat, and all around him hung the sweet scent of soap and his cologne.

She found a smile, and put it on; she wore it as she stripped herself of clothing. He opened his arms, and she went to him, pressing against his clammy skin. He pulled the blankets over them, and pressed his mouth on hers, pushing his tongue between her teeth.

"Wife," he said, releasing her. He was smiling in his pleasure, in his gratification-to-come; it was the same smile she had seen an hour before, when she had served him with his pasta. He whisked away his towel, and, fumbling with himself, pushed into her. She winced. He grasped her breasts—his hands were cold—and began to pump. While his pumping was slow, and grinding, she watched the wall; as his pumping gathered pace, she matched him with the movement of her hips, to hurry him along. He took his time, but she was determined, and, before he had intended, gasping, his face screwed up in a chimp-like grimace, he was done.

When he opened his eyes, her smile was there, and getting warmer. He put his arm around her shoulder, and pulled her close.

"Wife," he said. "My wife." He ran a hand across her naked belly; his palm was rough, like sharkskin. "I'm feeling lucky today. I have a feeling today could be our day. I came across a little bed of oysters while I was gone—only half a dozen youngsters—and I kept them for myself. Oysters do a man good; there's nothing better to boost vitality. So I've been thinking..."

His words were lost in yawning.

"You need to sleep," she said. Soothingly, she stroked his head.

"I only sleep when I'm with you," he said. A minute passed and he was gone, tipped into sleep and softly snoring.

For a while, she held him close; the heat of sex had warmed the bed, and she was comfortable. In the hollow of his collarbone, his skin was glossed with sweat; from beneath the arm thrown back on the pillow, like a wolf through the forest his true scent came stealing, negating soap and cologne in maleness and musk. It was pleasant to her, and, dog-like, she sniffed it. But beneath the musk, something else was there: ever-present, unmistakable—the reek of fish.

She slipped from the bed and carried her clothes to the bathroom, washing away the sticky remains of his secretions before she dressed. Quietly, she lifted a silver-embellished icon of St. Elizabeth—elderly and pregnant—from its place on the wall above the television. Listening for the sounds of Andreas's sleeping, she unfastened the clips securing picture and frame, and removed its back. Sealed in their foil packets behind the cardboard icon, the small, white pills hidden there rattled treacherously. From a packet part-empty, she pressed a tablet from behind its seal.

She thought of Andreas all alone on some rocky beach, eating oysters to enhance his potency, and knew the magic of the oysters was no match for the opposing chemistry of the tiny pill she held. She hesitated, as she hesitated every day; she considered her uncle's words, and doubted his assertion that a baby was the key to peace of mind.

She hated to deceive Andreas; it was unkind, and made her a dissembler she had no wish to be. It was her heart that made her do it; her heart clung hard to dreams of possibilities which could never become realities if her freedom was lost.

She swallowed the pill, and stealthily replaced the icon and its secrets on the wall. The shadows in the room moved as clouds passed across the sun, and St. Elizabeth's face was changed; but whether she was smiling more, or frowning, Irini couldn't say.

❖

Towards four o'clock, the sun was already going down, drawing the light from the valley, and from the room. She sat a while in the shadows, fighting the beginnings of an uneasy restlessness, and a need for action; but the hands of the clock had all but stopped moving, and there was no activity she could think of to speed them on towards the time when she might sleep. She made more tea, and sat with it at the window, watching, as the afternoon dragged itself into evening, unable to think of anything to do which would hasten its end, or put her out of its misery.

Andreas stayed at home for a week. The catch had been good; the fish was all sold; he had money in his pocket: no need to put to sea. For two days, he slept, leaving the bed only to sit at the table, and eat, until the redness left his eyes and the disorientation of sleeplessness cleared from his head.

Then each day, they visited his mother's house, and talked about the weather and the price of fish and livestock. They put on stout shoes, and hiked the rocky mountain path to Profitis Ilias to gather oranges for marmalade. They visited the harbor chandler's, and drank coffee in the *kafenion* where the old men chewed the fat. They walked down to Nikos's, and sat with him for an hour or two as he spun them all the gossip he had heard.

But after seven days, Andreas was nibbled by the same

restless boredom that in his absence gnawed at Irini. It was time for him to go.

He began his preparations. He sent Irini to buy tinned meat and fish, fruit and coffee; he sat on the quayside, sewing up the rock-snagged holes in his nets.

But before he could leave, foul weather set in.

Winter was in its last days; the almond trees were already fluffed and pink with blossom. The extreme nature of the storm-force winds was unexpected. The sea exploded over the harbor walls and overran the harbor, flooding shops and houses with dirty saltwater. Screaming winds toppled power lines, and the power-station employees refused to go out to resurrect them. The electricity supply became intermittent, then deteriorated almost to nonexistent. The phones were out, and no phone-company employee would leave home to investigate. All shipping was forbidden to leave port; with no boats in and no boats out, soon there was no fresh produce to be had. In the grocers' shops, women scavenged the emptying shelves for tinned milk and pasta, which they boiled up on gas stoves and served slathered with margarine and a scraping of hard cheese. The wind shook the houses so mortar dust dropped on every surface, falling into the food as it was cooking, seasoning the food with grit as it stood on the table. Sleep was difficult; the old houses creaked and groaned, their doors and windows rattled and banged in the wind, and the wakeful lay listening for the crash of falling tiles, the crack and snap of falling trees.

Andreas anchored the boat well offshore and brought home the antiquated oil lamps from the cabin. For warmth, he fetched the brazier from the outhouse and lit it with last summer's charcoal. Then, he slept. He slept in his clothes; taking off only his boots, he wrapped himself in blankets like a caterpillar in a cocoon and dozed and snored in the dismal bedroom.

On and on he slept. At the roadside, the eucalyptus trees, tattered bark peeling white like sunburned skin, creaking and groaning, withstood the wind; Irini sat at the window, sometimes hearing the clock of St. Thanassis toll the daylight hours as the furious wind drew breath, and waited for the storm to pass.

Five

The fat man walked away from the *kafenion,* in the direction of the Seagull Hotel. As late morning drifted into the torpor of winter siesta, the seller of fruit and vegetables was sealing up his cartons of unsold produce, hauling the boxes of oranges and under-ripe tomatoes into a stone-floored storeroom already stacked with nets of brittle-skinned onions and stiff paper sacks of potatoes. The blue-painted shutters of the chandler's shop were closed; the door of the pharmacy, firmly shut, was secured with a rusting padlock.

He passed the door of his hotel, and, rounding a bend in the harborside road, found himself in a square paved with cobbles, bounded on three sides by tall, narrow buildings. With doorways built for barrows, and wagons, the buildings' past use as warehouses was clear; but all were now derelict, with rafters rotting beneath missing roof-tiles and cracks in the walls wide enough to take a man's fist. Behind a grimy window, almost obscured by heavy drapes of cobwebs, a FOR SALE sign sagged against the casement, discolored and water-stained with the damp of years.

At a corner of the square was a kiosk, a small hut bright with advertisements for soft drinks and cigarettes, its doorway hung with cards of plastic cigarette lighters and racks of tourist maps, its shelves packed with chocolate bars, camera film and chewing gum, and, discreetly displayed behind the till, packets of Italian condoms. On a shelf at the front of the kiosk was a telephone, metered for public use; behind the narrow counter a teenage girl, pretty but determinedly unsmiling, sat cross-legged on a high stool, the phone receiver pressed between her shoulder and her ear.

As the fat man approached she said one word into the receiver.

"Wait."

The fat man smiled at her, and asked for a pack of his brand of cigarettes.

The girl regarded him for a moment, as if contemplating refusing him service. She sighed, laid the receiver on the counter, then picked it up again and spoke into it.

"Just a minute.

"We don't stock that brand," she said to the fat man.

"You would be surprised," he said, "how many tobacconists say that to me. And often they find, if they look carefully, that they do have a pack or two, after all. So I would be much obliged, my dear young lady, if you would humor me, and check."

Again she sighed, and, turning her back on the fat man, began a desultory search amongst the stocks of cigarettes. At the very back of the highest shelf, concealed behind the popular brands, the unfamiliar name was there, copper-plated across the age-discolored paper wrapping which bound the packs together. The girl blew dust from the wrapping and ripped it open, slapping a box of his cigarettes onto the counter, where the platinum-haired starlet on the lid smiled her coy and easy smile.

"And two boxes of matches," said the fat man, himself still smiling.

She laid them on top of his cigarettes.

"And I think I might take one of those maps. If you would be so kind."

She reached up, and slid one of the thin documents from the display rack. She placed it on the counter beside the cigarettes and matches, and looked at him with narrowed eyes.

Reaching inside his jacket, he took out a wallet of soft calfskin and chose a high-denomination note. He handed it to the girl.

"I'm so sorry," he said. "I don't have any less."

She pressed four buttons on the till, and when the drawer popped open, lifted the coin box and hid the note he had given her beneath it. She released a pile of thousand-drachma notes from a spring clip, and counted out several; she scrabbled amongst the coins, and put a small pile of bronze on top of the notes.

She picked up the phone receiver.

"I wonder," he said, smiling, "if you might have such a thing as almond chocolate? With whole nuts, rather than chopped."

She glared at him, and laid down the receiver. She found a bar of pink-wrapped chocolate prettily decorated with almond blossom, and placed it before him. He handed her back one of the notes she had given him.

"Could you change this for me?" he asked. "I like to make sure I keep plenty of change on me. For tips."

She pressed two buttons on the till, and the drawer sprang open. She replaced the note he had given her within the stack, and scrabbled again amongst the coins. She placed a larger pile of bronze on the counter.

He scooped up the coins and dropped them into the pocket of his jacket.

"Thank you very much," he said.

She picked up the receiver.

"I'm here," she said. "*Kalé?* Are you there?"

It was clear she was hearing only the monotone of a line disconnected. Smiling, the fat man wished her good day.

By the kiosk was a litter bin. The fat man slid open first one matchbox, then the other, tipping the matches from both tinkling into the bin. He slipped the empty boxes into his jacket pocket.

Opening up the map, he might, he found, have saved his money. The map was simple as a pirates' treasure map—land surrounded by water and a single road, snaking up from the harbor where he now stood, up the mountainside to the upper village. Here the road divided, one branch running down to the hamlet of St. Savas, the second winding through the foothills to the monastery of St. Vassilis at the island's far tip. Beyond these settlements, through the higher mountains, broken lines denoted dirt tracks and footpaths, the only access to outlying smallholdings and isolated chapels. At the foot of the map were a few lines of information — the island's dimensions, and its highest point — and a list of every church, chapel and deserted monastery to be found there. One hundred and thirty-two, noted the fat man, almost every one dedicated to a different saint or martyr. And below the places of worship, a paragraph — a sentence — boldly titled "Getting About."

"There is a regular bus service from the main port to the small port of St. Savas," he read.

And there, he decided, was as good a place as any to begin.

The bus — a minibus, with rust-riddled wheel arches and tires with no tread — was already waiting at the bus stop. The driver, a man with a doleful, sagging face, leaned on the sill of his open window. The stubble of his unshaven cheeks was gray beyond his years, and as he watched the fat man's approach, no interest showed in his bagged and bloodshot eyes.

On the rearmost seats, two women whispered to each other like conspirators, hugging bags of warm bread loaves to their breasts.

The fat man stood at the driver's window. Close up, the stink of last night's Scotch was strong on the driver's breath.

"Good afternoon, friend," said the fat man. "Is this the bus for St. Savas?"

The driver bent his head. Yes.

"What time do you leave?"

"From the port, every hour, on the hour. From St. Savas, every hour, on the half-hour. No buses between two and four." He recited the simple timetable like a chant.

The fat man climbed into the bus and squeezed himself with some difficulty into the seat behind the driver. He filled, quite easily, two-thirds of a seat made for two; on the unoccupied portion he placed his holdall.

He tapped the driver on the shoulder.

"How much to the end of the line?"

"One hundred drachma." The fat man produced a coin from the change in his pocket, and handed it to the driver.

An elderly man with a parcel of whitebait wrapped in newspaper hauled himself, panting, into the seat across the aisle from the fat man. He lay the parcel on his knee; the fluids from the fish—from scales, fins, bowels, bones—were already soaking through their wrapping, darkening patches of the fabric of his trousers.

"Good day, all, good day," he said, turning to see who else was on the bus. "Now then, George," he addressed the driver, "I've nearly killed myself running to catch you, and you're still sitting here as if we've all the time in the world. Fire her up, man, and let's be on our way."

"Another two minutes yet, by the clock," said George, and he, the old man, the two women and the fat man craned their heads towards the clock tower at the end of the harbor.

"He's right, Vassilis," said one of the women. "Two minutes yet."

"Well, bugger me," said the old man. "I needn't have killed myself after all."

"That's what you get here," said the driver, morosely, not taking his eyes from the clock. "Those that're early want you to leave the rest behind. Those that're late blame you for not waiting beyond your time. There's no winning with these people."

The fat man smiled, politely, sympathetically, but, unsure whether it was he whom the driver addressed, said nothing. So the three men sat a while in silence; behind them, the women whispered secrets which would soon be known to all.

Across the water rang the lonely, hollow note of the first afternoon hour.

The driver started his engine, and the bus moved slowly along the harbor front and labored up the steep, switchback road which wound across the island to St. Savas's Bay.

High above the port, the fat man looked down through his window onto the rain-dulled blues of the harbor waters. Above the road, a line of cylindrical windmills crowned the rocky ridge like the crest on the head of a lizard, the weathered stone of their walls a chameleon match for the rough mountain slopes. But, unused for decades, the mills were falling into ruins; their canvas sails were long stripped from their frames, the once-conical roofs were all open to the sky.

Beyond the mills, the road began to descend. The driver took the blind bend at speed; the fat man closed his eyes, feeling the twists in the steep lane in the lifting of his stomach. The lane leveled; the driver braked, and brought the bus to a halt.

The fat man opened his eyes.

The bus stood in a stone-paved square; amongst the houses which lined it were a tiny general store, and a small hotel where a winter of dead leaves lay on the patio. Outside the store, the grocer's wife paused in the picking-over of a box of aubergines, and watched the passengers descend, as if she were expecting someone.

Hugging their bread loaves, the women paid the driver in small coins and climbed down from the bus.

"Is this St. Savas?" the fat man asked the driver.

"No, no, not yet," answered the old man, fumbling in his trouser pocket. "This is the village. Stay where you are, sir, stay where you are. St. Savas is a little way yet."

"Well," the driver snapped at the old man, "are you coming with us, then, or are you getting off?"

"I'm just looking for my fare," said the old man. He looked into the palm of his hand at what his fumbling had produced, and chose three twenty-drachma coins for the driver. Handing them over, he stood and tucked his sodden parcel beneath his arm. The lap of his trousers was dark where the fish-reeking water had soaked them.

"Keep the change," he called, as the bus pulled away.

"Silly old fool," muttered the driver.

They wove through the narrowest of lanes, between houses so close an outstretched hand would touch them as they passed, to the head of a wide, shallow valley, where the lane once more became a rural road. Rattling downhill, the fat man looked out on the tatters of an agricultural heritage: groves of squat, silvered olive trees, their crops all unharvested; the wheat terraces, brilliant with ungrazed meadow-grass and thistles; the collapsed boundary walls of small vineyards where the vines were no more. They passed beneath a line of shivering eucalyptus trees, and by the Half-way House, and soon they reached the sea again, where the driver turned right, and halted. He switched off the engine and leaned tiredly on the sill of his window, as if the fat man were not there. The cooling engine ticked and popped; tiny waves tumbled the sharp gray stones of the roadside shingle.

"Thank you, friend," said the fat man, climbing out of the bus and slamming the door.

But the driver did not answer.

The fat man took the curving path which followed the line of the sea. At the boatyard, chickens scratched amongst the upturned boats and discarded paint cans; a smoking brazier held the ash of a recent fire. The fat man paused to inspect the joints and plane-work on the newly assembled ribs of a rowing boat, and poked, frowning, at a half-finished fiberglass repair on the hull of a two-man speedboat. Overhead, a white gull wheeled. Picking a strand of drying seaweed from the sole of his left shoe, he walked on until he arrived at a tall house at the path's end. On the door lintel was fixed a painted sign, with writing so badly cracked and faded it could not be read. At the back of a terrace patchworked with stones taken from the sea stood a single table, and four chairs; at the table sat a man wrapped warm in heavy clothing, his face hidden by the peak of a sheepskin cap.

"Good afternoon," said the fat man, politely. "I wonder if I am in the right place for a cup of coffee?"

Nikos pushed the peak of the cap off his face and regarded the fat man.

"A stranger in paradise," he said. "It's not the season for strangers. But coffee we can manage, winter or summer. How do you take it?"

"Greek coffee, no sugar," said the fat man. "Thank you."

Nikos hauled himself out of his chair and limped into the kitchen. Beneath the chair he had vacated, a ginger cat with watering, inflamed eyes licked the thin hair of its flank. Beyond the boatyard, the bus turned the corner and disappeared up the harbor road. The wind drew ripples in the rainwater pools lying in the hollows of the terrace stones. The fat man shivered.

Nikos brought coffee, and water, and a clean ashtray to the table, and sat down with the fat man. He held out his hand.

"Nikos Velianidis."

"Hermes Diaktoros. Hence the winged sandals." The fat man pointed to his tennis shoes. Nikos smiled, as if he might have understood the joke.

The fat man gestured at the bay and towards the mountains, whose peaks were hidden in lowering clouds.

"It's very beautiful here," he said. "Peaceful. A spot like this would suit me very well."

"Would it, now?" asked Nikos. "Well, sir, I'll tell you something. If I had a thousand drachma for everyone I'd heard say that, I'd be a rich man now. You know what they say. The grass is always greener."

"Sometimes, it's true," said the fat man.

"We have a lot of foreigners," said Nikos, "who think they'd like this life. A life of ease. It's too much ease that drives them home again."

"It's certainly very quiet."

"It wasn't always like this. This island was a center of industry, once."

"Really?" The fat man peeled the cellophane from his new pack of cigarettes and offered it to Nikos, who took one. Nikos held up a gold lighter which burned with a small, steady flame, and the fat man leaned towards him to light his own cigarette. "May I say that, frankly, I have seen very little here of what I would term industry."

"Sponges," said Nikos. "They were the heart of an international business. We fished them, cleaned them, packed them and shipped them. There were thousands of people living here, all making a good living out of sponges. We were merchants, and exporters on a grand scale." The fat man thought of the derelict warehouses he had seen in the harbor square. "Now, we are importers. Germans, English, Dutch. We trade in ice cream and cold beer and sunbeds. Seasonal, but profitable. Six months' hard labor, six months sitting on our arses waiting for the next wave to roll in." He drew on his cigarette. "But you," he said, "if I may say so, are not typical of our clientele. We don't get too many from Athens."

"News travels fast."

"Listen," said Nikos. "You can't pick your nose here without everyone knowing about it. And I expect the Chief of Police's nose is out of joint now you're here."

The fat man took a sip of his coffee and replaced the cup carefully in its saucer.

"The state of Mr. Zafiridis's nose," he said, "is not my concern."

"I don't suppose it is," said Nikos. "Though he's an interesting man, nonetheless."

He folded his arms across his belly and waited for the stranger to take his bait. The fat man smiled, and bit.

"In what way could he possibly be interesting? I found him lacking both charm and intelligence."

"He is charmless and stupid, of course," said Nikos, wafting away the fat man's observations with his cigarette smoke. "But he's a man with a secret."

"Yes," the fat man concurred, flatly. "He is."

Nikos looked at him.

"You know?"

"Yes, I know. Presumably, so do you. Weren't you about to tell me?"

Nikos stubbed out his cigarette.

"I must swallow my pride," he said, "and admit that I don't. So if you know his secret, please satisfy my curiosity. The Chief of Police is an enigma I have puzzled away at for some considerable time. I know he is not what he seems. But the man is like a hermit crab: the more you try and winkle him out, the deeper he conceals himself. He's a man with something to hide. Unfortunately, he is also a master at hiding it. If you know, indulge me, as a curious old man."

For a few moments the fat man hid his mouth behind his hand and looked at Nikos, assessing, considering.

"I wonder," he said, finally. "Are you the kind of man who can be trusted with another man's secrets?"

"I never break a confidence." Nikos bent and stroked the cat beneath his chair, concealing the light blush which the lie brought to his skin. The cat sniffed at his hand, then stood and ambled towards the kitchen door.

But the fat man seemed to take him at his word.

"Mr. Zafiridis," he said, leaning back, relaxed, in his chair. "His secret is quite an unusual one, even amongst our nation, where lying is a way of life. He is not Mr. Zafiridis of Patmos, as he pretends, but a certain Mr. Xanthos, from Sifnos."

Nikos smiled in delight.

"An imposter!"

"Just so. He and the real Mr. Zafiridis met on a ferry out of Piraeus. Mr. Xanthos was heading home to a wife he disliked and some embarrassing problems with the tax man. Mr. Zafiridis was on his way here, to take up his new post as Chief of Police; but he, too, had a lot on his mind—in particular a certain young lady who had proved unworthy of him, but not before she had spent every drachma he had. The two men got talking, and then they started drinking; Mr. Zafiridis, especially—the real Mr. Zafiridis—became very drunk. They talked of Mr. Zafiridis's work, and he made the statement several times that a trained monkey could be a perfectly adequate Chief of Police. In fact, he was quite correct: one has only to look at your own 'Mr. Zafiridis' to see the truth of this statement. Then the real Mr. Zafiridis, maudlin drunk but rather rashly nonetheless, expressed a wish to die. Without his paramour, he said, life was not worth the living. Our 'Mr. Zafiridis' took him at his word, and helped him over the side twelve miles off Halkidiki. But not before he helped himself to the real Mr. Zafiridis's papers. He presented himself here as the new Chief of Police—and has been here ever since."

The fat man drained his coffee cup.

Nikos's eyes were bright with excitement.

"How has he got away with it?" he asked. "And what happens if someone who knows the *real* man comes looking for him?"

The fat man licked a fingertip, and rubbed with it at a blemish on the trim of his right shoe.

"The false Mr. Zafiridis is not bright, but he is cunning. He is adept at making himself scarce when danger threatens. But his life here has not been comfortable. He spends a great deal of time looking over his shoulder. Chance, and Fate, are always there, ready to take a hand; and Chance is one thing in life no one can make provision for. In the end, his sins will find him out. His time will come. Sooner or later."

Nikos frowned.

"How do you know all this?"

The fat man smiled.

"It's quite simple. I read his mind."

Nikos smiled back.

"It's a good story. A very good story, in fact."

"You could dine out on it for months, no doubt."

"But is it true?"

The fat man shrugged.

"It may be. It may not be. You choose. After all, does it really matter, to you?"

There was a brief silence, and Nikos had the uncomfortable sense of being chastised. But his curiosity pricked again.

"So, if it's not Mr. Zafiridis you're after, what *is* your concern here?" he asked. "If I am allowed to inquire."

The fat man looked out across the sea. The tiny silhouette of a ship moved slowly on the distant horizon, passing them by.

"I am here," he said, "to protect the interests of a young lady named Irini Asimakopoulos."

"Ah." All animation left Nikos's face; it fell into sadness made poignant by welling tears he tried to wipe away like tiredness.

"You knew her."

"Irinaki mou," sighed Nikos. He signed the triple cross, and laid his hand over his heart. "Yes, I knew her. The dear girl was my niece."

"I'm sorry."

"Can I offer you a nip of something?" asked Nikos, suddenly. "Metaxa, ouzo? Whisky?"

"A small whisky, then."

Nikos limped into the house, and for some minutes the fat man was left alone. When Nikos reappeared, he carried two tumblers and a bottle of Johnnie Walker Red, three-quarters full. He slammed the glasses down on the table, unscrewed the cap from the whisky and poured out two generous measures.

He sat down, and held up his glass to the fat man.

"To Irini, God rest her," he said.

"To Irini," agreed the fat man. They clinked their glasses together, and drank.

"Tell me about her," said the fat man, quietly. "I want to know how she died."

Nikos looked at him with troubled eyes.

"I'm not sure," he said.

"But what do you think? What does your gut tell you?"

"My gut tells me many things, none of them pleasant. My gut tells me that, on the balance of probabilities, her death was not an accident. If only because, in all the years I've lived here, I've never known anyone fall off the mountain. Not by accident. Not on foot, anyway. That idiot Stefanos from the wine shop in the harbor, he fell off it in his truck, but he was drunk at the time. And even he walked away from it. Not a mark on him."

The fat man took another sip of the whisky, and waited until he felt the warmth of the spirit hit his chest.

"Mr. Zafiridis told me it was suicide," he said. "Did you know that's what they were saying?"

Nikos nodded, slowly.

"Might they be right?"

"You're the detective."

"But you knew her."

"I thought I did. I knew her as a little girl. I worked abroad, for many years; when I came back, she was all grown. We're not from here, you know. We're from the mainland. Not far away, but far enough..."

"Far enough for what?"

"Far enough for these small minds to think us foreign. Anywhere not here is foreign to them."

"But does that matter, if you fit in? Did she fit in?"

Nikos hesitated.

"Let me tell you my view on life. Everyone wants to be happy. Happy Ever After. But life's not like that. We all know that. Just some people accept it better than others. Happiness is something that comes along in little bits, not in ever-afters. The day your kids are born, you're happy. Ecstatic. Two days later, when you haven't slept and the brat won't stop bawling and your wife's in tears, you're miserable. You're so miserable you want to throw the kid at the wall, walk out the door and never come back. But it's too late. You can't put them back where they came from. So you soldier on. And sure enough, the kid brings you more bits of happiness. The first time my son called me 'Papa,' I cried, I was in tears. Then they throw up all over you. All in all, you wouldn't be without them, but there are sacrifices to be made. Sometimes, those sacrifices are... significant. Do you see what I'm saying? What people should be looking for is... shall I call it 'contentment'? Knowing that, on balance, highs and lows taken into account, they're probably better off where they are than anywhere else. Not looking over the fence all the time to see what the other guy's got that you haven't. That way lies heartache. Settle for what you've got."

"That's one point of view, friend," said the fat man. "But what would happen if everyone settled for their lot in life? What about Man's great discoveries—medicine, literature, art? Without people who refused to settle, we'd still be thinking the world was flat and the seas awash with dragons. We'd still be waiting for some other guy to invent the wheel."

Nikos smiled.

"Touché," he said. "Anyway. Irini had done things the wrong way around—married, then decided she wasn't ready to settle. She had the idea that she could persuade Andreas the money he'd been saving for years was best spent seeing the world. He didn't see it that way. All he wanted was a quiet life—a house of his own, a couple of kids, dinner on the table. But she was stubborn. If there was something she wanted to do, she wouldn't give up the idea, and if there was something she didn't want to do, she didn't do it. She wouldn't go to church, said it bored her. But it bores everybody, doesn't it? Bores the pants off me. No one goes to church because they *enjoy* it. The women here go to church, it's what they do. Gives them an interest outside the home. It's their social club. But she wouldn't go."

"She wasn't happy, then?"

"In the beginning she was. Andreas was a good match, in many ways. I wouldn't have had her tied to anyone who wasn't right for her. He's a simple man, uncomplicated. He makes enough to be comfortable. He's no debts, and he pays his bills on time. So when my sister was looking for a match for Irini, I vouched for him. My sister and I arranged the marriage together."

"And Irini was happy with your choice?"

"She showed up at the church. I took that to mean she was happy enough."

"Our friend Zafiridis seems to have discovered almost

nothing useful in investigating Irini's death, but I have inferred from him that your niece was late in marrying—that she was, in fact, for these parts, almost an old maid. Was there a reason for that?"

Nikos hesitated.

"There'd been someone else," he said at last. "Someone she'd waited for. Someone she wasted a lot of time on."

"A broken heart, then."

"A broken promise. He'd had her heart and all her wits some years before. But by the time he left her on the shelf, it's my belief she cared no more for him than he did her."

"Is it possible, then—forgive me—that Andreas was a port of last resort for her?"

Nikos studied the back of his hand; behind his knuckles was a dark, oval bruise whose origin he couldn't remember. He rubbed at the bruise with his thumb.

"You didn't know Irini," he said at last, "so it's understandable you might think that. But Irini believed that life as a spinster—and you and I both know what stigma that role carries—was preferable to life with Johnny Anybody. My sister had a man in mind for her—from a good family, wealthy and well thought of—and Irini refused to look at him. She turned him down. My sister was mortified. It caused her great embarrassment, and created a rift between her and Irini that never properly healed." He stopped, and looked into the fat man's face. "This is private business," he said. "I'm telling you this because I trust you to do the best you can for my Irini."

"You have my word on it," said the fat man. "And you may count absolutely on my discretion."

Nikos took a sip from his glass.

"Things got difficult," he said. "To save face, the intended man's family put it about that it was they who'd turned Irini down, rather than the other way around. People made up their minds she'd been putting it about. My sister blamed Irini for destroying the whole family's reputation. And, when the rumors started flying, needless to say no other candidates stepped forward for her hand."

"Except Andreas."

Nikos bowed his head.

"Except Andreas. He was prepared to take my word that there was no history a man wouldn't want in a wife. They met; they liked each other. It was hard for her at home, I know; but no, Andreas wasn't a port of last resort. They got along. He's straightforward, he's uncomplicated, and very skilled in his work, and she admired that. They could have been happy ever after."

"So if she was happy at first, what changed?"

"I really couldn't say," said Nikos, wearily. "Maybe nothing. That's common enough ground for growing unhappiness, isn't it—nothing changing?"

"Could she have been unhappy enough to commit suicide?" asked the fat man.

Nikos considered.

"I don't think so. But what do I know? What can anybody know about another's state of mind if they choose to hide it? But a suicidal state of mind is a hard thing to conceal. Especially here."

"Is it true she was having an affair?"

Nikos laughed. "Well, well," he said. "The grass hasn't been growing under your feet."

He picked up the whisky bottle and poured another measure into each glass.

"So is it true, Nikos?" persisted the fat man.

"There're only two people who could ever know the answer to that question. One of them's dead. Better ask the other. *Yammas.*"

The fat man picked up his glass and echoed the toast.

"*Yammas.* But will the other tell me the truth?"

"In his place, I wouldn't."

The fat man smiled, and sipped his whisky.

"What's he like, this Theo Hatzistratis?"

"You've got a name, then?"

"Yes."

"Well done. Quiet fellow. Not a womanizer. But then, what do mothers say to their daughters? Never trust the quiet ones."

"Do you think there was anything between them?"

"Maybe. She was bored, and the Devil finds work for idle hands. And other body parts. But if she was screwing him, she did wrong. She married Andreas in good faith, promised him fidelity. Then she sees something she likes the look of and she's off, making a fool of him. Worst thing a woman can do to a man, cuckold him. If she'd been my wife, I'd have killed her."

The fat man raised his eyebrows.

"Figure of speech," said Nikos.

"What about the lover? Is he married?"

"Yes, lovely wife, a good girl. They've got a daughter. But men get bored, don't they? You can't blame him. It's different, for men."

"Are you married, Nikos?"

"Widowed."

"Were you faithful to your wife?"

Nikos laughed. "Me? Never! I'd find it easier now. The mind is willing, but a man's flesh won't comply. And I suppose you're going to tell me I'm an old hypocrite. So I am. Hypocrisy is part of human nature. Don't do as I do, do as I say."

"Perhaps she and Hatzistratis cared for each other."

"Pah!"

"You're not a sentimental man, are you, Nikos?"

"Sentimentality is for fools."

They were quiet for a while. The fat man looked at his watch. No bus between two and four. He had a long walk ahead of him.

"Where can I find the husband?" he asked. "And the lover?"

Nikos told him, in detail, how to find the two men.

The fat man drank down the last of his whisky, then leaned forward to press for an answer to his last question.

"How did she die, Nikos?" he asked.

"I loved her," he said. "She was like a daughter to me. I miss her. Have another drink before you go."

"Thank you, no. I must be on my way. But we'll talk again." He stood, and pushed his chair beneath the table; taking money from his jacket pocket, he laid it beside his empty glass.

"Good day to you, Nikos," he said, and turned to walk away.

But the old man grabbed the sleeve of his jacket and held him back.

"I'm going to tell you something," he said, quietly, "but you didn't get it from me."

"You may rely absolutely on my discretion," said the fat man.

Nikos regarded him with uncertainty; but the fat man held his eyes with his own.

"Trust me," he said. "You must, for Irini's sake."

Nikos turned his head to left and right, scanning the seafront and the pathway to his house for unwelcome listeners, for witnesses to his given confidences. There was no one.

He beckoned the fat man to bend close, and spoke into his ear.

"Go to Profitis Ilias," he said. "There's a man who lives in a cabin there, right on the mountain. They call him Mad Lukas, and you'll find him rather strange. But he knows something that'll interest you. He saw something. Someone. Go and ask him who it was he saw, up there in the mountains—in just the spot where her body was found."

Six

Still the furious wind blew, ripping across a sky of clearest blue. At the roadside, the eucalyptus trees creaked and groaned; at the window, Irini caught a single chime above the wind's howl as the clock of St. Thanassis struck ten. In the bedroom, Andreas slept. And then, a huge crack, and a sudden, shivering rustle of dry leaves whose whispers seemed to rise in panic; a dulled thud as split wood crashed down on concrete, and the storm-felled limb lay a barrier across the road, the narrow leaves on its broken branches fluttering like faded, tattered pennants in the wind.

She ran to the bedroom. Andreas lay on his back, mouth open, his breathing profound and slow. His unshaven face was ridged with softening folds; in sleep, he had the vulnerability of a child, or of great age. It seemed a shame to wake him; and so, returning to the kitchen, she pulled on her warmest jacket and walked out into the storm, alone.

The bitter wind went for her eyes; it peppered them with dust and grit which stung until the tears ran, and spread her hair across her face like a veil. She stood, wind-whipped and shivering, holding her hair as best she could off her face, beside the fallen branch. It was, she knew, far beyond any strength of hers to move it from the road, and, deciding she must disturb Andreas after all, she turned towards the house. But, above the whooping wind, she caught a sound which stopped her: the sound—and the danger—was moving closer, in the faint but growing rumble of a vehicle approaching.

The bends in the road were blind; the drivers, in the main, were not.

But Theo Hatzistratis was searching for the number of the mainland lumberyard; last time, they sent the wrong lengths of timber, all too short. He wanted to speak with Malvilis, and check that the order was right; he wanted to talk to Buscotis, the warehouse man, and tell him to make sure that, first boat out when the storm passed, it would be here. The number was scrawled in pencil on a paper napkin; the napkin was in the pocket of his jacket, which lay on the passenger seat. He turned the jacket over, and looked down to guide his hand to the pocket. When his eyes switched back to the road, the road was blocked.

The brakes needed attention; he had known it for weeks, but time was too short to hang about the garage workshop watching Stavros on his back beneath the truck, losing his wrenches and his temper and making the problem worse than when they'd started.

He stamped on the brake, pumped it, pressed it to the floor. There was a sliding, a spraying of gravel, a squealing of tires. He closed his eyes, his arms braced on the wheel in readiness for the impact, but all he felt was a light, playful shove of a bump as he made contact.

He opened his eyes. The front of the truck was buried amongst the gray-green leaves and twigs of eucalyptus. Beyond, a woman watched him with startled eyes; she held the closed fingers of one hand over the "o" of her mouth.

He switched off the engine. As he climbed out of the truck, she gathered her magnificent hair—*hair for burying your face in*—and, pulling it impatiently over her shoulder, held it there. The wind was behind him; it caught him in the back, and made him take a step towards her.

He knew her, knew who she was, though he didn't know her name. He knew she was Andreas the Fish's wife, the woman Andreas had fetched himself from the mainland. Now, he could see she was worth fetching. She was a woman a man could admire. Savor. Caress.

The wind nudged him again, propelling him forward; as he took another step, he found there was no resistance in him at all.

I blame the wind for everything: the wind fetched down the branch, and laid it like a trap across the road. I didn't know him, I had never seen his face before; and yet as we faced each other, something passed between us—a flicker of recognition, understanding, a tiny charge of emotion which made us, somehow, conspirators. But in a heartbeat it was gone, and I was left looking at this man who was a stranger to me. He was tall, and younger than Andreas. He wore a full beard, untrimmed, a mourning beard; his black eyebrows were heavy, as if he might have exotic ancestry, Arab blood from the palm-fringed oases and scented harems of the Mussulmen. He had two heavy creases above his nose, which made me think maybe he frowned too much; but then he smiled at me, and those deep frown-lines just melted, and softer lines, from too much smiling, appeared at the corners of his dark and lovely eyes.

And then I realized that I was staring, so I lowered my eyes, but I could feel his still on me. He was bolder than he should be, like the boat-builders; except with Theo, somehow I didn't mind.

He called out, "Yassas"; *he had to shout to lift his voice over the wind.*

"We have a problem here," he yelled, and he kicked hard at the branch, expecting—I suppose—that it would rock, and give. But the branch was solid, rigid, and his face crumpled in pain, and he swore at himself and his own stupidity. And then he smiled at me, and I couldn't help myself—I laughed.

He shouted something else to me, but the wind carried his words away and I couldn't understand him, even if I watched his lips. So he parted the leaves, and stepped across the branch, and stood so close to me I could smell the scent of wood on him, the freshness of pine resin, and cigarettes on his breath. And on his hand I saw a wedding ring, a heavy band of white gold tight on his finger.

I told him I had seen the branch fall, that I had watched it from the window.

He asked me where Andreas was, and I told him he was sleeping. He called Andreas an idle dog, and said that he would get him out of bed.

He walked away from me. His thighs were long, his walk was supple, fluid. I watched him go. I watched him open my house door, and enter it as if it was his own, and I felt no objection to his intrusion.

She stood alone in the road, waiting, until the two men came out of the house together. Andreas was fastening his jacket, and laughing. The stranger pulled the door closed behind them.

It was the same, always: now there were two of them, she was visible to neither one. They did not speak to her, but stood a little distance away, gesturing, conferring, while the wind brought scraps of their talk to her ears.

"If we could borrow a winch..."

"...tie it to the back of your truck..."

"...in the workshop...ten minutes..."

It was cold, and the wind was a torment. Irini went inside to watch them from the shelter of the kitchen, but by the time she reached her chair at the window, they were out of sight, gone walking away down the road to the bay.

When they returned, she was making the batter for a lemon cake, beating margarine and sugar to a pale cream. Above the wind, an engine with a holed exhaust roared; a banana-yellow truck, badly rusted, pulled up outside the house. Crouched in the back, ducking behind the cab for shelter, Andreas and the stranger were red-cheeked from the cold, their hair comical in wind-teased peaks. In the cab sat the two boat-builders from St. Savas. The short one, the one with the missing fingers, looked over at the window where she stood and, seeing her there, raised his hand in friendly greeting, as if he never murmured those things to her when Andreas was away.

Andreas vaulted down onto the road. From the bed of the truck, the stranger lifted a chainsaw—a brute of a machine, heavy, long-bladed, jagged-toothed—and passed it to Andreas, then jumped down himself.

The four men stood together, heads cowed against the wind, and talked. She watched Andreas gesture above his head and point out the long, pale scar where the branch had been ripped from the trunk. They prodded at the branch with their toecaps, and made theoretical slices through it with the sides of their hands. They folded their arms self-importantly and discussed the possibilities. They spat on the ground and interrupted each other. They ridiculed the boat-builder with the missing fingers and called him *malaka.* And finally, they appeared to agree to a plan.

Andreas held up the chainsaw and peered at its workings, but one of the boat-builders—the one with rotten teeth—was impatient, and snatched it from him. Holding it before him, its brutal blade at the center of the group, he yanked at the starter cord, pulling it to its full extent. Nothing. He yanked again. Nothing. He lowered the saw, and the stranger pointed to a small, black button on the motor. The boat-builder pushed the button, held the saw up level with their faces, and yanked a third time at the cord.

As Andreas, the stranger and the boat-builder with the missing fingers leapt back, out of range, Irini heard the roar of the chainsaw. The boat-builder lowered it to the branch; and in a spray of sawdust and woodchips, the first log fell away.

They swaggered laughing into the kitchen, pulled chairs up to the table and sat themselves down. Outside, on the verge where pink cyclamen had bloomed, a stack of logs had grown. In the road, the wind skimmed the tops off the hillocks of soft sawdust and spirited the fine powder upwards, and away.

Andreas slammed an ashtray down on the table and spoke to Irini over his shoulder.

"Make us some coffee, wife," he said.

They leaned back in their chairs, legs splayed wide,

fumbling in their jackets for cigarettes and lighters. Andreas, finding his first, offered around a red-and-blue-banded pack of Assos: cheap Greek tobacco, rolled into cigarettes so badly made that sometimes the filters came off in the smoker's mouth. Irini watched Andreas pinch off the loose, white tip of the cigarette he was about to light. If they had been alone, he would never have removed it, because she would complain. Unfiltered cigarettes made his cough worse, and she would nag him for his early morning hacking and hawking and spitting which spattered mucous leavings in the bathroom sink.

The air was thick with cloud-gray smoke. She lit the gas burner, spooned aromatic coffee and damp sugar into the water-filled pot, and set it on to boil. From the parlor dresser, she fetched four of the pastel-flowered porcelain cups which had been a wedding present from her sister and wiped them clean.

The men grew loud as they talked, stimulated by their little adventure, excited by the glut of small-time news the storm had brought.

"It's taken the roof off Petros's new bathroom," said the boat-builder with the rotten teeth. "He came to us for a tarpaulin. I lent him one, but that's gone as well. He didn't tie it down right. I told him not to skimp on the rope..."

"What about old Pantelis the Tomato Man?" asked Andreas. "It blew him over! He's broken three ribs. And his wrist. But there's no boat to take him to the mainland to get it plastered..."

"Stavros the Draper, his boat, that fiberglass one he

bought last year, slipped its anchor," interrupted the boat-builder with the missing fingers. "Ran onto the rocks, broadside. Lot of damage. *Lot* of damage. Serve him right for trying to avoid dry-dock fees, tight old bastard. He said last autumn we charge too much. I said to him, no skin off my nose, your money'll be going into my wallet now anyway..."

Irini watched the thin wisps of steam rising from the surface of the coffee, waiting for the moment when it would boil and rise, frothing, to the brim of the pot. Across the room, Theo watched her, shyly, or slyly, the direction of his eyes hidden by his heavy brows. The coffee boiled, and she lifted it from the heat, pouring it carefully into the delicate cups. As she poured the last drops into the last cup, she glanced towards him; somehow it was no surprise to find him watching.

Andreas pushed his chair back from the table and stood up.

"Let's have a drink!" he said. "I think we've earned ourselves a drink, lads."

Irini placed the coffee before the men. No one thanked her. Andreas grabbed a bottle of good Metaxa from the shelf and took four glasses from the cabinet, then stood a glass before each man and splashed in a shot of brandy.

"Yammas!" he said, sitting down and holding up his glass. "Good health!"

But as they raised their glasses to their lips, there came a hammering at the door.

Andreas drank down half the brandy in his glass.

"Get the door, wife," he said.

Irini crossed to the door, and, with her foot behind it to prevent the wind taking it from its hinges, opened it a few inches; but the man standing outside was impatient.

"Let me in, for Christ's sake!" he said, and, putting his hand to it, pushed the door wide open. The wind swept through, ushering in a flurry of dried leaves and sawdust. Irini closed the door. The men at the table lowered their glasses, and regarded the visitor in silence. Squat, and bald except for the curled, gray hair above his long-lobed ears, he wore the clothes of a young man: a jacket in fine Italian leather, a linen shirt open at the neck. On his right hand, the nail of the little finger was long, and filed square: the mark of a man above manual labor.

The visitor smiled around at them, showing teeth filled here and there with gold.

"Well," said the visitor, "here's a pretty gathering. Having a party, are we, fellas? Irini, my dear, how are you?"

In greeting, he took her fingertips limply in his own, and brushed a soft, smooth-shaven cheek against each of hers. His skin smelled sweet, of violets, and Nivea lotion.

"Mr. Krisaxos," she said. "Welcome. Can I get you some coffee?"

"No, no, my dear, thank you." He looked in turn at the men around the table. Still none of them spoke. "I'm looking," he said, "for the idiot who's blocking the road with their truck. And I see the culprit right there, don't I, Nephew?"

Theo, coloring, stood up from his seat.

"Sorry, Uncle Louis," he said. "I'll get it shifted."

Theo walked towards the door; as he passed his uncle by, the older man squeezed his shoulder, in a way which might have been avuncular affection, or reproach.

"Yassas," said Theo, and passing quickly through the doorway, he was gone.

"Well," said Louis Krisaxos. "We can't all drink the day away. Some of us have work to do. Don't get too drunk, gentlemen." He pushed up the sleeve of his jacket to show the gold watch on his wrist. "My word, is that the time? Sorry to disturb you. Irini, come and have coffee with Anna. She'd love to see you."

They watched the door close behind him.

"Old faggot," said the boat-builder with the missing fingers. "He'll screw anything that moves. He's got a hot date with a soldier's backside; I'll put money on that."

"A date with his own right hand, more like," said the boat-builder with the rotten teeth. And they all laughed; except Irini, who removed the stranger's coffee cup and glass from the table and took them to the sink to wash them.

The boat-builders drained their glasses.

"Back to work," said the one with the rotten teeth.

As they left, the boat-builder with the missing fingers called out goodbye, but as Andreas closed the door behind him, she gave no answer.

A spatter of soot and brick dust fell from the chimney breast into the fireplace.

"Can't stand that man Krisaxos," said Andreas, taking a cigarette from the pack. He put it to his mouth and lit it. "He thinks he's a cut above us all, now he's made his pile."

"Your mother says he's a good businessman," she said.

"He's no businessman; he's a thief, a crook. That old queen will tread on anyone to get where he wants to be. His blood is bad: that family's got more skeletons in its closet than the rest of this island put together. Trust me, they'll all come crawling out one day to bury him. And I'll be glad to lend them a shovel to do the job properly." He drew on his cigarette, and flicked a few flakes of ash into the ashtray. "He wants a good dose of what they gave his father. A shot of the old medicine, that'd sort him out."

Irini ran water into the sink.

"What happened to his father?" she asked.

"He was rotten to the core," said Andreas. "Tassos, they called him. His appetites were warped. They had to put a stop to it."

Irini left the sink, and went to sit beside him at the table.

"Tell me," she said.

He poured himself another finger of Metaxa and held out the glass to Irini. She took a sip of the mellow, brown liquor; Andreas drank down half of what remained.

"Friend Louis is a faggot, pure and simple," he said. "He doesn't try to hide it anymore. But his father's perversions were far worse, and the family kept the secret very close. Some say he practiced first on Louis and his sister. There was talk, from time to time; the neighbors heard things. But children grow, and old man Tassos liked them very young. He started on his niece's daughter, a tiny thing just six years old. He got her in the house with promises of chocolate. When the niece got to him, he'd got his trousers around his knees, and the child was crying, half-undressed."

"My God," said Irini. "Did they call the police?"

"Police?" He knocked ash from his cigarette. "What would they have done? Old man Tassos had a bit of money; he'd have paid a lawyer to lie on his behalf, and walked away. No, there was no need for the police. The child's father went for him with the grandfather, and dragged the dirty dog out of hiding in the cellar. They tied him to the plane tree in the square, and left him there a while to let the crowd gather while they fetched a big, old rooster; just to make the pervert sweat, they slit the bird's throat in front of him. And when they'd got him gibbering and begging, the child's father had the honor of daubing his head with tar, and they pulled the feathers from the rooster and covered old man Tassos's head in them.

"When they put him on a mule and paraded him around the town, they took him past his own house so his wife could see. She spat on him from the window, and took the kids — our friend Louis and his sister — straight home to her mother. She divorced him, of course. Her family wouldn't stand the shame."

"What happened to him, in the end?"

"Ah, now — there's a question." Andreas drank down the last of his Metaxa. "After they let him go, he stumbled off and wasn't seen again. Some say he's here to this day, holed up in some back room in some relative's house, still too ashamed to show his face. But I think he's long gone, years since, somewhere far away, yearning like all exiled Greeks to come back home. He'll never come home. He'll never dare."

There was silence as he drew on his cigarette, and exhaled.

"Anyway. Just watch that one," he said. "He's got his eye on you."

She laughed.

"What would that old goat want with me?" she asked. "I'm not his taste."

But as Andreas replaced his jacket on the peg and went to switch on the TV, it seemed to Irini that it might not be Louis Krisaxos he'd meant.

Seven

Clean Monday, the first day of Lent: a day of austere feasting, to clean the stomach and prepare the body for deprivation. In a sky without cloud, Irini had expected the sun to give some warmth, but even in the sheltered lee of the chapel wall, on the mountainside the damp chill of winter remained. Amongst the rocks, scrawny ewes grazed the new growth of herbs and grass, their fattening lambs pulling at their teats; at the hill's foot, where the dry riverbed ran, the children aimed missiles—rocks, sticks, a broken-strapped sandal—into the branches of a walnut tree, trying to dislodge the last few nuts (they grew high, and would never be within their reach) of its crop.

Andreas's mother, Angeliki, had cleared a level patch of sandy ground, pitching the largest stones into the spreading bushes of thyme, uprooting a twisted branch of oregano and sweeping away the scattered sheep-droppings with its fragrant leaves. Now, she spread a patchwork quilt, and hunted in the thyme bushes for the heaviest stones she had thrown away to weight its corners. Strathia, Irini's sister-in-law, had lost, briefly, the scowl she wore around her children; bending into the back of the truck, she hauled out the coolers which contained the picnic. Beneath her dress, her thighs were pale, and slack; at the backs of her knees, thick veins ran.

Irini spread the Pyrex dishes and Tupperware bowls at the center of the quilt, and laid out the fasting foods: no oils, no fats, no meat, or fish which bled. They had brought olives, fat, sour, green ones and the shriveled, milder black; there were carrots, cauliflower and hot peppers pickled in brine, baby beetroot in jars, gherkins in vinegar, fish roe in tubes. There was an octopus Andreas had caught, and black-striped, whiskered prawns. There were scallions and Kos lettuces Angeliki had pulled from the garden, peppery rocket, pink radishes and the pale-mauve globes of turnips. Irini had boiled potatoes, and sprinkled them with salt and lemon juice; Strathia had steamed fresh mussels with bay leaves and onions. There were slabs of sticky, sweet vanilla halva swirled with cocoa, and flat, dimpled loaves of Clean Monday bread, and—wrapped in water-soaked towels to keep them cool—bottles of chilled retsina and lemonade.

But Angeliki was fretting.

"There won't be enough. We should have brought more bread. Strathia, we've forgotten the salt."

"It's here, Mother."

"Your father won't like those mussels cooked with bay leaves. He can't stand the taste of bay."

"Let him eat something else, then."

"This lettuce is all holes. You can't keep the snails off it, not with all this wet weather. I did wash it, though; I have given it a good wash. But I don't think your father'll eat it with holes in the leaves."

The scowl returned to Strathia's face.

"For heaven's sake, Mother," she said.

Crouched over the stack of fallen branches they had broken for firewood, the men—Andreas, his father Vassilis, Strathia's husband, Socratis—were poking dried twigs and grass into its base. Andreas lit a cigarette, and put his lighter to the fire. Smoke billowed around them, masking them, and cleared to reveal them, like shadows on a day of scattered clouds: here, then gone. Socratis pitched a root of thorny capers into the growing flames; it spat a shower of crackling sparks high into the air. One falling spark, still glowing, caught Vassilis on the back of his hand; as he, cursing, flicked it away and licked the stinging burn, Andreas and Socratis laughed.

Andreas was still smiling as he walked back to the women; he put his hands on Irini's shoulders and kissed the tip of her nose. Beneath the wood smoke which was already in his hair, he smelled familiar, safe. She placed her hands on his waist (it was thickening a little, as he grew older), and made them partners, ready for the dance.

Through the fabric of his clothes, she pinched the softness of his body.

"What's this?" she said, teasing, smiling.

"My wife's cooking," he said. He touched his lips to hers.

"It's time for a drink. Strathia, find the cups. We'll have a glass of wine."

"I don't want wine," said Angeliki. "It gives me a headache."

"You'll have a headache anyway, no doubt, by the time we're done," said Andreas. He winked at Irini, crazing the skin around his eyes. "You'll have a glass of wine, and like it."

Strathia was handing around the paper cups.

"Well, just a small one, then," said Angeliki.

When the fire burned down to red-hot embers, Socratis spread the octopus on the grill and placed it over the heat. Beneath the walnut tree, the children probed a nest of ants with stalks of grass; from behind the chapel, where goats foraged, came the hollow rattling of bells. Slowly, the octopus flesh changed from dull pink to deep red; its juices dripped, hissing, into the embers.

Socratis drank from his cup, and flicked a crawling insect from the end of his nose with the pad of his thumb. He had a boxer's nose, bent and misshapen; it fitted his reputation as a hard man. Before their marriage, he battered a rival for Strathia with an iron bar; the rival limped now, and his vision in one eye was blurred. But as time had passed, Socratis and the rival had shaken hands, and shared a drink together, many times. Socratis was not a man for grudges. Not if he prevailed.

Across the valley, at the horizon, a man appeared at the wall of an abandoned olive grove. He leaned, like a biblical prophet, on a long staff and stood, like a sentinel, looking down on them. Socratis, shading his eyes with the flat of his hand, squinted to identify the watcher and, having done so, grunted, and silently prodded the embers with a stick. Andreas's eyes were not as good as they had been, once; from this distance, he could not identify the figure.

"Who's that?" he asked.

Vassilis hawked, and spat on the ground.

"Lukas," he said. "Let's eat. When he gets here, there'll be nothing left."

The watcher raised a hand, and waved; the echo of his shout was indecipherable.

"Where're your manners, Father?" asked Strathia. "Call him down."

"D'you think there'll be enough, if he comes?" asked Angeliki, doubtfully.

"For God's sake, Mother," said Strathia. "Andreas, call him down."

Leaning on his staff, the figure began to pick his way down the hillside. His gait was uneven—not quite a disability, but a limp.

"No need," said Vassilis. "He's halfway here already."

Strathia handed Lukas a cup of wine, and he, glancing to where Socratis poked the fire, thanked her. He placed the cup between the insteps of his boots—thick-soled, black boots, scuffed, and dull with dust, bought cheap from a demobbed National Service soldier—and, lifting the patch which covered it, rubbed at his left eye with a dirty finger. He had acquired his flak jacket and khaki trousers as part of the same deal with the soldier, but the trousers fitted badly, and were held up by a leather belt buckled tight around his ribcage, so the crotch of the trousers was too high up in his own. Because he wore the trousers so high, there was a gap where his shins showed pale pink scars between his trousers cuffs and the tops of his boots. In his solitary life, he took no care of himself, and had become too thin; he ate voraciously when food was offered, but spent too many of his evenings in the company of drunkards in the village ouzeri. He smelled bad, of his unclean self, and of his goats. But he was not without his vanity: he took pride in his hair, which hung in knotted, sun-bleached dreadlocks on his shoulders. His pride was that his hair was touched just once a year; he had one aunt who loved him, and every Easter Day, she was permitted to wash it, and cut half from its length.

He bent to pick up his wine, and drank, eyes lowered.

"Will you eat with us?" asked Strathia.

But Lukas declined.

"I've to be getting on," he said. "I've twenty goats to water, up at Agia Anna."

Vassilis broke the crisp-crusted end from a loaf, and bit into it, saying nothing.

"The goats'll wait a while longer," said Strathia. She offered him a bowl of olives, and the loaf from which her father had taken the end. "Eat," she said.

Lukas broke a piece of bread, and took a handful of the olives. With a pair of tongs, Socratis lifted the roasted octopus onto a plate, and carried it to Angeliki, who placed it at the center of the gathering.

Socratis, grinning, slapped Lukas on the back. Lukas flinched.

"How're you doing, Cousin?" asked Socratis. "Not married yet?"

Angeliki cut the legs from the octopus, and sliced its body; the inner flesh was starkly white against the red and black of its seared skin. Dousing it with lemon juice, she sprinkled it with flakes of dried oregano pulled from a bush.

"Eat," she said. "Everyone eat. Strathia, call the children."

"Leave them," said Socratis. "They can eat later."

For a few minutes they ate in silence. Irini watched Lukas tear off a hunk of bread and dip it in the octopus's lemon-sharp juices, then smear a second piece with cod's roe.

"So," said Vassilis, "forty days to your haircut, Lukas."

Lukas's mouth was stuffed with half-chewed bread.

"I may not bother, this year," he said. He put his hand to his head, and fingered one of the dirty dreadlocks.

"If it gets much longer, you'll fall over it," said Andreas.

"Come on, Lukas," said Strathia. "Let's have the news. What are they talking about, downtown?"

As she spoke, a faint blush stole across Lukas's face. He reached for the wine bottle, and refilled his cup.

"I don't know much," he said.

"Sure you do," said Andreas. "Come on. Fill us in."

Socratis stood.

"I'll put some of those prawns on the grill," he said.

"It's hungry work, listening to his monologues." He wandered away to the fire.

"Well," said Lukas. He speared the tip of an octopus leg with his fork, and bit into it. "You'll know all about Manolis Mandrakis's wife, no doubt."

"Which Manolis Mandrakis?" asked Strathia. "Do you mean the house-painter?"

"Yes," said Lukas, "the young one."

Irini knew him. She knew his wife, too: a tall, thin, morose girl who provoked public disapproval by wearing trousers.

They waited. Lukas unwrapped the sticky halva, cut a piece and put it in his mouth.

"Well?" prompted Andreas.

"Well," said Lukas, "Mandrakis caught her with the Chief of Police."

Angeliki drew in her breath.

"Never," she said.

"It's true," said Lukas. "He found them half-naked in the back of her father's shop. He's got that butcher's next to the ice factory."

Angeliki crossed herself, quickly, three times.

"Mandrakis didn't dare lay a finger on that police scum, of course," Lukas went on. "Just told him to get out and close the door behind him. Then he shut himself in with his wife and beat the shit out of her."

There was silence.

"He's divorcing her, of course. Her family are in a terrible state. The mother's got heart problems; she got palpitations and had to have the doctor."

"My God," said Andreas.

"That son-of-a-bitch policeman wants sorting out," said Vassilis. "Why didn't Mandrakis get his brothers onto him? He's got enough of them."

"One of the brothers is a bar owner," said Lukas. "Needs his drinks license. That bastard would have shut him down."

As the afternoon faded, the wine bottles were emptied. The men drank ouzo, and talked; Lukas lay on his back in the shade of the chapel wall, sleeping. The acid of the food, the pickles and lemon juice, the dry wine, had given Irini a sharp pain in the stomach. She stretched out, feeling the sun on her legs and arms, and closed her eyes. She thought of the morose face of Mrs. Mandrakis, and imagined it pummeled, and bloodied; and she wondered if the girl had cried and screamed, or if she had submitted quietly to her punishment, knowing that no one would come to her aid.

Eight

Irini, mindful of her duty, went calling on her mother-in-law. She went reluctantly, driven in Andreas's new absence by a yearning for companionship. There was an awkwardness between the women (the story was an old one: no woman could ever be good enough for him), and she expected to be received, as always, coolly. But she had chosen her time badly. Her mother-in-law was unctuous in her welcome. She described Irini's arrival as fortuitous.

"Come in, Irini," said Angeliki, "come in. Your father-in-law is wanting some help."

She was a tiny woman, fine-boned and fragile in her mind. For many years, the doctor had prescribed her Valium. The drug had left her vague, and forgetful, so the house was always littered with chores half-done: half the brasses polished, half the potatoes peeled, half the laundry ironed and put away, and often two trips in a morning to the baker's to fetch the bread she had already bought. There was today a smell of scorching: at the stove, water boiling over in a forgotten saucepan hissed on the hot-plate. In the yard, a goat was forlornly bleating.

Angeliki handed Irini a folded cotton apron and a plastic bucket.

"Put your apron on," she said. "You'll not want to get it all down your clothes. It makes such a mess, if you're not careful. He'll be ready to start. I expect he was waiting for me." She placed her tiny hand in the small of Irini's back and guided her through the yard door. Her touch was delicate but insistent, like that of a mouse's paw. Irini moved quickly, to be free of it.

Dangling from the branches of a lemon tree, the goat was strung up by a rope tied around its back feet. An old billy, it stank of goaty musk and the piss which fear had drained from its bladder. Stretched out, its cloven hooves hung inches from the ground it couldn't reach. It spun slowly at the end of the rope, a full turn clockwise, then anticlockwise, watching the earth through the black slits of its strange, yellow eyes. Its wretched cries were neatly spaced, like a pulse; it had perhaps been hanging there some time.

Her father-in-law crouched close by, sharpening a hook-tipped hunting knife on a flat stone wetted with spittle. Though the sun had no strength in it, his face was red, his sparse-haired pate and bald forehead moist; from beneath his shirt (the fabric strained across his dome-round belly) she smelled a similar goat-like musk: much milder, sweeter, but, essentially, the same. He scowled at her, as if not pleased to see her, but Irini knew he was indifferent whether she assisted, or Angeliki. To him, one woman was as useless as the next.

"Come to help?" he said. "Bring the bucket, then; let's have the bucket."

He pulled the sharp edge of the blade across the cushion of his thumb; it drew a stinging line of blood. Standing, he arched his back, complaining at the aching in his kidneys. He'd had trouble passing water this morning, he told her. He ought to see the doctor. Behind him, the goat bleated; it sounded like derision.

Irini felt the urge to comfort the goat, to stroke its head. What was the point? She gave Vassilis the bucket.

"Let's get on, then," he said. "Are we ready? Step away."

He knew men who, at this moment of playing God, as the instrument setting the soul adrift, sending it back whence it came, would bless the animal, wish it God speed. *All mad*, he thought. *Faggots*. It was a beast, that's all; he felt no more for it than he would for an orange he bit into.

The goat, sensing its time was here, began to bleat in panic. Irini gazed up into the branches of the lemon tree, focusing on the brilliance of the fruit, the gloss of the leaves, the structure of the branches. There was a light, tearing sound, and a splash of liquid in the dirt. The bleating became irregular; each wavering cry was interrupted at its middle by the goat's desperate sucking at the air it couldn't breathe. Soon, nothing.

Vassilis stretched, complaining, up into the tree and sawed, grunting, through the taut rope. The corpse dropped; warm blood spattered her shins and shoes.

"Fetch that tablecloth, Irini. Quickly." He pointed to a sheet of blue-checked plastic by the yard door. She spread it where the blood was worst. Vassilis took hold of the forelegs and heaved the carcass onto the plastic.

Complaining, he knelt beside it. With the point of his knife, he made the first cuts at the inside legs, delicate incisions to separate skin from flesh. He sliced, carefully and shallow, down the belly. Then, tugging gently, he peeled off the pelt, expertly, in one piece, like tearing Fablon from its backing, revealing beneath a layer of creamy fat, bubbled with air pockets, crackling like static.

He handed the warm pelt to Irini.

"Hang it over there, on the line." He waved a gory hand towards the washing line, where two white bed sheets hung billowing in the breeze. There was no line left, and Irini's hands were too bloody to unpeg and fold the sheets, so she hung the skin over the lowest branches of the lemon tree.

"Bucket!"

She knelt beside him. He turned the flayed beast on its spine.

"Get the legs," he said, "and hold it steady."

But it was hard; the greasy flesh slipped under her hands. The goat's strange eyes were still bright, but bulged in the stripped skull; its little teeth grinned a rictus grin.

Vassilis cut deep, from chest to scrotum, the stinking guts bursting through the incision as it opened. Irini let go of the hind legs to steer the guts into the bucket, but, one-handed, she couldn't control them. They spilled like water; like live things, they slithered over the rim.

Vassilis swore, and cursed the goat. At his armpits, his shirt was damp with half-moons of sweat, and the smell of his musk was potent. He lifted the spilled guts into the bucket, then plunged his hands into the body cavity, feeling around with the knife to cut them free, scooping out what was left—the gray ropes of shit-filled intestine, the spongy lungs, the beast's still heart.

"You're done," he said. "I'd better fetch the saw."

At the yard well, the steel can they used to draw water stood empty on the well's stone rim. Holding the blue nylon string, she dropped the can into the narrow shaft, where, unseen in the dark, it slapped the surface of the water and, filling, began to grow heavy. She hauled up the can, and splashed cold water over her rank, sticky hands.

Angeliki brought a teacup, and a bottle of washing-up liquid; scooping water from the can, she rinsed the soap from Irini's hands as Irini rubbed at them. There was blood behind her nails, dark as dirt; though she rubbed and rinsed and soaked her hands there, the blood remained.

"Have you heard from your mother?" asked Angeliki. "We haven't seen her for a while."

She handed Irini a towel; its pattern was faded, its fabric almost brittle from over-washing.

Irini wiped her hands.

"I spoke to her two days ago," she said. "She's going up to Athens to see my sister. She likes to spend time with the children."

"Grandchildren are such a blessing," said Angeliki. "She'll have more time for you, I expect, when your little ones come along."

"I used to go with her," said Irini, "before I married. I miss the children too. And I love the city. My sister used to take me dancing, sometimes. One night I danced so much, my feet bled."

Angeliki sniffed.

"The city's dirty," she said. "All crowds and traffic. And I don't know what kind of man your sister's married to—what kind of man lets his wife go dancing with her unmarried sister? Who was your chaperone?"

"He was," said Irini. "My brother-in-law loves to dance."

Taking the towel from Irini, Angeliki folded it square, taking the time to match corner exactly to corner.

"Andreas was never a dancer," she said, "and I've never thought much of married women who dance. It wouldn't surprise me if all that dancing was at the root of your problems down below. And I'm surprised your sister's managed to make time to have children if she's out dancing every night."

"Not every night," objected Irini. "Once in a while."

"Even so. There's not many women here who'd compromise their reputations for a night kicking up their heels."

"I think that's a great shame," said Irini. "An evening's dancing once in a while would be marvelous for all of us. It would break the monotony."

"I don't know what you mean by monotony," said Angeliki, huffily. "We're all perfectly happy as we are, thank you."

❖

Walking the road home, she held her share of the kill at arm's length. The sharp spike of a roughly sawn rib had punched a hole in the plastic bag; through the hole, blood dripped, marking her trail downhill, showing exactly the route she had taken: where she had veered to the left, where she had stepped onto the verge to let a motorbike pass.

As she came within sight of the house, she caught the sound of an engine. A red truck rolled past her; the driver blew his horn and waved. Irini didn't know who it was. By the time she had remembered Theo and turned to wave, he had already disappeared around the bend in the road.

Days later, Irini was returning home from St. Savas's Bay. She walked down there often while Andreas was away; it had become her habit to go and look for the boat returning to port, even when she knew it was impossible he would be there, when he had been gone only a day or so. She walked slowly, idly reviewing the vegetation in the verges, sometimes picking a few edible leaves for salad or wild flowers for the table. At the end of the quay, she would sit a few minutes on the same bollard, scanning the horizon for the boat she knew she wouldn't see; then, not seeing it, she would wander along the narrow beach, half-heartedly looking for shells on the gritty sand and for octopus in the shallows. Often, she would pay Nikos a visit; sometimes, she went the other way, towards the mountains. When the clock struck twelve, she would head back up the road, impelled by convention to be in the house by lunchtime.

This time, as the red truck approached, she turned to face it. She saw his dark face smiling behind the windscreen, and his hand raised to her.

She raised her hand to him. And as he disappeared around the bend, she found she was smiling, too.

Here's how it started: innocently. I saw her on the road sometimes, walking. She seemed, not lonely, that's not the right word; self-contained, perhaps. She looked as if her mind was somewhere else. She always walked alone, and she always seemed to be walking for the sake of it, aimlessly. Killing time. I waved to her. I smiled. I didn't feel it was wrong, but I knew in my heart that it was something to be hidden, because if I had anyone with me in the truck I would pretend I hadn't seen her. She was cautious at first, a little mystified probably as to why I was so friendly in this place where men and women may not be friends. The first time she smiled, a little part of me came alive with a kind of happiness I had not known before. You will say, of course, that I should have seen the danger. But once a candle has been lit in the darkness, who wants to snuff it out? And what danger is there in one candle? One candle's worth of light isn't much to ask in a life, surely?

I was only playing. I was in control.

But that little candle flared up, and something caught fire.

Who could have guessed that one little candle burning in the dark would one day ignite—destroy—the fabric of my whole life?

The way I was drawn to her was a mystery. I never understood it, but, almost from the moment I first saw her, more than anything in the world I wanted to hold her hand.

In the beginning, he did no more than intrude, from time to time, on her thoughts. As one workman shouted to another out of sight, as the sound of hammering echoed down the valley, she would wonder, *Is that you?*

But then the changes began. There were unnecessary trips out of the house, to fetch groceries she didn't need or to take walks she didn't want, because she might see *him*. She took care with her clothes; she put on lipstick. He became, slowly, insidiously, the highlight of her days. He preyed on her thoughts, occupying far more of them than he had a right to. And in those thoughts grew a strengthening undertone of lust. She wanted to know how he looked without his clothes. Sometimes, when the sun was hot, he rolled up his shirt sleeves and dangled a naked, taut-muscled arm down the side of the truck as he drove. She wanted to reach out and touch it.

All this, this far. And, since the day of that fateful storm, not a single word spoken between them.

I saw her at the carnival. I went with Elpida and Panayitsa; Panayitsa was dressed as a Turkish princess, all chiffon and gold braid. And she was there. I'd seen her old man: he was selling fish on the harborside, making what he could before the people stopped eating fish for Lent. Amongst the folks in their Sunday best, he looked a scarecrow: his clothes were filthy, and he hadn't shaved for days. But he was going home to her.

I'd hoped she might be there. I had Panayitsa by the hand; I was afraid of losing her in the crowd. She was whining; she was cold, but she wouldn't wear the coat Elpida had brought because it hid her costume. So I bought her cinnamon doughnuts to shut her up. She was eating them, dripping honey and powdered cinnamon everywhere. Elpida had gone to find her mother; she was going to be mad at me for letting Panayitsa get in such a mess.

Suddenly, in the crowd I saw her. She was walking towards me, her eyes on my face. Then she was next to me, about to pass me, and she looked at me and smiled, such a pleased-to-see-you smile. She said my name, she said hello, and I smiled and said hello too. And then for a long moment she looked into my eyes and I remember thinking, how lovely your eyes are. In that moment, I understood that there was nothing innocent left in my feelings for her, nor in hers for me. I had a hard-on. When she walked away, she left me on fire.

Nine

The morning after he first met Nikos, the fat man was feeling under the weather. The malady from which he was suffering was self-inflicted. As evening fell, he had gone walking in the unlit, narrow backstreets and alleys which ran behind the main harbor, and found a taverna open for business. He had dined in the company of men: two old bachelors and a widower, a married man bored at home, two scowling youths with nowhere else to go. They had sat at decrepit tables between sacks of sprouting potatoes, cartons of paper napkins and crates of domestic wine and mineral water, calling out their conversation to each other, looking out onto the dark, deserted patio where in summer the visitors sat late over Greek salads and souvlakia. Now, the dried, dead, wind-scattered leaves of an overhead vine scuttered around the legs of the stacked-up patio chairs.

The fat man was hungry, but the chef was not in the mood to cook.

"It's out of season," he said. He was an underweight, unsmiling man, much in need, thought the fat man, of a decent meal, for his disposition as much as for his physique.

"Pork chops. That's it, take it or leave it." He picked at the inside of his nose with a long fingernail.

"Pork chops are fine," said the fat man, "as long as the pork is fresh. And I'll have an ouzo, well-watered, if you'd be so kind." He found a seat at a table in the corner, beside a door marked "WC." Beneath the door blew a draft which chilled the fat man's ankles and brought the faint, sharp smell of the urinal to his table.

Reluctantly, the chef threw a pork chop onto the smoking charcoal grill and, turning up the heat beneath a pan of well-used oil, peeled several poor-quality potatoes, digging out the black eyes and worm holes with the point of his knife.

The fat man sipped his ouzo and ate his chop; after he had eaten, he sat on a while, listening to the banter between the chef and his customers. He ordered another ouzo, and bought one for the chef, and the gesture—or the alcohol—worked magic. Small dishes of delicacies began to find their way to the fat man's table—a few sea urchins soused in olive oil and lemon, a plate of stewed wild bitter greens, some toasted bread with garlic sauce for dunking, a chunk of fried, salty-fleshed moray eel. The fat man sat, nibbling, listening, drinking, until the evening had slipped well into night. He paid his bill, and left a generous tip beneath his plate; then, weaving dangerously close to the deep, black water, he had wandered back along the harbor front to the cold discomfort of his hotel room.

And so this morning, an aching head and a precarious stomach caused him to lie dozing long after the clock at the harbor's end struck six. The water in the shower was only lukewarm, but he let it run over his scalp until the aching was reduced; shivering, he dried himself with the single hand-towel the hotel had provided.

He dressed with care. He took from his holdall a shirt of peacock blue, and put on his suit, the sheen of whose extraordinary gray cloth seemed at once to shift from lavender to teal, the perfect foil for his shirt. From a small jar, he took a fingerful of pomade fragrant with orange-flower and rose attar, and stroked it through the damp disorder of his curls. He ran the tip of a steel file behind his fingernails, and polished each one with a chamois buffer. He cleaned his teeth with powder freshened with cloves and wintergreen. His shoes he daubed with a full coat of whitener; while they dried, he stood in stockinged feet on the balcony of his room and watched the view.

The morning was bright, but cold. The fat man made his way to Jakos's *kafenion,* and found a seat amongst the workmen fortifying themselves for the day's work with strong coffee and cigarettes. The fat man drank one coffee, then ordered another. He lit a cigarette, but his hangover objected in a surge of nausea. The fat man, knowing better than to persist, stubbed it out.

In ones and twos, the workmen drifted off, to building sites and cargo boats, to sweeping roads and painting houses. As the last workman left the *kafenion,* Jakos picked up his empty cup and well-used ashtray and carried them inside. The fat man heard the rattle of china in the stone sink, but then Jakos returned to the doorway, and, leaning on the doorpost, gazed out across the sea, as if his heart and thoughts were very far away.

"What do I owe you?" asked the fat man.

Jakos turned his eyes towards him, and raised his chin.

"Three hundred," he said. "Just give me three."

The fat man placed a five-hundred–drachma note beneath his saucer.

"Maybe you can help me," he said. "There's someone I need to find."

"Who might that be?"

"One Thodoris Hatzistratis. You'll know him, I'm sure."

"I know Theo," agreed Jakos. His eyes returned to the distant horizon, where the pale sky met the sea. "But he won't be pleased to see you. He has a carpenter's shop, opposite the chandler's. Close by the taverna where you ate last night." The fat man understood his meaning; the grapevine's sources had been at work. "You'll find him there, about now. But don't let on it was me who told you where he was."

"I never disclose my sources," said the fat man. And, wishing the café owner good morning, he set off in search of his quarry.

He found the carpenter's shop without difficulty. It occupied the ground floor of a dilapidated building; the workshop windows were opaque with dirt, and lengths of timber—some blond and freshly cut, some weathered gray—were stacked against the walls. Its doors were craftsman-carved, but years unpainted and black-spotted with the holes of woodworm; an ancient lion's-head knocker snarled over a huge and ornate keyhole.

The fat man pushed at the doors, and found them locked. He stepped up close to the window; with the tip of his index finger he rubbed a small, clean circle in the grime and put his eye to it.

"Can I help you?"

The fat man stepped back sharply from the window, and turned to face the man who stood behind him. He was dark-complexioned, with the heavy eyebrows which suggested Arab blood; he might have been handsome, but his face had been spoiled by the lines of perpetual frowning.

And he was frowning now.

The fat man gave him a genial smile, and held out his hand.

"Might you be Theo Hatzistratis?" he asked.

The younger man didn't take his hand. He held an antique key whose shaft was the length of his palm and whose loop end was so large, it made a key ring for a dozen others. He inserted this key into the ornate keyhole, and turned it.

"What's your business with me?" he asked.

The fat man dropped his hand.

"My name is Diaktoros, Hermes Diaktoros. I'd like to speak to you, if I may."

"About what?" Theo pushed open the workshop door. From within, the fat man smelled sawdust, and varnish, and the cloying must of damp.

"I've been sent from Athens," he said, "to investigate the death of Irini Asimakopoulos."

Theo stood for a moment with his back to the fat man, looking into the workshop. When he turned, his face wore a puzzled smile.

"So why do you want to speak to me?" he asked.

The fat man was feeling unwell, and had no appetite for diplomacy, or being messed with. So he laid it on the line.

He said, "Because she's dead, and you were having an affair with her."

The smile left Theo's face.

"That's a damn lie," he said, coldly.

The fat man took a step closer to Theo. "Where's the lie?" he asked. "She's dead, isn't she? Undeniably rotting alone up there in the cemetery. Isn't she?"

Theo turned away from the fat man, and pulled the workshop door closed.

"I think she was in love with you," persisted the fat man. "Maybe very much in love. And I think you might have been in love with her. Maybe you still are. Are you, Theo?"

Theo turned the ancient key to lock the door and removed it from the keyhole.

"I didn't even know the woman," he said. "So I suggest you take your investigation elsewhere, and stop troubling innocent citizens like me."

And, slipping the keys into the pocket of his jacket, he sauntered away.

◆

It was the fat man's experience that nothing settles an abused and angry stomach better than the smooth, sweet softness of a custard slice.

At the baker's, he chose an almost perfect example, heavily dusted with icing sugar and cinnamon. He ate with relish, powdered sugar falling on his lapels and down the front of his shirt. He folded exactly in half the paper bag his confection had been supplied in, and tucked it in the front pocket of his holdall for later disposal, then took a blue, paisley-patterned silk handkerchief from his top pocket and used it to flick the sugar off his clothes. He put the handkerchief away, picked up the holdall, and, closing his eyes, squinted as if thinking hard, or trying to recall something to memory. Opening his eyes, he set off purposefully towards Jakos's *kafenion*.

Theo was there, alone at a table for two. The fat man sat down at his table. Theo stared off to one side, pretending, like a child, that the fat man was invisible.

The fat man leaned forward, and spoke low.

"I don't care, Theo," he said, "if you look at me or not when I'm talking to you, just so long as you listen. I have a job to do. That job is to find out who killed Irini Asimakopoulos. She may have killed herself. Or you may have killed her. Or someone else may have done it. I will find out. But it won't end there, because I don't just want to find out who killed her. I want to know *who was responsible for her death.* Which is not necessarily the same thing.

Responsibility is the key here, Theo. So I'm going to leave you alone for a while to think long and hard about your part in this tragedy—because I *know* you played a starring role, my friend—and the next time I see you, we'll have a proper heart-to-heart."

He stood up from his chair.

"A word of advice," he said. "Don't piss me off. I get nasty when I'm pissed off."

The fat man walked away, whistling, in the direction of the bus stop.

Ten

In a hundred different ways, she gave herself away. It was in the time she took to style her hair, and put on the make-up she had rarely worn before; it was in the money that she spent on lotions for her face and body. It was in the dowdy clothes she threw away, and the new, more flattering outfits she bought to take their place. It was in the way she neglected all the chores, and didn't care what food was on the table; it was in the time she didn't spend with him, and in her absence when his boat returned to port. It was in the way she went earlier to bed, so she could feign deep sleep when he came to join her, and in her disinclination to be touched, or kissed, or held, at any time of day. But it was clearest in her eyes, and their expression; they showed her love for him was fading, that her emotion was being channeled to a newer passion, somewhere—someone—else. It was, for him, the cruelest cut: to see affection shrink, and be replaced by cold indifference, and contempt.

When Love began to show her ugly face, Irini failed to recognize her, and so allowed her in. In her quiet life, the spark generated by the interested smile of an ordinary man — a man of no consequence — assumed a disproportionate importance, and Love, scenting opportunity, quick as a rat nipped through the open door.

It was hard to determine when or where the shift took place. Somehow, though, this man became sole occupant of her thoughts: first thought, when she awakened; last thought, before she slept. Slowly, lingeringly, she lost her heart, and all her freedoms — freedom of thought, freedom of action. Over herself, she had no control.

Failing to heed old Nikos's wise advice, she unwrapped the pretty, shining gift brought by the stranger in her dream. The comfortable armchair of her marriage was abandoned. All those quiet, dull — peaceful — days when she had walked, sewn, baked, complained of nothing to do — they were a memory now. Her time was taken up in sitting at the window, waiting for him to pass, afraid to move, afraid to miss the moment.

Pandora-like, she lifted the lid on Love's Box of Delights, and discovered that the flavors of Love are many. He met her eyes and smiled; she dipped into Ecstasy and Euphoria. How sweet they were, how she came alive at their taste! Her step was light; there was magic in the morning. He turned his head, pretending he did not know her in the street; she tasted bitter Despair and Devastation, and descended into blackness. Life was not worth the living, because he did not love her.

She tried Hope and Delusion, the brightest-shining offerings in the box of fool's gold. One day they would be together, she knew they would. Their love would last forever, of course it would. Their lives would be happy ever after; they would go away together, and start a new life. Of course they would.

She tasted Dreaming, that potent soporific. Dreaming led her gently to her chair near the window and abandoned her there, gazing out, for hour upon hour, watching, waiting. Dreaming sat next to Compulsion and Obsession in the box, and, taken together, they were a fatal combination; they rendered her inert. Compulsion and Obsession gave her neither rest nor peace, chaining her in the grooves of new habit until Hope left her late at night, releasing the sentinel to her bed.

But not to sleep. For there, in the deepest, darkest corner of the box, was the largest of the Delights, glowing red like hot coals. But this coal would not be cooled with water. This delight would have to burn itself out; Time and Habit are its only remedy.

It was Passion, dangerous and despicable, uninvited and presumptuous. Passion travelled straight to her groin and lodged there, glowing, a hot stone demanding the cooling touch of ice only one man could bring. Its heat spread through her body until she was on fire with the desire and need and longing to be touched, licked, shafted by him, only him, a longing so intense that soon it wiped out all the other delights, spreading through her existence like a virus, like rampant weeds in an untended garden, until she was no more than hot, lustful flesh demanding to be sated. In the night, she burned.

Andreas, not a complete fool, smelled the rottenness which had invaded their home. He was not to blame, he knew, for the changes in his wife. He himself had not changed. *She* was changed. Love, playing its dirty tricks, made her more attractive to him; she dressed well, wore perfume, had a light in her eyes which was not there before. But when he wanted her, she would not open her arms to hold him; like a port whore, open-eyed and uninvolved, she let him go through the motions, and afterwards left him alone in the bed, lonely and degraded.

He knew who was responsible; he named the offender, and made accusations which she laughingly denied. He had no proof. It drove him mad. When he began to shout, she curled her lip in distaste, and turned away.

"Where are you going?" Andreas's low voice came from the dark doorway of the room where she thought he was sleeping.

"Out."

"What for?"

"There's no milk."

He nodded very slowly, watching her, his lids low over his eyes. Lifting his hand to his mouth, he cleared his throat; the hand was shaking, vibrating with too much whisky and too little sleep. He looked disheveled, unkempt. His face had the red imprint of creases from the blanket he had used as a pillow; his shirt was crumpled, and stained, the fly of his trousers was part-unzipped.

He came towards her. She had her coat half on; she made to put her left arm in its sleeve.

"Just one moment, *madame*." His sarcasm was new; it

was pronounced and unnerving. "Come here." He beckoned to her, exaggeratedly, with his index finger. His eyes were red with alcohol and disturbed sleep. "Come here, *wife*."

He was making her uneasy; she didn't move.

"I won't be long," she said. It was lightness that was needed; she said it lightly.

He shouted, "Come here!"

She didn't know what had made him angry, or what would appease him. There had been outbursts lately—a plate smashed, a fist slammed on the table—small eruptions of the rage which had been growing in him, quietly, but steadily. She feared him then, but contempt made her foolhardy, and she goaded him—*Go on then, hit me, it's what you want to do*—instead of offering appeasement.

But this was going to be different, because he was somehow not the same.

She tried appeasement now; she began taking off her coat.

"If you don't want me to go," she said, feigning petulant indifference—innocence—"I won't go."

"I said come here!"

He lunged for her, grabbed her hair at its roots, close to the scalp, and pulled, forcing her head towards his face. He pulled her, whimpering, by the hair, across the kitchen to the store cupboard, slammed back the cupboard door.

"Let's look, shall we?" His reasonableness was counterfeit, touched with madness. "Let's look together, and see if we have any milk."

Her face was twisted with the pain from her scalp; in

her mind, she could see the next few minutes. And part of her said, "Don't fight him, just take it; it won't be so bad." But the pain from her head *was* bad, very bad, and the strength of his grip made it clear he could do to her whatever he liked. It was his to choose if she lived or died, and the terrifying violence coming off him was about to explode.

Because she knew what he was going to find in the cupboard. Because her obsession, her addiction, her need to find *him,* see *him,* had made her careless, and there was a price to pay for carelessness. Still the moment seemed a long time coming; he seemed to stand there minutes, hours, reviewing the shelves, before he found what he, too, knew was there.

He took the first tin of milk, the kind they used for coffee, and threw it across the room. It hit the wall, denting the plaster, and fell to the floor.

"There's no milk." Childishly, he mimicked her voice, her innocent assertion, her lie. "There's no fucking milk, she says! Here!" He pulled a second tin from the shelf, threw it at the wall. "You lying fucking bitch! A cupboard full of the fucking stuff and she says there's no milk!" He looked again in the cupboard. She began to cry, quietly, at the horror of it, at the stupidity of her attempted deception, as he found a liter carton of UHT milk, brightly patterned with a red-and-white cow. He held the carton up in front of her face; then, without warning, brought it down on her head. She screamed. He struck her again, on the back, then dropped the milk, deciding he preferred his knuckles. He held her face straight before him and punched. She felt her lip split, and the warmth of the blood as it reached her tongue. Where he had hit her, she expected pain, but her face felt numb. He hit her again, on the side of the head, so her ear sang. She dropped to her knees, fell onto all fours, and tried to crawl. For a moment, he held her back by her hair, until a clump came away in his hand, and he let go, to hold it up and look at what he had done. Sensing escape, she scrambled towards the underside of the table, but he kicked her hard up the backside, between the cheeks. She screamed again; or perhaps she had been screaming all along. He bent to grab her foot and, pulling her flat onto her face, dragged her back, full length, to the center of the floor where he could get at her. He kicked her in the ribs, and on her right side, something gave with excruciating pain. She curled into a ball, as small as she could make, forearms protecting her bleeding scalp, and he kept kicking, and kicking, and kicking, panting with the effort he was making. Then consciousness began to fade; an unknown voice inside was chanting, *Soon be over, soon be over.* Then the kicking stopped.

She stayed where she was, curled tight, arms around her head. She waited, not moving, trying to get a sense of where he was, what he was doing, what he was thinking. Minutes passed, in silence. The fear of renewed attack began to leave her.

She lowered her arms and opened her eyes. She could see his legs; he was still standing just in front of her. She raised her eyes further. His head was bowed onto his chest, his fists were clenched, and he was weeping.

Unsure which way to move to stand with the least

pain, she pushed herself onto her knees and sat back on her feet. Dazed, and faint, for a long while she remained still. He took a tentative step forward, but she held a hand up to him, and he stepped away. Wincing, clutching her ribs where the pain was worst, she grasped a corner of the table and heaved herself to her feet. She limped into the bedroom and lay down on the bed.

She heard the creaking of a floorboard as he appeared in the doorway, and turned her face towards him. His eyes were soft, sorry and swollen.

"Irini," he said. "Irinaki. Are you all right?" She turned her face away. He sat down heavily on the bed, and tried to take her hand; she pulled it away.

"Can I get you anything?"

"Just leave me alone," she said. Her voice sounded strange, unlike herself.

"Irini . . ." His eyes filled again with tears. "Irini, I can't take anymore. I can't stand it, the thought of you and him . . ."

She shouted, "Leave me alone!"

He stood, and paused a moment in the doorway, afraid to say more out of fear of the loss of her he was certain to provoke. She heard him shuffle away, like an old man, into the living room, and the creak of the sofa as he lay down.

She thought because of the pain and shock that she wouldn't sleep; but sleep must have come, because he woke her. He was out on the roof; he was sitting where on summer nights they used to sit together, holding hands. He was out there, alone in the cold, and he was singing. No words were decipherable—maybe there were none—but the notes of his voice were clear, and the hopelessness of his song clearer still. His soul was in it, and his heartbreak, his loss, his grief and his devastation: all were there. Without words, the lyric shone through: he loved her, he needed her, he couldn't bear the loss of her, yet she no longer wanted him. He knew he had lost her, and he was singing his pain to the mountains.

She wiped tears from her eyes. His anguish evoked in her an answering heartache she had not anticipated, a heartache which threatened to dispel the self-righteous anger she felt against him for the violence he had done her, and that anger was her only defense against her shame, and guilt. His pain was unbearable to him, and she was its cause; she had mistreated him and destroyed the life of quiet affection they had enjoyed together. She had let herself love another man. Andreas knew it, and to spare him disgrace, she must take the disgrace on herself, and leave him. It was impossible now that she should stay.

For some time she lay crying—for herself, for Andreas, for the sadness of their tragedy—until she thought of going to him, and trying to make things right. But as that thought came to her, Love put the Other into her mind, and reminded her that any kind or decent act towards Andreas—any reconciliation—would have unpalatable consequences.

She could not, would not, leave *him*. The answer, Love whispered, lay in duplicity. For Andreas, she might feel deeply sorry; but she should use that residual tender feeling to make their life together bearable, until the time was right for the lovers to declare themselves.

Still Andreas's song of love for her went on. Draining the last finger of whisky, he hurled the empty bottle into the night; somewhere on the hillside rocks it smashed, and he, despairing, sobbed.

Irini told herself that she was torn between the old love and the new, but didn't leave the bed they shared to comfort him. She told herself that it was for the best. But her heart, not fooled, allowed her no illusions; the light of truth shone brightly there, and showed her to herself for what she was—the ruthless, selfish creature Love had made her.

Eleven

The fat man paid George the bus driver his fare, and asked to be set down where the road began its downward gradient, just below the windmills. As the bus climbed slowly up the winding road, the fat man looked down on the almost deserted port. Around the headland, a vast, three-decked ferry slid slowly through the cobalt waters towards the harborside.

Beyond the windmills, George pulled off the road and braked to a stop. The fat man struggled from his seat, and, thanking the driver, climbed down from the bus, which set off downhill towards the heart of the village.

Below the road was a strip of grassy meadow where three milk-goats, each tethered by a foreleg, grazed; across the meadow lay a footpath, a muddy track worn through the grass, scattered with the droppings of the goats.

The fat man, thinking of his newly whitened shoes, hesitated; as he did so, a vehicle came into view below the windmills, making its way towards the village. The car was gray; on its side, it bore white lettering: *Astinomia*.

The fat man waited until the car rounded the bend. As

its driver caught sight of the fat man, he slowed the car, and brought it to a halt.

The Chief of Police wound down his window, and smiled a smile which didn't reach his eyes.

"Good morning," he said. "I'm surprised to see you still here. I thought you'd be catching the ferry that's just docked."

"Chief of Police, you do me a disservice," said the fat man. "I could hardly leave without notifying you of my findings."

"Still determinedly detecting?" smiled the Chief of Police. "Might I ask what you have detected, so far?"

"In truth, very little," answered the fat man. "But it is early days yet, early days. Tell me, which of these houses is the Asimakopoulos house?"

The Chief of Police raised his chin and laughed.

"So that's what brings you up here," he said. "Hot on the trail. The husband as prime suspect, I suppose. Don't trouble yourself. He didn't do it."

"What makes you so sure?" asked the fat man. "Because he told you so?"

"I'm telling you, don't waste your time. He's not the type."

"Anyone can be the type, if they're pushed to it," said the fat man. "The *crime passionel.* Spontaneous crime. Opportunist crime. I'm sure it's an area of which you have experience."

The Chief of Police looked at the fat man for a long moment, then shrugged.

"Talk to him if you like," he said. "He didn't do it. No one did it. It was suicide."

"So which is the house?"

"You can't see it from here. Ask the neighbors." He depressed the clutch, and put the car in gear.

"By the way," said the fat man, "you say you hail from Patmos."

The Chief of Police frowned, and flicked a speck of dust from his trouser leg.

"My people are from Patmos, yes," he said, uncertainly.

"I have good friends there," said the fat man. "Perhaps you know them?"

"Patmos is a large island," said the Chief of Police. "One can't know everyone. I'll wish you good hunting, Detective. I have business to attend to."

He let out the clutch, and drove away. The fat man set off across the meadow, painstakingly picking his way through the mud and the goat dung.

The path emerged on an alleyway paved with stones, interrupted all along its length by steps, a couple going up, three going down, to follow the contour of the hillside. At intervals, houses had been built on plots hewn out of the rock; beyond their terraced gardens, they faced the lower slopes of the mountains across the valley, where the white-walled cemetery lay. Above the clay-tiled roofs, darting swallows called. A cowering mongrel dog approached the fat man, and, head down and fawning, sniffed his shoes. The thin hair of its coat was in patches scratched away, where fleas had been tormenting it; a sore beneath its eye was weeping creamy pus. The fat man bent to stroke its head, but the dog slipped away, disappearing behind a derelict house where down-headed thistles grew high around the doorway. He whistled to the dog, and called to bring it back, but from the empty house came only silence.

The fat man continued along the street. A small child played on a trio of steps, running a yellow dumper-truck along their length, parking the truck in a garage he had constructed by setting flat stones across their perpendicular. The truck's axles were rusted from being left out in the rain; the boy's face was streaked with the red dirt of the mountains, and mucus ran from his nose to his upper lip. As the fat man approached, the boy watched him with mistrustful eyes, swiping away the tickling mucus with the sleeve of his sweater.

The fat man gave the boy a broad smile, and crouched beside him so their eyes were level. The boy's eyes were clear and brilliant blue; his face was solemn.

"Hello, son," said the fat man. "That's a fine truck you have there. They didn't have trucks like that when I was a boy."

The boy regarded him silently.

"May I see it?"

Abruptly, the boy whisked the truck out of sight behind his back, setting his lips in a line of defiance.

"You're very wise, son," said the fat man. "Never trust a stranger with your valued possessions. Do you like chocolate?"

The boy did not reply. The fat man unzipped his

holdall, and from somewhere within produced a bar of milk chocolate, wrapped in silver foil embossed with colorful, juggling clowns.

The boy met the fat man's eyes with his own.

"This is for you," said the fat man. "But you have to ask your mother first if you may have it."

The boy blinked.

"Go on," said the fat man. "Go and ask her. I'm sure she'll say yes."

The boy dropped the truck clattering to the pavement, and ran into the open doorway of a nearby house. The fat man picked up the truck, and thoughtfully spun the little plastic wheels, front, then rear.

"Can I help you?" A girl, no more than seventeen, stood in the doorway, holding the boy in her arms. Her sleeves were rolled to the elbows, and her hands were red, and damp. On her fingernails, the burgundy polish was chipped and flaking; the fingernails were bitten to the quick.

The fat man lay the truck down on the steps, beside its garage, and held up the chocolate.

"I offered this to your son," he said, "but I told him he must ask you first."

The boy pointed to the chocolate, and wriggled to be put down. The girl, hesitating, held him firm.

"I'm looking for the Asimakopoulos house," said the fat man. "Perhaps you can point me in the right direction."

The girl loosened her hold on the child, and, sliding to the ground, he ran to the fat man, hand outstretched. The fat man gave him the silver-wrapped bar, and the boy sat down on the steps, tearing at the foil.

"Say thank you, Petro," said the girl; but the child said nothing. He broke off a piece of chocolate and chewed it, wiping his nose again on his silvered sleeve.

"It's three doors down," said the girl. "The house with the green door."

"Many thanks," said the fat man, taking a step in the direction she had shown him. But the girl did not go back to her chores inside the house; she folded her arms, and stood watching the boy fill his mouth with chocolate.

The fat man hesitated.

"I wonder," he said, turning back to the girl, "will I find the family at home at this time?"

"Oh, they'll be there," said the girl. "Angeliki, she's mostly there, if she's not shopping."

"My business is with Andreas Asimakopoulos," said the fat man. "I was told I'd find him here."

"Oh," she said. "Him." She unfolded her arms, and called to the boy. "Petro, don't you get in a mess with that chocolate!"

"I'm sure Mr. Asimakopoulos is very upset by the death of his wife," said the fat man. "Isn't he?"

The girl tossed her head, giving a suggestion of the flirt she had been, before she was roped to domesticity.

"He makes a show of being upset," she said. "How genuine it is, only he knows."

"Did he not care for his wife, then?" asked the fat man. "I was given to understand he did."

"Who gave you to understand that?"

"People," said the fat man, evasively. "People hereabouts."

"He beat her," she said. "He used to drink too much, then go to work on her. Are you from the insurance?"

"What insurance?" asked the fat man.

"That's what I think happened," she said. "He took out life insurance, then bumped her off to collect it." She picked up a broom which leaned against the outside wall, and began to sweep the pavement before the door. "Don't pay. I wouldn't pay, if I were you. He doesn't deserve a single cent."

"I'll bear your words in mind," said the fat man. And winking at the chocolate-smeared boy, he walked away.

The ruby-flowered geraniums in their terracotta pots were in need of dead-heading, and no one had swept up the dry, yellowing leaves they had dropped. The fat man knocked, a second time, and from within the Asimakopoulos house, he heard a woman's footsteps, light but slow.

Angeliki Asimakopoulos opened the door only a crack; her face remained in shadow. There was a glistening of spittle at the corner of her mouth.

"Mrs. Asimakopoulos?"

"Yes?"

"My name is Hermes Diaktoros. I've come from Athens."

"I don't want to buy anything," she said. Her voice was slow, and blurred. "I never buy at the door."

"I'm not selling anything," said the fat man. "I'd like to speak, if I may, with your son Andreas."

"I don't think he can see anyone at the moment," she said, tentatively. "I'm sorry, but..."

"I wanted to talk to him about his wife. About Irini."

"They said there'd be no more questions," she said, uncertainly. "Mr. Zafiridis told us—"

"I don't work with Mr. Zafiridis," interrupted the fat man.

"I don't think Andreas will want to talk to anymore policemen. My husband says we're none of us to talk to the police again."

Behind her, a man spoke, too low for the fat man to hear his words.

She glanced over her shoulder, back into the house.

"It's just a salesman," she said.

But the fat man called past her, "Andreas Asimakopoulos, is that you? I'm here to give you my assistance! I'm here to investigate the death of your wife!"

There was silence, then the scraping of a chair pushed away from a table. A large, black-haired hand removed Angeliki's delicate one from the door's edge, and her face was replaced there by a man's. The five-day stubble of his beard was growing through gray; his eyes were red, and the skin beneath them sagged with the weight of misery.

"I'm not answering any more questions," he said, withdrawing behind the closing door.

"Wait," said the fat man. "I've come from Athens to help you. I'm here to find out who killed your wife."

The door reopened, and Andreas stood before the fat man. Bitterly, he smiled.

"You want to know who killed my wife?" he asked. "Come in then, and I'll tell you."

The shutters on the windows were all fastened; the light was dim, the room chilled, as though it had long been given up to melancholy. There was whisky on the table, a bottle three-quarters empty, a glass one-quarter full. Andreas motioned the fat man to a chair.

"Drink?" he offered. "I'm just having a little eye-opener myself. First of the day."

"Please just wait a moment, Andreas," said the fat man.

Angeliki stood uncertainly behind his chair, twisting her hands. The fat man turned to her. The buttons on her blouse were misfastened; one button at her neck was spare, one buttonhole at her waist unused.

"I wonder, madam," said the fat man, "if you'd be good enough to make us coffee. I take mine without sugar. You'll know how your son takes his, I'm sure."

Silently, she left them. Andreas put his hand out to his glass, but the fat man covered its rim with the palm of his hand.

"Wait," he said. "Before you take that drink, you and I must talk."

Andreas ran his tongue over his lips.

"Say what you have to say quickly, then," he said, "because I'm thirsty."

"I want you to tell me about what happened to Irini. Everything you know about her death."

Andreas threw back his head, and breathed a sigh which seemed to carry a lifetime's misery.

"I already told Zafiridis," he said.

"Zafiridis won't talk to me. He and I are not on the same team."

Andreas smiled.

"Don't give me that," he said. "Police is police, wherever you come from."

"I'm not a policeman, Andreas."

Andreas sat back upright in his chair, and looked at the fat man indignantly.

"If you're not the police, what the hell's my wife to do with you?"

"I work for a different authority," said the fat man, "a higher authority. Call me a private investigator, if you like."

"Her family sent you, then. You're acting for them."

"I'm acting in their interests, certainly."

"They think I did it, don't they?"

"What they think is immaterial—you'll find me totally impartial. I intend to discover for myself exactly where the responsibility lies."

Andreas placed his elbows on the table and put his head in his hands, hiding his face from the fat man. Around his neck, half-hidden in his graying chest hair, a crucifix glinted gold.

"There's no point in any investigations," said Andreas, wearily. "She's gone. That's it. It's nobody's business but mine. Leave me to grieve in peace. And for Christ's sake, give me my drink."

But the fat man moved the tumbler away.

"Mr. Zafiridis did tell me your wife's death was

suicide," said the fat man. "But I don't think she killed herself. I think someone else did." He paused. "It's true that some think that someone was you."

Andreas raised his head, and regarded the fat man through his tear-blasted eyes.

"Well," he said, "they can all just go fuck themselves. I loved my wife very much. I had no reason..."

He stopped.

"You were going to say," said the fat man, "that you had no reason to kill her. No motive. But I'm afraid you did, Andreas. You had the strongest motive a man could have to kill his wife. Jealousy."

Andreas gave a small bark of laughter.

"If you've come to blackmail me," he said, "you're wasting your time. I already paid Zafiridis, and I gave him plenty. He'd keep our name clean, he said. He said there'd be no more questions. Now you're here, so it looks like money poorly spent, wouldn't you say? Well, I'll tell you what I told him. I didn't kill her. She jumped off a cliff because that bastard used her and threw her away. I know who it was, and his time will come, believe me. He might as well have put a gun to her head and pulled the trigger himself. He's the guilty one! If you're looking for a killer, he's your man. Go and talk to him about the death of my wife."

"Be assured," said the fat man, "he is high up on my list. Where were you when your wife died?"

"I wasn't with her," he said. Slowly, he shook his head. "That's all I know. I wasn't with her, and I should have been."

"Were you there when the... when Irini was found?"

Andreas flinched from the memory. Noise, dust. Decay.

"Yes," he said. "For my sins, I was there. I reported her missing when I came home from Plati. She wasn't there. I thought she'd gone. I thought at first she'd gone with him."

"How did you know she hadn't?"

"Because I saw him. While I was making a fool of myself, asking around after my own wife's whereabouts, I saw him going about his business as if nothing was going on. And I was glad to see him, so glad, because I knew then she wasn't with him. So I thought then she'd gone to her mother's, and I called, sure she'd be there, but she wasn't. It was her mother who called the police."

"Why didn't you call them?"

"Because I had inside knowledge, didn't I? I didn't believe it was a police matter. I knew how things stood between us. I knew it was a miracle she hadn't gone before."

"Did you ever beat your wife, Andreas?"

There was a rattling of china as Angeliki carried in a tray from the kitchen. As she slid it onto the table, the tip of her tongue poked her lip in concentration, like a small child doing its best. She lay coffee and water before the fat man, coffee before Andreas.

"He won't drink it," she said. "It's whisky or nothing, these days. He'll drink himself into an early grave."

Andreas lowered his head back into his hands, but Angeliki, oblivious of her gaffe, went on.

"Try the water, sir," she pressed the fat man. "It's from

our own well. It's the sweetest water anywhere. Go on, try it."

Obligingly, the fat man took a sip from his glass. The water was cold; it held the taste of stone.

"It's excellent," said the fat man, politely. "Fit for the gods."

Satisfied, smiling, she left them. Thin wisps of steam rose from the coffee. Cautiously, the fat man sipped at it. It was sweet.

Andreas's eyes were on the whisky bottle.

"Did you beat her, Andreas?" asked the fat man, quietly.

"Oh, they'll all be running to tell you that," said Andreas, bitterly. "That's how they see me, now. The wife-beater who drove his wife—like Mother says—to an early grave. Do you think that's where I wanted her?"

"No, I don't," said the fat man. "So why don't you tell me how it was?"

"I loved my wife; that's how it was. We were happy. *I* was happy. I thought she was too. Just goes to show..." He sniffed, and rubbed at his nose with the back of a hard-skinned hand. The fat man thought of the small boy, playing with his truck in the street. "Things changed. Not overnight, but fast enough. One day she can't do enough for me, the next when I walk in a room, she walks out. There were new clothes, and make-up—and she was never home. Always out and about, walking, walking. When she wasn't walking, she was mooching by the window, looking for *him*. Look. I'm island born and bred, but I'm not a fool. I knew there was another man; I could smell him. It was like he was in the house with us, all the time. I couldn't stand it, the way she was, the way she despised me. She didn't want me there, in my own house. I did beat her. Once; it was only once."

"Once too many, my friend," said the fat man, sternly. "There can never be any place for violence between a man and a woman. By beating her, you desecrated the love you say you had for her."

"Do you think I'm not sorry? Well, let me tell you: I regret it more than anything I've ever done. No man was ever sorrier. It was the lying, and the thinking she was going to be with him; it maddened me, it made a madman of me. I didn't do it again. I left her alone, after that. I took myself off, spent my time at sea, came home from time to time to see—what a jerk I was, a total jerk—I came home to see if things had changed. I thought she'd get it out of her system. I thought I'd come home one day and it'd all be over. I prayed it would, and I was fool enough to think God was on my side." He gave another mirthless laugh. "God! What a yellow-bellied cuckold I was! I thought the best way was to leave them to it, for a while. Get out of the way. What I should have done was take the old man's shotgun, and shoot him like a dog. Straight through the heart..."

"Why didn't you?" asked the fat man.

Andreas glanced at the whisky glass just out of reach, and at the coffee cup before him. He picked up the coffee, and drank from it.

"My mother makes bad coffee," he said, "always too sweet. Irini made good coffee. Just so." He let his head roll back, and stared at the ceiling where threads of cobwebs dangled.

"So why didn't you shoot him?" the fat man asked again.

"Don't think I didn't want to," said Andreas. "I thought about it, night and day. I thought if I caught them together, I'd shoot them both. When I was fishing, it's all I thought about: killing him. There's nothing noble in why I didn't do it; it was cowardice, saving face. If I'd shot him, everyone would have known that bastard was screwing my wife."

There was silence. Andreas lowered his head and rubbed at his eyes with the heels of his hands.

"I don't believe you," said the fat man, quietly.

"Well," said Andreas, smiling. "That's your problem, friend."

"I don't believe," went on the fat man, "that there was nothing noble in your not seeking him out. I don't think you're a coward, Andreas. I don't think you'd have shot him, but if you'd taken your fists or a stick to him, no one would have blamed you. I think there was something else." Andreas drank again from his cup, but said nothing. "I think you didn't lay hands on him because you knew if you did, you'd disgrace her. You'd have had to divorce her, wouldn't you? Send her back to her mother, bags packed."

Andreas laughed.

"You got me," he said. His eyes were bright with tears. "Bang to rights. Guilty as charged. Pity me. A man—less than a man, a man without balls—who loved his wife so much, he'd take back another man's leavings. That's me. Poor fool that I am, I believed that if I waited around long enough, she and I could pick up the pieces. Only there are no pieces to pick up, are there? Pass me that glass now, friend."

"A moment more," said the fat man.

He bent to the floor, and, unzipping his holdall, took out a small Ziploc bag of herbs—dried flowerheads, seeds, small twigs and leaves—which he laid before Andreas.

"I said I wanted to help you, Andreas," said the fat man, "and I do. I believe—in spite of your attack on your wife—that you have a good and faithful heart." From the depths of his grief, Andreas sighed. "That heart is shattered, I know. Love has been cruel to you—almost impossibly so. Sometimes, the Fates cannot be excused, or forgiven. Your grief is unbearable to you, and so you seek comfort in a glass. That is natural. But drink will kill you, and I have something better. These," he patted the bag, "are herbs you will not know. I have gathered them on my travels. They will help you sleep, and calm your mind. Make tea with them, and drink a little—only a little—when you feel the need, when the pain in your heart is worst. And when you're feeling able, go back to sea. Do your work, and wait for time to pass. You will find love again; you have my word. One day, you'll tie up in a port not far from here, and she'll be there. Not Irini; none of us can bring her back. But she would want you to be happy—loved—again. And you will be, Andreas. In time, you will be."

Andreas turned to him; the fat man put an arm around his shoulders, and for a moment held him close.

"Courage, son," he said. "Have courage."

The fat man stood. Quietly, he left the house. In the street, the wind was freshening; behind the mountains, high banks of rain-filled clouds were swelling. Of the small boy and his mother, there was no sign. As the fat man pulled the door closed, a cockerel crowed; as its cry died away, from behind the door the fat man caught the sound of Andreas's weeping.

Twelve

"Theo? Theo!"

He broke off tracing the pattern on the kitchen tablecloth with his forefinger. Blue squares.

"Have you?" Elpida stood impatient at the stove, stirring; she had that look of whining ill temper he so disliked. From one pan came soft sizzling, and the savory smell of onions browning in hot oil; from another, steam, and a low bubbling. Where his finger had traced out the squares, a fat fly crawled.

"Have I what?"

"Got any money?"

"What for?"

"Have you been listening, Theo?"

He hadn't been listening; his mind had been elsewhere. He had been thinking, planning, scheming. Turning things over in his mind. He had been dreaming, of the woman he wanted. Hard-core dreams. He had another hard-on he didn't want Elpida to notice.

"What do you want money for?" he asked.

"Shoes."

"You've got too many shoes."

"For God's sake, Theo. Not for me. For Panayitsa."

He wanted no trouble. He leaned away from the table; sliding his hand into the pocket of his jeans, he pulled out all that was there—two thousand-drachma notes, and a few coins—and laid the money on the table.

"Is that enough?" He was impatient. This kind of trivia was anathema to him, these days.

"No." She looked confused, and annoyed; he knew the price of shoes. What he was offering her wouldn't cover a quarter of it.

He didn't want to be around her; he was restless in this house. He believed he was concealing it, but he was wrong. He hated to look at her, because she had changed for him, and he had lost sight of any qualities he had ever valued in her. And this kitchen, which he had known intimately all his married life, he saw with carping eyes—a long, low-ceilinged room ruined by faults. The pine-boarded floor sloped by so many degrees, he had—some years ago, on a day when they were happy—shored up the far side of the stove with wooden wedges so the saucepans as she cooked were on a level. Everywhere was cleaned, every day, because that was her life's work; there were no spiders in the corners where the sunlight never reached, no dust gathering in the grooves between the floorboards. They lived with the scents of compulsive domesticity always in their nostrils—laundry soap, bleach, starch, the ammoniac stink of Brasso—and the irritating touches her mother had taught her: the showy ornaments and gaudy icons, the doilies of hand-crocheted lace on every surface. And there, hanging above the fireplace, the great buffed and burnished copper pans that had been her grandmother's, symbols of the continuity of their line and of their calling. He thought them ugly. A memory came to him of Elpida polishing the pans, black-handed, proud, and smiling. He despised her for her pride now, and his guilty heart cringed.

To him, the room stank of poverty and scrimping, of making-do. The flimsy curtains were strung on a length of fishing twine suspended between two nails knocked into the flaking plaster. The tabletop was a piece of wood sawn from a cast-out door; beneath the blue-squared tablecloth, the depressions cut to take the hinges were clear. The seats of the four cane-bottomed chairs had gone into holes, so Elpida had made cushions to cover the damage, cutting the covers from old clothes, stuffing them with the remnants of a torn bed sheet.

He looked, and saw it all as a stranger would see it.

Is this all we have? he thought. *Is this all I've done?*

She said, "You can eat now, if you want."

He didn't give a damn about food.

"I'll eat later," he lied. He stood, and took his jacket from the peg. "I'm going out."

"Why are you going now, when the food's just ready?"

He had no answer; he didn't know. So he said, "I'm going to the bank."

"The bank closed an hour ago," she said.

No answer. He was gone.

She stirred the boiling chick-peas, caught one with a

spoon and, popping it in her mouth, bit on it. It was soft. She turned off the burner. Outside in the street, she could hear Panayitsa's shrieks amongst the others as the children played.

She opened the door and called out, "Panayitsa! Time to eat!"

But her shouting had no impact; the children yelled and sang and shouted as they played on, into the afternoon.

Outside, beneath the window, tires scattered the loose stones and gravel of the unmade road. A car slowed, and stopped. Above the idling engine, a tape was playing, traditional music, *rembetika,* slow and sad.

Elpida crossed to the window. In Theo's space, a silver Mercedes was parked. In its time, it had been a showpiece; its upholstery was soft, red leather, its trim walnut veneer and highly polished chrome. Now, it was a curiosity, the kind of car tycoons drove in black-and-white, after-midnight movies. Elpida knew the car, and its driver. Everyone knew Michaelis Kypreos.

Kypreos switched off the engine; the music stopped. The talismans dangling from the rear-view mirror—a turquoise-studded crucifix; a small, laminated icon of a rosy-cheeked madonna; a sachet of pot-pourri—became still.

Elpida switched off the iron, kicked off her slippers and put on her yard shoes. A length of straw was stuck to one sole with drying chicken shit.

Kypreos stood in the road, hands on his waist, looking up at the window. He was a big man, and ugly. *Face like an octopus's underside*, the people said. They didn't say it to his face. Kypreos had money, and influence. The people didn't like him, but his money bought their respect.

Kypreos began to shout up at the window.

"Carpenter! Carpenter! Are you there, God damn you?"

Elpida ran a hand through her lank hair and went out into the courtyard. As Kypreos strode towards her, she opened the door wide.

Kypreos was the kind of man who was never satisfied; he always wanted more. He had made his money somewhere in Africa, and packed up and left when the region's natives looked like winning their rebellion. In Africa, he said, he'd had a string of supermarkets; but the people talked about gun-running, and illegal interests in diamond mines. In Africa, he said, he had servants in his house. He had a mansion here, with gold taps in the bathroom; he slept (the people said) with his pretty young wife in a water-bed big enough for four. His wife, the people knew, was having an affair with a ferry-boat captain; but none of them had the temerity to tell Kypreos.

Kypreos had invested in some land up the coast. He was going into the tourist business, building apartments for rent to a German company he'd done a deal with. Theo got talking to him and persuaded him to give him the carpentry work—doors, windows and shutters. It was a big contract; for Theo, a coup. But Kypreos had his own ideas about how much he would pay.

"Listen," he said to Theo, as they discussed terms, "I'll do you a deal. Finish the job by mid-March, I'll give you 50 per cent on top of the price we've agreed. Finish after the first of April, I'll pay you half. If you work fast, you'll come out the winner."

They shook hands. Kypreos had clapped Theo on the back, and walked away, laughing, believing his money was safe — for when had anyone known any of these tradesmen finish a job on time? But Theo was smiling, and confident.

"I've made up my mind to get it done ahead of time," he told Elpida. "I want to see Kypreos's face when he hands over the cash."

From time to time, she'd ask him how it was going.

"I'm working every daylight hour," he'd said. "I'm working like a madman to get done."

"Where's Hatzistratis?" Kypreos was always loud, but today, he was shouting. There was rage in his reddening face, and in his tight, hard eyes. "Where is the idle son of a bitch?"

He stood too close to her; he smelled of fresh sweat, and warm leather, and the aniseed of ouzo. The neck of his shirt was unbuttoned too far, for a man of his age and corpulence; resting on the rise of his fat belly, a great, gold medallion embossed with the star of Macedonia hung on a heavy gold chain. Kypreos told the people the medallion had been worn by Alexander the Great, and some of them believed him; the truth was, he'd had it made by a goldsmith whose brother owed him money.

"He's not here," said Elpida. "He went out, over an hour ago."

"Well, where the hell has the son of a bitch gone?" shouted Kypreos. "Time is money!"

"I don't know," said Elpida. "I don't know where he's gone. If you want to come in and wait..."

"I haven't time to sit around waiting for carpenters!" roared Kypreos. "You can tell him if that job's not finished tomorrow I'll get someone else to do it. I've got the glazier waiting to go to work on the window-frames and half of them are still stacked up against the wall. He's not even been near the place for four days. He told me he'd be finished three weeks ago. And you can tell him if the job's not finished tomorrow, he'll not get one cent out of me."

She left her shoes outside the kitchen door and, in stockinged feet, wandered to the parlor sofa, where she lay down. At her temples, a headache threatened. Kypreos's words flew around her head, forming questions which had no answers. Theo hadn't been there, working; when he'd said he'd been there, he hadn't.

So where had he been?

And the money—he'd blown all that money. All the things it would have bought, all the worry it would have dispelled. Now, there'd be nothing. Not one cent.

The pulse at her temples grew stronger, and an ache

began, behind her right eye. If she'd known where he was now, she would have...killed him. But it was not the small voice which whispered of the possibility of betrayal, and faithlessness, which roused her; that, she preferred to ignore. He had lost them a winter's worth of wages, and that made her angry—so angry, it kindled into flame a smouldering ember of rebellion which had long lodged in her heart.

Eleni found her, still lying on the sofa, fingers pressed to the pulses in her temples.

"Are you sick?" she asked. She bent over her daughter and put a hand on her forehead, feeling for fever as if Elpida were a small child. Her mother's hand was cold; Elpida could smell vinegar on her breath.

"You don't look well," said Eleni. "I'll make you some tea."

"I don't want tea, Mama. It's just a headache. It'll pass."

"Is it that time of the month? Tea will do you good. I saw your ironing, in the kitchen. I'll bring it through here. Then you can stay where you are."

Elpida laid her hand across her eyes.

"You don't need to do the ironing, Mama," she protested. "For God's sake, let it wait."

But Eleni didn't hear her. She was already in the kitchen, making tea.

"Why have you bought this starch?" Eleni held up the bright yellow can and examined the small, white rectangle of its price ticket; the reading of small print was harder by the day, and, even compressing her eyes into a squint, the figures remained blurred. "I've told you not to buy this starch. Buy Evrika, I've told you. It's much better. This stuff, the nozzle gets clogged up. And I'm sure it's more expensive. Why pay more than you have to?"

"I like the smell of that one."

Elpida sipped the green-scented sage tea. It tasted bitter; her mother had infused the leaves too long. The pain had moved to the bridge of her nose, and she drew her eyebrows together to relax the tautness in the muscles of her forehead, creating an expression of bad temper.

Eleni rolled her sleeves up to her elbows. Elpida watched her bend to the plastic-lattice linen basket and take out one of Theo's crumpled shirts, spread the wrinkled sleeve on the ironing-board and spray it lightly with starch. Eleni lifted the iron. The tendons in her forearm tightened, and the blue veins there and at her wrists stood raised along the bloomless, winter-white skin. Elpida thought her mother had a physique, a strength, which didn't suit a lady—beneath the mottled fat (her mother was still gaining weight, despite the doctor's instructions), she had a laborer's arms. Elpida looked down at her own hands. They were chapped, and red; on her fingertips and the fleshy mounds of her palms, the skin was dry and hard, and discolored brown from the juices of chopped onions.

She listened to the quietness, to the sliding of the iron over cotton, the *psst-psst* of the starch spray, the hiss of steam. The steam released the freshness of laundry blown dry in the wind; it evoked nostalgia, memories of afternoon hours at home when she sat at her hated homework as Eleni ironed, and watched her.

"Kypreos was here a little while ago," she said.

"Oh yes?" Her mother folded the shirt, deftly tucking the sleeves in behind the torso. She laid the shirt on the end of the sofa. It might have been slid into polythene packaging and sold as new.

"He was looking for Theo."

"Wasn't he at the building site?"

Elpida didn't answer.

"Elpida?"

"He hasn't been there for days."

Eleni stood the iron on its base and took a small, pink T-shirt from the basket.

"So where's he been?" she asked.

"I don't know, Mama." Elpida pinched the bridge of her nose, but the pain stayed the same. "Kypreos said if the work's not finished tomorrow, he won't pay anything at all."

Elpida pressed the T-shirt's sleeves: right, left.

"I thought that job was worth millions," she said.

"It is. What should I do, Mama? If I say anything to Theo, he'll yell at me."

Eleni lay the folded T-shirt beside the cotton shirt, and picked out a pair of red-striped underpants.

"You leave him to me," she said.

"Mama," said Elpida, "why do women have to get married?"

She had dared to ask herself recently if she even liked him, or if he liked her. She knew exactly how he saw her:

malleable, pliable—the creature he had made her. His method had been simple, and she had been... in love, or fearful? Each time she failed to please him, to anticipate his wants and wishes, he dragged a suitcase from beneath the wardrobe and laid it on the bed. His message was clear: please me, or go back to your mother. She could not let the family's good name be smeared by such disgrace. She learned to do as she was told.

He had been a bastard, but not from the first day; from the eighth. Day eight of their marriage, early in the morning. Cigarettes and ashtray on the table. Coffee on the stove. It was her mother's doing, her mother's parsimony. *Economia.* "Use half a spoon of coffee in the pot, Elpida," she had said. "Then the packet will last twice as long." He had told her for a week to make the coffee stronger. She had resisted, because that was what her mother had told her to do. She served his coffee. He tasted it, and replaced the cup in its saucer. Then, slowly standing, he had pulled on his jacket, calmly lit a cigarette, put his cigarettes in his pocket and, with the back of his hand, swiped everything, all the new wedding-day gift china laid for breakfast, off the table to the floor. She remembered the crash of china shattered, the fast drip of coffee from table to floor, the bang of the door as he slammed it behind him. She had been terrified he would never come back. She had wept as she cleared up the mess, and cried all morning before Eleni found her.

But when she told her the story, her mother had laughed.

"Kori mou," she had said, "all men are like that. Your

duty is to do things his way. Take care, or he'll be running home to his mother, and think of your shame then."

The meals she had prepared for his lunch and dinner that day had congealed and been scraped into the chicken scraps hours before he came home. He wouldn't speak to her because there was nothing to eat. She had made him an omelet—he had sat at the table and watched her do it—and when she put it in front of him, he had stood up and, smiling, slipped it into the trash.

Now, consciousness was pricking. She felt cheated, conned, because she had kept her half of a deal which was bringing her no return. She had made a bad bargain. He was remote, preoccupied, disinterested. Uncaring.

Eleni took a pair of Theo's trousers from the basket.

"Getting married is something women do," she said. "They've always done it."

"But why have they?" asked Elpida. "The men don't love us. They don't think much of us at all."

He didn't love her. As she spoke the words, she knew them to be true.

Her mother laughed.

"No, sweetheart," she said, "they don't love us. Marriage isn't about love, or romance. Marriage is about security, and family, and having someone to provide for you. But mostly, it's about children. *That's* why women marry. Because then our men give us the greatest gift any woman can have, *kori mou*. They give us our babies. *That's* where we get our love from, sweetheart, and our respect—from them. Nothing else matters. Women will put up with anything, for the sake of the children."

Thirteen

Andreas had gone without saying when he would return. There had been no kiss goodbye, or fond waving from the quayside, just a door quietly closed and footsteps fading in the road outside. On her pillow, he left a note. *I am giving you time to think*, it read. *I love you. Your husband, Andreas.* As if she wouldn't remember who he was.

Twelve days slipped by. At first, his absence made her glad; it freed her to obsess, and indulge in her compulsions. But the days were long, and lonely, and the night noises—the scrabbling of vermin, the sighing of old timbers, the whisperings and rustlings in leaves and grass—affected her in a way they never had before.

Then, it began to rain. It rained heavily, and constantly, throughout the night; when morning came, the rain persisted, falling steadily from heavy clouds so low they hid the mountain peaks. The day was melancholy, tedious, and cold; she went nowhere, spoke to no one. Evening came early, and still the rain was falling. Irini made hot soup, and as she spooned thin noodles from the bowl, she thought of Andreas, and wondered where he was.

⯌

The room was dark, lit only by the trembling shadows cast by the television. The game-show host offered insincere condolences to his contestant, and with the onset of the signature music, the credits rolled. Beneath the rain on the roof tiles and the spattering of water leaking from the gutter, the street door opened quietly. The audience was still applauding, and as the game-show host, waving, smiling, bid Irini a very good night, an unheard figure crossed the kitchen and stood for a moment, watching her. Next, said the announcer, would come the news, followed by the weather for farmers.

"Irini."

His voice was altered, hoarse, and low, but she knew it; still, she was so badly startled her heart began to race. She turned to him. He made a ghastly apparition. His rain-soaked clothes clung to his limbs like leeches; his face was luminous in its pallor, and the blue phosphorescence of the television lit only its bones, so its cavities were black as the grim sockets of a skull.

Andreas...

It was the strange half-light, and the shock of being surprised that created the illusion; but for a moment, she believed it was his spirit who stood before her.

He's drowned himself, she thought. *Now he's come to take me with him.*

But the smell this ghostly Andreas brought with him was familiar. It was of fish, and stale tobacco—and the sour, acrid stink of vomit.

"Is that you, Andreas?" she asked. She was unsure. "Turn on the light, for God's sake."

The figure reached out with a slow hand and pressed the switch. In better light, his face was gray. To warm himself, he held his arms hugged to his body, but still he shivered, swaying slightly, as though still moving with the rhythm of his boat at sea. Passing her, he went unsteadily into the bedroom, where he dropped onto the bed and lay with his hands clutched on his stomach. There were spots of fever on his cheeks. Closing his eyes, he pinched the bridge of his nose against the pain of his aching head.

He put out his hand to her, and she took it in her own. His hand was icy, mottled purple.

"Irini," he said, "I need something to warm me. I feel cold inside."

She squeezed his hand; unlacing his boots, she pulled them from his feet.

"Take off those wet things," she said, and from the chest of drawers she handed him clean clothes. In the bathroom she found only one aspirin in the bottle. She made chamomile tea, and carried it to him on a tray with water and the single aspirin.

She plumped up the pillows at his back, and helped him sit to take the aspirin, and sip his tea.

"I had to come home," he said. "I was too ill to stay away." She recognized his words for what they were—apology—and felt the prick of self-reproach.

"How long have you been ill?" she asked.

"Two days. I ate some..."

He pressed the tea cup on her and hauled himself from the bed. Leaning on the wall for support, covering his mouth, he stumbled to the bathroom, and shut himself inside.

When he returned to the bed, his face was damp with sweat. He lay back on the pillows; his breathing was fast, and shallow. When she offered him the tea, he shook his head. He closed his eyes.

"You'd better get Mother," he said. "She'll know what to do."

She leaned over him and put her lips to his hot forehead.

"I'll be straight back," she said.

The rain had stopped, though water still dripped from the branches of the eucalyptus trees, and runnels ran in new channels they had cut in the stony dirt of the verges. By torchlight, the surface of the road glistened. The night was fresh with stirring greenery; in the gardens, snails were creeping out to feast. Except for the distant barking of a dog, the village was silent; in many houses, the windows were already dark.

But at her mother-in-law's, the lights still blazed. At the table, four men sat, each frowning at a hand of cards. At the center of the table was a pile of money, notes and coins, and an ashtray full of ground-out butts. By Vassilis's elbow was a tumbler of Metaxa; by his feet, the bottle was almost empty. Before the other men were glasses of retsina; scattered on the tablecloth were the hard half-shells of roasted pistachios. The men glanced towards her, but none spoke. Vassilis's color was high, and on his upper lip were tiny beads of sweat. He slammed a card down on the table: the ten of clubs. One of his opponents, slyly smiling, slid another banknote into the pile.

Silent in the corner sat Angeliki. The rose-pink cardigan she pulled around her shoulders was stained with drops of oil; her hands were busy with a piece of lace. The work was fine, white and delicate.

She left her chair to greet Irini.

"Welcome, welcome," she said. "Sit, sit." Anxiously, she looked around for a chair for Irini. The men occupied them all. "Sit here," she said, "sit in my chair. I don't mind standing. I've been sitting all day."

"Andreas is sick," said Irini. "He's asking for you. I've come to fetch you to our house."

"Mercy!" said Angeliki. She crossed herself. "I'll come. Of course I'll come. Do you hear this, Vassilis? Andreas is sick. He's asking for me. I'm going down to see what wants doing."

Deftly, Vassilis folded his cards into a stack and held them against his chest.

"What's wrong with him?" he asked.

"Oh," said Angeliki, "I don't know."

"Don't you think you'd better find out what's wrong with him, before you go running down there? Irini, what's wrong with him?"

"I don't know," said Irini. "He's got a bad headache. His stomach's bad. I think it's something he's eaten."

"He's poisoned, then! Good Lord above! Or maybe it's cold, cold in the stomach. It could be that. Has he been out in this rain?"

"Get your coat, woman," said Vassilis, "and go, instead of standing here prattling. You're always prattling. Sotiris, lay one down." He spread his cards back into a fan.

Angeliki was animated by the crisis, and by a rare sense of being wanted. Her face shone with purpose. In the street, she led the way, light-footed.

"Have you lemons in the house?" she asked. "And alcohol? We'll be needing both. If you don't have them, run up to Panayiotis's, and buy some. Get plenty of lemons; lemon juice is the thing for stomachs. I'll walk down and sit with that poor boy. And Irini—don't be dawdling and gossiping on the way."

Irini went quickly through the dark streets. The sinister yowling of unseen cats echoed down the alleys; by the builder's yard, a sleek rat scuttled into hiding. At the grocer's, the door was open onto the pathway, spreading yellow light onto the pools of rainwater which had formed in the hollows of the pavement stones. Beside a chiller cabinet low on stock (dry-ended half-rolls of mortadella and salami, an uncut wheel of hard cheese, a block of paper-wrapped feta), Panayiotis sat on a high stool. He was a miserly man: unappetizing as the cold meats were, he wouldn't spoil his customers with fresh until these were sold. The back of the shop (where he kept the cleaning products and the paper goods—soap powder, bleach and napkins) was in darkness; if Irini went that far, he'd stand, and switch the light on for her, and switch it off as soon as she had made her choice. He glanced at her, and, wishing her good evening, turned the page of the cheap paperback he was reading; its cover showed a Stetsoned cowboy in black silhouette against a sunset, and the author's name: Zane Grey. Amongst the canned carrots and the bottled garden peas, a small transistor radio crackled commentary on a soccer game.

Irini chose six lemons from the crate behind the door, and laid them on the scales; behind the boxes of at-home hair-dye, she found a bottle of medicinal alcohol and a packet of aspirin.

Panayiotis placed a chewing-gum wrapper inside his book to mark the page, and, slipping from his stool, took a pencil from behind his hairy ear. On a paper bag, he totted up her bill. Irini had no money. He sighed, and took an exercise book from beneath the counter; he rif-fled through the scribblings and the lists until he found her name. She watched as he carefully wrote the date, and the total she now owed; he must be watched, as he was prone to adding on a little extra.

She wished him good night. Panayiotis took up the paperback Western, and began to read.

The way home was deserted, the silence of night dis-turbed only by the trickling of water in the drains and gutters, and by her own footfall. The village was left behind. A rising wind was thinning out the clouds, and for a moment, the brilliance of the full moon's luminescence lit the valley, casting strange, crouching shadows from the thorny shrubs and cacti.

She was almost home — around the bend, the house would have been within sight — when she heard the sound of an engine behind her. She didn't look back, but stepped onto the muddy verge, out of its way. She waited for it to pass, watching the verges bloom in its headlamps, like green light spilled in the darkness.

But the vehicle didn't pass. It slowed, and pulled up alongside her, and the driver leaned over and pushed open the passenger door.

It was him.

She gazed at him, at his face half-hidden and beautiful in the shadows, and felt his eyes on her face. Her hands trembled; her heart beat too fast. The gods were, at last, being kind, and the moment she had longed for (for so very, very long) was here; but now, at the instant of commitment, she hesitated. She looked along the road, afraid of being seen, but there was no one. The time was here, and it was tempting, delicious, irresistible; it was shameful, and immoral, and betraying.

She had the bag of lemons in her hand, her anchor to the mundane.

She placed it in the footwell of the passenger seat, and climbed into the truck.

She pulled the door to, and closed them in together. At last, they were alone.

He reached over and gently squeezed her hand, as if he had shared her fantasies. She felt herself touched by divinity, and looked down at her hand, surprised to see it unchanged. Neither of them spoke; after all this time of waiting, what words could be spoken that would not debase the moment?

When he kissed her, she knew dreams do come true. She had grown hot so many times imagining this kiss, and now his lips were pressed on hers and his tongue was in her mouth. *I have died*, she thought, *and this is heaven.* She wanted to absorb him, take him into her, touch every part of him. She stroked and pulled at his hair, ran her hands over his muscled back and shoulders. She pulled his shirt up over his back and stroked his naked skin. Their breath was deep and fast; they nibbled, licked, sucked at what bare flesh they could find. He bit her neck; she pulled his hand up to her face, and sucked his fingers. His hands were on her thighs, and then between them, parting them; she spread them gladly. He pushed up the clothing from her breasts, and put his mouth to her hard nipples, then came back to her face, bit her lips and kissed her as if their lips would never again be separated. The gods were kind; their lips could not be separated, ever again, as they lost themselves in bliss.

Did seconds pass, or minutes? Neither could have said. For them, the world was burning, and suddenly the sky was lit by fire, transforming the scene of their consummation into white heat; their love was making its own white light, the better to see, and know, each other.

No. The light flooding the cab was from the headlights of a car pulled up behind them. The driver leaned on his horn.

"Shit," he said. She straightened her clothes and

smoothed her hair; he slammed the truck into gear and pulled off the road. The car eased past them, the dragon's eyes of its red tail-lights fading into the night.

"I'd better go," she said. He sighed.

As she opened the door, he said, "We'll work something out." He grasped her hand, and pressed it onto the hot hardness of his erection.

She used the same hand to pick up the bag of lemons. When he passed her on the road, she kissed the air he drove through.

Andreas had shut himself away in the bathroom; Angeliki was at the sink, rinsing a bowl with bleach. The house smelled both sanitary and sour, of Andreas's sickness.

Nothing mattered. He loved her, he wanted her, he burned for her, and the thrill, the ecstasy, the memory of his touch would carry her through anything—even the nursing of poor Andreas.

Fourteen

The bus was very late, and the wait at the quayside was long. The short bench beneath the wooden bus-shelter was already occupied, by a serene young girl who nursed a sleeping baby boy on her breast. Beside her sat a scowling youth with one arm bandaged and cradled in a muslin sling; his face was raw with weeping grazes.

The fat man seated himself on the steps of a stone staircase leading down into the water and watched the fish swim at his feet. A shoal of tiny, glittering fry moved as an entity, a tumbling ball shape-shifting like a cell seen through a microscope. The fledgling fish moved fast, but synchronously; they darted here, there, here, and there were no stragglers, no dissenters, no breakers from the pack, swimming together because their lives depended on it. It was a mindset, thought the fat man, adopted by far too many people: safety in conformity, running always with the herd. He thought of Nikos, and his view that everyone should settle in life for what they'd been given; then he was troubled about the old man, and wondered if he was well. He had promised Nikos another visit, before he left this place; he would go today, if the main business of his day left time.

By the time the bus arrived, a small crowd of passengers had gathered. They ushered the serene girl before them, to take her choice of seats; as she climbed aboard, her dreaming baby boy made little sucking movements with his lips, like kisses blown towards his doting mother.

A woman with a paper bag of pharmacy medicines spoke to the driver.

"You're late, George," she said. She didn't care (nothing was pressing), and the driver offered her no reason, but silently took the coins she held out to him.

The fat man squeezed into his preferred seat at the driver's back. The scowling youth was last to board; he offered George a note to pay his fare.

The driver looked the young man in the face, and smiled, unpleasantly.

"Well, well, well," he said. "So here you are, back with us after all this time. Where's that motorbike of yours, Sostis?"

From the base of his neck to the roots of his hair, the young man colored.

The driver slipped the banknote in his pocket, and began to pick out the smallest of his small change.

"D'you know," he said, still smiling, "I saw a bike just like that brute of yours only yesterday. But it can't have been yours. This one was in a ditch."

The youth's jaw tightened; he held out his hand for his change, but the driver held the many coins tight in his fist.

"So where is your bike today, Sostis? In the shop? Out of petrol? Here." He let the coins fall into the youth's hands. "Let it be a lesson to you."

The youth moved away to an empty seat.

"You can't tell 'em anything," said the driver. He released the handbrake, and the bus moved off. "They always know best."

On his mother's breast, the baby gave a gentle sigh.

The bus drew into the village square. The grocer's wife paused in her rearrangement of the pastel-colored broom handles which stood against the window of the tiny shop; she watched the passengers descend, as though waiting for someone she knew. At the hotel, the winter-fallen leaves had all been swept away, and an aluminum ladder leaned against the outside wall, where new paint was drying on the pale-blue stucco. Alone on the patio, an old man in a navy-blue seaman's cap rested on a solitary paint-splattered chair; he clutched a posy of white-petaled marguerites, and at their heart, a single garden rose, pink and fragrant. As the passengers descended, the old man limped across the square towards the bus.

The fat man touched the driver on the shoulder.

"I wonder, George," he said, "if you could advise me. I'm looking for a goatherd called Lukas. You'll know him, I expect."

George gave a snort, as if blowing a stray insect from his nostril, and rubbed a knuckle into his red eyes.

"Oh aye," he said, "I know Lukas. What in God's name do you want with him?"

"I want," said the fat man, evasively, "to find him."

"The boy's touched!" George tapped his forefinger to his temple. "Have they not told you that?"

"No," said the fat man. "No one's told me that."

The last of the passengers was gone; none remained except the fat man.

The old man put one hand on the doorpost, and one foot onto the bus's step, then waited, panting, for the impetus to haul himself aboard.

The driver put his foot to the accelerator, and revved the engine, chiding the old man.

"Come on, Nikolas, for God's sake," he said. "We're late enough already, without hanging about for you."

The fat man left his seat, and took the old man by his elbow to assist him. Beneath the thin cloth of his jacket, the skin slipped loose over the ends of bones.

"Allow me, sir," said the fat man.

The old man smiled at him. The craters of his cheeks sank in his vacant gums; the remnants of his hair were like blown cobwebs. The fat man lowered him into a seat across the aisle from his own.

"You'll be going to the cemetery, will you, Nikolas?" asked the driver.

"Yes," said the old man, "the cemetery, if you please." Anticipating the short journey, he smiled on, like a child at the promise of a treat.

George eased the bus into the narrow lane on the

square's far side. He raised his voice almost to a shout, to compensate for the thundering old diesel engine, and for talking with his back to his passengers.

"I don't know why you don't stop up there," he called. "It'd save us carrying you, when the time comes." As the smile left the old man's face, the driver laughed.

The fat man laid his palm on the old man's forearm, and leaned across to speak into his ear.

"Don't listen to him, friend," he said. "I see a good few years left for you, yet." He touched a conspiratorial finger to the side of his nose, and winked. "Your flowers are glorious," he added, louder. "Your wife's a lucky lady."

But the old man shook his head.

"I never married, sir," he said. "I never was blessed, that way. I'm taking these for a very good friend of mine, who passed away just recently."

"Not recently," challenged George. "A year ago, at least."

"Time passes," said the fat man. "As I get older, the years fly by. And you were telling me, driver, how I'd find this Lukas."

"I hope you've got your walking shoes on," called George.

"I have on my trusty winged sandals," replied the fat man, and held out his right foot. The tennis shoe was freshly whitened; the laces were new, and unmarked. The old man looked down at the shoe, and smiled. "So if you would tell me where I'll find him, I'd appreciate it."

"He has a house—hut—smallholding, God knows what you'd call it, up by Profitis Ilias," George said. "I can't take you that far. The road's no good, for this old bus. I could take you as far as St. Anna's. Take you about half an hour to walk from there. Maybe less. But you'll not find him at home at this time. He'll be out with the herd."

"He'll be home for his lunch, no doubt," said the fat man. "And by the time I get there, there won't be long to wait."

Where the road began its descent to St. Savas's Bay, George took the other fork, towards the mountains, winding beneath the spreading branches of a line of pomegranate trees, passing the half-built houses at the village boundary.

At the cemetery gates, the fat man took the old man's arm and helped him to the ground. The old man took his hand, and pressed it firmly between his own.

"God bless you, sir," he said. "God bless you for a saint."

The fat man waved away his thanks.

"It's absolutely nothing," he said. "No more than anyone would have done."

George put his foot to the accelerator, and revved the engine.

As the bus wound slowly up the mountain, the cemetery came back into view. The fat man watched as, far below, Nikolas picked his way amongst the tombs of marble, until, finding his friend, he removed his cap and, kneeling, bowed his head, laying down his wilting posy on the cold, white stone.

⁂

A mile and a half beyond the village, an ancient chapel looked down onto the sea. Its roof was circular, tiled in terracotta green with lichen; over its low doorway hung a bell, whose coiled rope hung on a meat hook driven into the wall.

"St. Anna's," said the driver. "Follow this road a little ways, until you come to the mule track, off to the right. That'll take you to Profitis Ilias. After that, you'll find your goatherd's house, the first you'll come to. The only one you'll come to! It's hard to miss, even for a stranger."

"My thanks to you, George," said the fat man. "How much do I owe you?"

The driver considered.

"Three hundred would be fair," he said. "Just give me three."

The fat man laid a thousand-drachma note on the dashboard.

"Keep the change," he said.

As the rumbling of the engine died away, the fat man listened to the sounds of the never-silent mountains. The wind stirred the pine trees into whispering; a screaming jay took flight, the beating of its wings echoing off the rocky hillsides which dropped away to the ocean.

He reached the mule track quickly; his stride was long, and for such a large man, he was exceedingly fast on his feet. Wide enough for one pack-laden donkey, the track's construction was of even-sized, square-hewn stones, laid in a pattern of precise geometry. It was a masterpiece of both artisan's craft, and art; it was a testament to the patience and time-to-spend of another era, an era which, in this place, was only just slipping over the horizon. Here was a piece of the heart of Greece, of Greece the immutable, of timeless, ageless Greece—mountains against a clear sky, a glimpse of sapphire sea, the scent of herbs carried on the wind. And stillness; except for the rustling of wind-stirred grasses, the stillness was profound—yet the fat man found himself listening for a sound not quite heard, for music dying away, as if ancient pan pipes might have played here, only moments ago.

The mule track led him over the inland hills, to the monastery of Profitis Ilias, whose white walls had for centuries enclosed communities of monks. The fat man, being curious, pushed open the wrought-iron gate leading into the chapel precincts. At the corner of the courtyard, honey bees crawled on a bush of rosemary in powder-blue flower. Outside the long refectory, a cup tied to a string lay on the well-cover, and the fat man, opening up the well, hauled up and sipped a cup of cool, clear water. He wandered into the dim, cold chapel, where unsmiling images of Profitis Ilias stared down from smoke-blackened walls. The air was sickly with old incense; overhead, the paraphernalia of Orthodoxy hung: candle chandeliers and ornate brass incense-burners.

The fat man took a candle from an alcove, but put no payment in the offertory box. Lighting the candle with his cigarette lighter, he held it up against the dark, illuminating the wall high above the arched door. There, a medieval fresco filled the wall, its simple, brilliant colors still intact. It depicted the damned being cast into hell; at its top sat Christ, surrounded by his saints. None was smiling; none intervened as they looked down on a group of mortals (all naked, all labeled with some vice—lust, greed, pride, avarice) being ordered by a frowning angel into the gaping mouth of a fearsome, fish-like monster. The fish-monster swam in a lake of red and yellow fire; red devils armed with pitchforks and instruments of torture (whose uses were unthinkable) teased and prodded the hell-bound crowd. Above all this, Christ, like royalty confronting a bad smell, seemed to have noticed nothing.

The fat man lowered the candle to inspect the floor, a mosaic of black pebbles inlaid with white, arranged to depict the creatures of the deep—a bloated fish with water spouting from its thick-lipped mouth, an octopus, a leaping dolphin. The fat man smiled. The Greeks who built this chapel had been half-hearted converts to Christianity and hell-fire; they had been smart enough to hedge their bets. In this floor was their appeasement to the Old Ones; these images of ocean creatures were all tributes to Poseidon.

Not far beyond Profitis Ilias, he found the small stone hut where Lukas made his home. It was a lonely place; the view from the single window was of empty hills, and broad, unending sky. A young kid, still pretty in its soft baby coat, was fenced inside a pen of chicken-wire; it held a bandaged foreleg off the ground, and bleated at the fat man as he rubbed its fluffy forehead with a knuckle.

Towards the sea, a solitary eagle drifted in slow circles.

Beside the closed door there stood a wooden chair, painted blue, entwined with delicate, painted flowers and crawling with painted ladybirds. The fat man took a seat upon the flowers, and, waiting, watched the view.

From below, there came a sharp whistle, and a shout. The fat man had been sleeping; the hands of his watch had moved on half an hour. A long-legged dog ran amongst the hillside scrub, catching its rough coat on the thorny bushes. Behind, a man was following. His gait was uneven; not quite a disability, but a limp. Seeing the fat man, the dog stood and, sniffing the air, began to bark. The man planted his staff firm on the ground, and looked up towards the fat man. The fat man raised a hand in greeting, but the man, not responding, demanded silence from the dog, and came on up the hillside. His hair was dirty dreadlocks on his shoulders; his soldier's fatigues were worn and torn, his army boots were pale with dust. He stood close to the fat man; he stank, of goat musk and sour sweat (yet light within the stench, the fat man caught the scent of meadow hay, and the sweetness of fresh milk). He had a black cloth patch across one eye; the other eye was clear, and brilliant blue. With that eye, he surveyed the fat man.

"Help you?" he said.

The fat man held out his hand.

"I'm Hermes Diaktoros, from Athens," he said.

"I know who you are, now I've seen you close." He turned, to avoid taking the fat man's offered hand, and whistled to the dog; it came to him, and sat down panting at his feet.

The fat man lowered his hand.

"In a small place, word gets about," he said. "You know me already; and I know you too, Lukas."

But Lukas didn't answer. He put his hand on the dog's head, and scratched behind its ear.

"I wonder if I could trouble you for a glass of water," asked the fat man, invoking the obligation of hospitality. A request for water could never be refused.

Lukas pulled a heavy key from his pocket, and turned it in the lock of the wooden door. He went inside and closed the door behind him; moments later, he reappeared carrying a glass of water which he handed to the fat man. The fat man drank it down. Lukas snatched back the empty glass.

"Now leave," he said.

The fat man folded his arms across his chest.

"Before I go," he said, "you and I must talk. About Irini Asimakopoulos."

"I've no time for talking," said Lukas. "I've chores to do. Animals to feed." He looked across to the chicken-wire pen, where the kid forlornly bleated.

"I won't take much of your time," said the fat man. "Just a question or two."

Lukas put his hand down to his crotch, and scratched there. The dog rolled back onto its hips, and, lifting one back leg high, nibbled at an itch on its scrotum.

"You'll excuse me for speaking plain," said Lukas. "I'm well known for speaking plain. I don't talk to policemen.

Never. I don't trust them." He called out to the kid, whose bleating was both sadder and more desperate. "I'm coming, sweetheart," he said, and she seemed to understand, because the bleating ceased. He turned back to the fat man, and added, "No offense."

"None necessary," said the fat man, cheerfully. "You and I have much in common, Lukas. I don't trust policemen either. That's why I'm here."

"Word is, down town, you're big police. To ruffle Zafiridis."

"I may ruffle Zafiridis, if I get the chance," replied the fat man. "But I'm an investigator, not a policeman. I'm here to find out how Irini died. I think you'll find the police have closed their case." He slapped his thigh. "I almost forgot. I brought you something." He reached for his holdall, and, unzipping it, produced a loaf of crusty, fresh-baked bread which he held out to Lukas. "In case you didn't get to the baker's today," he said.

Silently, Lukas regarded the fat man. He took the loaf, and went inside the house. When he returned, he carried a baby's bottle filled with milk, and gave it to the fat man.

"If you'll feed Angelina, I'll see what's to eat with that bread," he said.

The fat man smiled.

They ate feta and olives with the bread. The fat man was patient, and ate without speaking; when the loaf was half gone, Lukas spat out an olive pit, and said, "So what's your business with Irini?"

The fat man said, "I want to know how she died. I want to know *why* she died."

Lukas shrugged, as if all was clear.

"Some people say it was an accident. Some say suicide."

"Do you believe that, Lukas? Do you believe she killed herself?"

Lukas didn't answer.

The fat man cast his eyes over the empty landscape.

"Living up here," he said, "I'll bet a man learns to notice the smallest thing. Things no one else sees."

"I've got good eyes," said Lukas. "Never needed glasses. Not like my aunt. Her eyes are bad. She needs an operation, but she won't let them do it." He ripped another piece from the loaf, and cut again into the slab of feta.

"Did you ever see Irini?"

Lukas bit into the bread.

"I saw her sometimes, lately," he said. "She'd fixed herself a garden, village topside. I walk by that way when I go to my aunt's. If she was there, I'd go and chew the fat. I gave her some tips on growing vegetables. Goat shit, I told her, that's the stuff for tomatoes. But she wasn't much interested in vegetables. She wanted to grow flowers. I can't see the point in growing flowers. You can't eat them, can you?"

"I see logic in your horticulture," said the fat man, "but not much madness. Why do they call you 'mad'?"

"That should be obvious." The dog lay quiet at Lukas's feet. He bent, and gently stroked its head. "Because I'm different. They can't understand why anyone would want to be different, so they say I must be mad. Maybe they should just call me 'Different Lukas.' But that wouldn't be the same, would it? It would point up their prejudice, wouldn't it? And people don't like to face their own shortcomings. And they can't understand why I live up here, away from them. But the reason's simple: their noise and their squabbles and their traffic and their damned church bells, *they* drive me crazy. Up here, a man can think. I keep my animals for company. Animals are kinder than people, in the main."

"Most people find company in marriage," said the fat man.

"That's another strike against me, then, as far as they're concerned. I never married."

The fat man brushed a breadcrumb from his breast.

"Why didn't you marry?" he asked.

"You married?" asked Lukas.

"No."

"Why are you asking me, then? Seems to me you must already know a good reason not to marry. But I'll tell you my reason. Men and women don't mix. Don't think the same way, don't want the same things. Women want houses, and children. Men want food and sex. Here, they all marry to have sex. How long does that last? Six months? A year? Soon as the woman's pregnant, she doesn't need her man. That's it. It's all over. Except they're stuck with each other for the next fifty years. Men and women should be kept separate. Meet up to fuck at weekends."

"And what about love, Lukas?" asked the fat man, softly. "There's not much love, in your ideal world."

"You know what I think?" Lukas leaned back in his chair, and held his hands behind his head. "Love's the worst affliction known to man. Life's greatest curse. I fell in love once." For a moment, he was silent, and turned his face from the fat man. "She's married now, to someone else."

"I'm sorry."

Lukas turned back to the fat man with a grin, but the muscles of his face were tight, and the grin did not fit with the sadness welling in the goatherd's eyes.

"No need for sorry, friend," he said. "I reckon I had a lucky escape. Life's easy; I take what I can get. Tourist season, there's plenty for all. If I ever thought I was falling in love again, I'd take the next ship out of here."

"I cannot disagree with you, Lukas, that such a course of action would be sensible," said the fat man. "But others are not so prudent. I've seen your cousin, Andreas. The loss of Irini has almost cost him the will to live. He's taken it very hard." He shook his head. "Very hard."

"I was at the funeral," said Lukas. "I saw him there."

"Irini's dead, poor girl, and your cousin's life's in tatters," said the fat man. "Don't you agree that whoever is responsible should be found, and punished?"

"Of course," said Lukas, vehemently. "Only a fool wouldn't want that."

"Then you must help me."

Lukas slammed his hands down on his knees.

"I can't tell you, dammit," he protested. "It's more than my life's worth to tell you anything."

"But you do know something."

Lukas hesitated. "I saw something."

"What did you see?"

On his shirt cuff, there was a length of cotton where the fabric was frayed. He rolled the thread, backwards and forwards, between his thumb and forefinger.

"It didn't mean anything at the time," he said. "I didn't know that she was dead."

The fat man laid a hand on Lukas's forearm, and applied a little pressure in a squeeze.

"Lukas, you have to tell me what you saw."

He looked the fat man full in the face.

"If I trust you," he said, "if I tell you, you must swear never to repeat it. You must never give my name. Or they'll make sure I'm not around to tell the story twice."

"I give you my word. Now tell me. What did you see?"

"The day after she disappeared, I saw the police car, the Suzuki."

"Looking for Irini?"

"You might have thought so. But it was very early, barely light. I wasn't far away. I'd some beasts penned up there, for milking, and I went to give them water. I saw someone get into the police car. He wasn't in uniform, but I knew him anyway. It was Harris Chadiarakis."

"Ah, yes." The fat man recalled the man: the bovine desk sergeant. "And what was Mr. Chadiarakis doing?"

"Nothing. Just got in, turned the car around, and drove off. I saw him, clear as I see you now, parked at the top of the cliff where she was supposed to have fallen. *But this was two full days before they found her.* When I realized *where* they'd found her, I was scared. I thought, the police were supposed to have been looking for her, but it seemed to me they knew where she was, all along. So I kept my mouth shut. Except I told Nikos. He told me to forget everything I'd seen. And if you say anything, I'm a dead man. But I see the misery of my poor cousin now, and if those bastards..."

"Lukas," interrupted the fat man, "listen to me. I'll make use of what you've told me, but no one will ever know where I got the information. That's a promise." He glanced at his watch. "I must be on my way. It's a long walk back to town. But I'll leave this for you. A little 'thank you' for information received." From a pocket tucked away inside his jacket, the fat man withdrew a pint bottle of golden liquor, unlabelled. He held it out to Lukas. "You've a good heart, friend," he said, "and you'll appreciate this. It's a little-known specialty, from the North."

Taking the bottle, Lukas unscrewed the cap, and sniffed at the liquor.

"It smells," he said, "of warm honey."

He made to put the bottle to his lips, but with a shake of his finger the fat man stopped him.

"It's not for every day," he said. "You must treat this liquor with respect. Where I come from, they use it as an antidote to love. So, if you ever find a woman getting a foothold in your heart, take a shot of that, and keep your heart where it belongs—with you!"

They laughed, and Lukas clapped the fat man on the shoulder. The fat man picked up his holdall, and crouched to tickle the mongrel beneath its chin.

At the first bend in the track, he looked back, and would have waved goodbye; but on the lonely hillside there was no sign at all of either man or dog.

The fat man walked briskly back to the road and headed in the direction of the village. Approaching the turn for St. Savas's Bay, he glanced at the gold-plated watch on his wrist, and decided there was enough light left in the waning afternoon to pay another visit.

At the seafront, the onshore breeze blew cold. Nikos's terrace was deserted, but the door to his kitchen stood open, and from within a radio played the primitive music of the islands: harshly scraped fiddles, a woman's nasal chant. The fat man stepped up to the door, and knocked. Immediately the radio was silenced.

"Nikos!"

He caught the chink of glass as a bottle was replaced amongst the liqueurs and whiskies. Then came a light belch and a profanity.

The fat man knocked again.

"Nikos! It's me, Diaktoros! Are you there?"

"I'm here." Nikos stood before him in the doorway; his smile was unconvincing, and the sagging skin beneath his eyes spoke of insomnia.

The fat man frowned.

"Forgive my bluntness," he said, "but you look unwell, my friend."

Nikos laid a hand across his belly.

"I have a bit of pain sometimes," he admitted. "It

comes and goes, but lately the coming has been longer than the going." He winced, and his face grew pallid.

The fat man took his elbow, and guided him towards the terrace chairs.

"Sit," said the fat man. "Rest. If you'll permit me, I'll take the liberty of making you some tea."

Nikos shook his head.

"No tea," he said. "I don't want anything. But help yourself to something from the shelf—whisky, Metaxa, whatever takes your fancy. Then come and sit with me; you'll take my mind off whatever's eating my guts. You'll be interested in some news I've had of our good friend Zafiridis."

He closed his eyes, and waited for the pain to pass. The fat man lay down his holdall, and turned his back on Nikos to hide the bag from view; unzipping one of its side pockets, he withdrew a cork-stoppered blue glass vial and concealed it in his hand. Inside the disorderly kitchen, he poured himself a generous measure of whisky, then filled a second glass with water from the slow-running tap. Uncorking the vial, he let three drops fall into the water glass, where they spread slow as smoke, tinting the water the lightest pink.

"I brought you some water," said the fat man, sitting down at the table, "because I hate to drink alone. *Yammas*." He raised his glass to Nikos, who, out of habit, chinked it with his own. The fat man sipped his whisky; Nikos took a deep swallow of water, and the fat man smiled.

"I've been to see Lukas," he said. "We had a most interesting conversation. A very *useful* conversation, in fact."

"I'm pleased to hear it," said Nikos. His pallor was lifting; there was a glow about his cheeks as if long-absent warmth was finally reaching them.

"You said you'd news of Zafiridis," prompted the fat man.

The pain in Nikos's stomach was easing. He sat back in his chair, stretched his feet in front of him and crossed his hands on his stomach.

"I have indeed," he said. "According to George the bus driver, our much esteemed Chief of Police has been having some trouble with his car."

The fat man frowned, remembering the police car in perfect running order.

"Mechanical trouble?"

"In a manner of speaking," said Nikos. "Someone removed all its wheels."

The fat man laughed, and raised his glass again.

"Here's to the thief," he said. He sipped at his whisky, watching Nikos closely as he too took a drink. "Do we have his name, or a motive for the crime?"

"As a matter of fact, we've both. And we know as well the criminal's punishment, which is, I'm afraid, no laughing matter. There's been a dispute, about money. It seems that, keen as he is in his official role to collect in fines and fees, Mr. Zafiridis is far from prompt in paying his own debts."

"All the more inexcusable," said the fat man, "considering how fond he is of collecting monies not due to him at all. My information is that, for a man in his position, he's made himself quite wealthy."

"It comes as no surprise," said Nikos. "The constabulary

is well known for it. But it's despicable then that he has failed to pay his rent for the best part of a year. His landlord is George Psaros, a man who's known to struggle for money. He was a farmer, in a small way, until some years ago. He lost a leg to diabetes. The house that Zafiridis rents from him is his only source of income. The family have helped the old man out as best they could. But last night his two sons had had a drink, and went to claim the debt in their own way. They spirited away the police car's wheels, and left a note naming the price of their return—the exact sum Zafiridis owes their father in unpaid rent."

"I approve wholeheartedly," said the fat man. "The plan has wit. But the humor is at Zafiridis's expense—and he's not a man to enjoy being laughed at." He took lighter and cigarettes from his pocket, lit a cigarette and inhaled. "How does it stand?"

"Janis, the youngest, has been arrested. They've got him in the cells at the police station. Petros, the elder, Zafiridis told to put the wheels back and sent on his way. And Petros has done it; he thought he'd made his point, and shamed Zafiridis into paying his debts. But now the Chief's threatening to send Janis Psaros to the mainland; he's charged him with theft, resisting arrest, assault, you name it. He's going to throw the book at him. And he still hasn't paid the rent."

"It seems to me," said the fat man, "that the man wearing the uniform is more of a thief than his prisoner. And why lock up one brother and not the other? Is Janis more guilty than Petros?"

Nikos shook his head.

"It has nothing to do with guilt. It comes down to Zafiridis's . . . *proclivities.* Poor Janis has made a very bad mistake in taking him on; he's played right into Zafiridis's hands. While Janis is gone—safely shut away in a mainland jail—Zafiridis will doubtless take advantage of his absence. For all I know, he may already have done so."

"Take advantage in what way?"

"Young Janis has a very attractive wife. It's my belief that Mr. Zafiridis will happily abuse his position to advance his suit with Mrs. Psaros, especially if the lady needs Zafiridis's influence. And if Janis goes to the mainland, she'll need all the influence Zafiridis can muster to get her husband out of *that* jail."

The fat man man's expression was thoughtful. He drew again on his cigarette.

"Our Chief of Police seems to have a taste for other men's wives," said Nikos.

"The inclination towards forbidden fruit is unfortunate, but for a man in a position of trust to force himself on vulnerable women is unforgivable. Has our friend made a habit of doing so?"

Nikos considered.

"One other, at least," he said. "Manolis Mandrakis's wife. Manolis is a house-painter—a bit slow in his mind, but a reliable worker. He caught his wife with our man in the back of her father's shop. There was a divorce soon after. At the time, why she had entertained Zafiridis was a mystery; his attractions are all in his own head, as far as I can see. But the rumor went around for weeks that she'd been coerced—that her father's business was at stake. Maybe the family put that rumor about to restore its honor. Or maybe it was true."

The fat man's cigarette was burned down almost to the filter. He inhaled once more, and reluctantly stubbed it out.

"I told Zafiridis more than once," went on Nikos, "he paid too much attention to my Irini. I told him it wasn't appropriate, but an old man's warnings made no difference to him." He sighed. "It doesn't matter now—she's out of harm's way."

"Out of harm's way, yes," said the fat man, "and we're a step or two closer to finding out who put her there. I persuaded Lukas to talk to me by giving him my assurance he could rely absolutely on my discretion. He seemed concerned there'd be repercussions for the help he gave me."

Nikos clenched and stretched the fingers of one hand, loosening the cold-stiffened knuckles.

"You mention help," he said, "and I have been wondering if I have kept something from you which might have helped you."

"Then tell me now."

"I thought it had no connection with Irini. The lark belonged to Andreas, after all."

"Lark?"

"Andreas had a lark that he was fond of. He called the bird Milo. He caught it himself, with lime smeared on a twig. Irini always said Milo would sing only for Andreas, and not for her. When Milo died, I assumed it was a grudge against him—someone short-changed, some other petty grievance. They can be like that here: the smallest offense gets blown out of proportion. But the thought's come to me, lately—I've too much time for thoughts, these days—would someone with no close connection to them know the bird was Andreas's, and not Irini's?"

"What makes you think there was a grievance? Caged birds die every day."

"Not in this way. The bird died of a broken neck. It was done by human hand—the cage door was left open. At the time, it seemed unkind—and petty, as I say. But now, when I look back on it, the action has an undertone which seems . . . sinister."

The light of afternoon was fading. Outside the hotel, a single street-lamp cast pale shadows on the road. For the first time in many days, the pain in Nikos's stomach was gone, and he felt sleep might come, if he lay down. He yawned.

The fat man stood.

"I'll do my best for Janis Psaros," he said. "And for his wife. But you must rest. A few hours' sleep will build your strength."

The fat man held out his hand, and Nikos took it; the fat man's grip was firm, and his hand was warm, despite the cold.

"I'll call again, before too long," he said.

"No doubt you'll find me here," said Nikos. "I shan't be going far. And I'll be glad, my friend, to see you. Your company seems to do me a world of good."

❖

That night, for the first time in weeks, Nikos slept soundly for many hours.

At the Seagull Hotel, the fat man's bed was hard, and cold, and he heard the clock strike eleven, and twelve, before he fell asleep.

At half past midnight, Haroula Psaros—lying awake, and not thinking of sleeping—heard a car pull up outside the house. The engine ran on until Haroula left the bed, and, pulling on a robe, crossed to the window and looked out; as she did so, the police car's headlamps were extinguished, and the ignition was switched off.

Delighted, she rushed to greet Janis. But as she unlocked the house door, only one door slammed shut on the police car, and only one dark figure walked through the courtyard gate.

"Mrs. Psaros."

The Chief of Police removed his cap, and placed it beneath his arm. His oiled hair glistened in the yellow lamplight; the citrus scent of his aftershave was potent, as if very recently applied. As he looked her up and down, he smiled.

She pulled her robe close around her, clutching it tight about her neck.

She did not return his smile.

"Where's Janis?" she asked.

"May I come in?" He took a step towards her, and she, feeling him too close, stepped back. "Janis, I'm afraid, is still at the station. There's paperwork. Formalities. I'm sure you understand."

"When will he be home?"

His smile grew wider.

"Now that," he said, "depends largely on you. By rights, tomorrow I should hand him over to the mainland force. He should be charged there. But I've been thinking. I'm a reasonable man; I can be very reasonable. With your help, all that unpleasantness might be avoided. So, may I come in?"

Her instinct was to spit at him, and slam the door; but Janis was still locked in some cold cell, and the ferry for the mainland was leaving early in the morning.

If they took Janis away, who knew when he'd be back?

"I'll come down to the station with you now," she said. "Give me a minute, and I'll dress."

"That won't be necessary," he said.

He took another step towards her; it brought him inside the door, and with the toe of his polished boot he kicked it shut. His fingers stroked the hand that held the robe and moved onto a tress of long, loose hair.

His touch revolted her.

"So lovely," he breathed. "So very lovely. Let's sit down, and make ourselves comfortable. We've a great deal to discuss, you and I, if Janis is to be home with you tomorrow."

Fifteen

When my brother Takis came for me, I was out in the yard.

The memory of that day will never leave me. I was on edge. Every moment, I expected trouble, because deep in my heart, I knew it was impossible I'd get away with it. I'd been seen with her, and it wouldn't be too long before the storm would break over my head.

I was spending a lot of time thinking, trying to make sense of what was happening to me, looking for a way out. I had finally learned the meaning of every crass love song; I knew why people sang of being set on fire. I was burning up. I had this balls-ache which wouldn't leave me alone, a permanent hard-on, wet dreams. Nothing relieved it. Only one thing could relieve it, and that was Irini. I spent all my time resisting the urge to go to her, search her out, do what had to be done.

But there was nowhere we could go, nowhere I could take her. The spies had every angle covered. I could have gone to her house while her old man was away, climbed through the bedroom window, but I was afraid. And I didn't want it to be that way. I had this idea of romance, this twisted notion of honor, that it shouldn't be something sordid, cheap, one eye on the clock, the other on the door. I dreamed of long, lingering love made in comfort. I wanted a vast, soft bed made with white sheets. I wanted to take my time. God knows I'd waited; I'd waited so long, and I wanted to savor it. Like fine wine, a gourmet dinner, I wanted to relax and taste and enjoy her, sleep it off afterwards with her in my arms.

There seemed to be no answer, no solution—no no-risk solution. And I wasn't sure—not completely sure—what I wanted to happen next. I wanted the best of all worlds. I wanted to keep my wife and child, and I wanted free access to my loving mistress. But I was never stupid enough to believe it would be that way. I've known enough philanderers come to grief on the rocks of discovery to know for sure my have-it-all preference was not in the realms of the possible. I needed to make a decision. I was going to have to choose.

Here's the punch-line. The joke is, my hesitation, my indecision, my cowardice, my fear of being caught, my inability to dive in and be damned with the rest, my need to be smarter than them, meant I got caught before the sin was even committed. I, poor fool, never tasted the full sweetness of the forbidden fruit. I never had her. I was technically innocent, guilty only of very serious intent.

I had been thinking about Aunt Sofia. The night before my brother came for me, I dreamed of her. I dreamed she was in a meadow, a walled meadow. It was spring, a glorious day, and the meadow grass was green, and sweet; I could smell it, in my dream. Aunt Sofia was picking wild flowers; she held a bouquet, all purples and blues and pinks, scented and fabulous. She looked happy, not like she does in life; in life, she always seems unhappy. She was singing to herself, and I wanted to go and join her, pick myself some flowers in that fresh, enticing meadow. But the wall around the meadow—a stone wall—was as high as my shoulder, so I needed to find the gate. I began to walk around the outside of the meadow, looking for a way in. All the time I was calling to Aunt Sofia, "Aunt, Aunt, show me the gate." But she couldn't hear me, or paid me no attention. She just went on gathering flowers. I went around and around and around the meadow, but I couldn't find a way in.

I couldn't say why, but it felt like a bad dream. It had made me nervous. It had put Aunt Sofia in my mind as I threw scraps to our scrawny chickens.

Aunt Sofia was widowed young. I don't remember Uncle Stamatis; he was long gone before I was born. The story was he was lost in the high seas of the Bay of Biscay. It was a story never questioned; mention Biscay, and see the fear in the eyes of the old sailors as they cross themselves.

Then, one night in summer, some years ago, my father sat drinking with old Uncle George. And as they drank, they talked, and I heard something to make me understand that our family's fable about poor, drowned Uncle Stamatis was no more than a myth.

Great Uncle George wasn't much of a drinker. He said it gave him a headache. But that Easter, he'd done some work at St. Vassilis, and one of the priests there had given him a couple of bottles of their old wine. Uncle George had decided this evening was the time to drink them, and my father had been given the honor of joining him. It's a fine wine they make over there, mellow, and rare, only a barrel or two a year. And Father and Uncle George gave it its due; they sat there some hours, drinking, and talking.

I was sitting in the courtyard eating some of the black figs Uncle George brought with him. They were halfway into the second bottle, when Uncle George made a joke about Aunt Sofia. Sofia the Widowed Virgin, he called her. Perhaps, he said, they should get Stavros, the simpleton who all the men say is hung like a donkey, to go and sort her out. Perhaps, he said, Stavros would succeed where Uncle Stamatis had failed. Who wouldn't have legged it, he said, from a frigid old witch like her? My mother came running out of the kitchen then, and told the old fool to shut his mouth, but I'd heard enough by then to work it out for myself.

It had passed me by for years: Aunt Sofia was the skeleton in our family's closet. To me, she was a melancholy woman, who came and sat each day in our house and said next to nothing. She was my mother's sister, but a stranger would have taken her for my grandmother. She was, to me, like an old, gray-whiskered dog which, though it's past working and expensive to keep, still no one has the heart to take out the back and shoot. Put it out of its misery. She looked like that was what she needed: to be put out of her misery. She was an inconvenience to us all, but it was my mother's duty to take care of her. That's what I believed. They said she was a little touched. Sometimes she'd have a "turn," when for days at a time she'd do nothing but cry, silently. We learned to ignore her; we lived our lives around her, waiting for when she'd go home. There was talk, only once, of the Leros asylum. My mother slapped that idea down. She wouldn't be tainted by the disgrace of insanity.

But it was concealing disgrace which had ruined Sofia. Her husband had deserted her. She couldn't keep her man. He took off and left her to fend for herself.

So my family dressed her up, in her prime, as something respectable: a widow. For the elderly, at the end of their lives, the restricted life of a widow is no hardship. For the young, childless girl that Sofia was, it was cruel. Dressed always in black, barred from social activity, shut up alone for much of the time in that old house high up in the village; all this out of respect for a man who didn't deserve it and who she knew, all the family knew, wasn't even dead. For over thirty years she played her part, and lived with the knowledge that he might, one day, come back to the island and expose her to ridicule and shame. They made her guard the family honor when they could have demanded back her dowry and had the marriage annulled for non-consummation. As a virgin, she might have found another man willing to take her on and gone on to have children, a daughter to care for her, and grandchildren for her old age, the pleasure of their weddings and baptisms. All that, they denied her.

So maybe it was sixth sense that made me dream of Aunt Sofia, because that's what my brother brought news of that morning—scandal, and my own disgrace.

He watched me for a while with that superior, insolent look on his face which always makes me want to punch him. He considers himself above such low, domestic chores as feeding chickens. Mr. Free Spirit, old Fast-and-Loose. They'll get to him, and I've heard it'll be sooner rather than later; my mother has her eye on someone for him, and he doesn't even know it. He lit a cigarette, but I recall he didn't offer one to me. I didn't speak to him, and I thought he'd go away.

He finished his cigarette and dropped the butt in the dust, grinding it out with his foot.

He said, "What have you been up to, then?" He had a sly look on his face, but then, he often did.

I didn't take his meaning at first. I thought he was making a casual inquiry, so I just said, "Not much."

"If you call screwing Andreas the Fish's wife not much."

It came like a smack in the mouth, a broadside. His crudeness was no surprise, but it made me angry. He is that kind of man, but his disrespect to Irini stung. He reduced her in a sentence to the level of a fast fuck, when to me she was . . . everything.

But there was worse. They'd put our names together, and the storm was breaking. I had to know what evidence they had against me, but I was too smart to ask. I needed to know who'd been talking. I wanted to know who knew, or thought they knew. It would be useless to protest I hadn't slept with her. I was guilty, at the very least, of being seriously involved with another woman. I wanted to know exactly how deep in the shit I was. I wanted to know if her old man knew, and if he was coming after me.

I knew my face must have said it all—I'd felt the blood just drain away, like water tipped out of a bucket—so I made an effort to recompose myself, keeping my head down, pretending to look for eggs in the stinking chicken hut.

And while I had my head down, I decided my reaction would be no reaction.

"Is it right, then?" he asked.

"Is what right?" I turned and looked him in the eye.

"About you and Andreas the Fish's wife."

I laughed. "Where do you get this shit from?" I asked him. "Now piss off, before Elpida hears you."

"Father's waiting to talk to you." He smiled, pleased to be the bearer of bad news. He might have been lying, so I ignored him.

"At the house," he said, "now."

I barged him with my shoulder as I walked, all unconcern, into the house. I told Elpida I had some business to take care of and that I would be gone for a short while. Of course she wanted to know what business, so I ignored the question. Takis followed me out to the truck and got in the passenger side. I lit my cigarette before I got in, because I didn't want him to see my hands shake.

As we drove up to my mother's house we didn't speak. He volunteered nothing, and he was the last person I would ask.

They were waiting for me. My father was there, of course, and Uncle Janis, and Pappa Philippas the priest and, to my surprise, Uncle Louis. My father, Uncle Janis and Uncle Louis were all sitting at the table, looking serious and smoking. They had empty coffee cups in front of them. Pappa Philippas's coffee cup was full, but he had a half-empty glass of whisky beside it, poured from a bottle in the middle of the table. As Takis and I walked in, he took a large slug of spirit. Aunt Sofia was sitting in her usual place, in the corner, behind the door. My mother was in the kitchen; I couldn't see her, but in the awkward silence I could hear the clatter of crockery and saucepans. And for the first time I could ever remember, she didn't come to greet me, or call out my name. That made my heart sink. It told me things were bad.

My father stared at the table and said, "Come in, son. Come in and sit down." He didn't want to look at me, but Uncle Janis did; he gave a sort of shrug, which said, "You'd better do as he says, but this is nothing to do with me." He poured more whisky into the priest's glass, then held the bottle up, offering a shot to me. I shook my head, and sat down near my father. Takis sat over by the window, smirking, waiting for the party to get under way. My father coughed, and flicked ash off his cigarette. He must have been thinking hard about where to begin. My mother had stopped rattling plates. The kitchen was silent.

My father said, "What's been going on, son? We've heard you've been sleeping with some woman." His choice of words was polite, and unnatural for him—out of respect, I suppose, for Pappa Philippas and the women. If we'd been alone, he'd have spoken plain.

"Says who?" I sneered. It was an uninspired and childish response, but then, they were treating me like a child. They were all looking at me. I knew my face was red, partly in indignation and outrage—how could they treat me this way?—but mostly out of embarrassment. Having my supposed sexual encounters aired before my family (especially my own mother) and the village priest was mortifying, like a nightmare where you're running around naked, and everyone else is clothed.

My indignation was at the hypocrisy of all these men, with the possible exception (though not necessarily, by any means) of Pappa Philippas. All of them had had women on the side. My father had had two that I knew about; Uncle Janis had had more than I could count. And Uncle Louis knew that I knew about his sexual adventures; his liaisons at the army camp were common knowledge. Did he think that I'd forgotten the occasion when I caught him with his pants unzipped, behind the bakery, and that boy walking away, still counting his money?

But how could I challenge them, remind them of their misdemeanors? My mother was eavesdropping in the kitchen. And yet I was confused. They all knew themselves guilty on multiple counts of the crime with which I was charged. So what was special about my case?

My father said, "Uncle Louis saw you kissing her."

Ah. The truck behind us on the road. I glared at Uncle Louis. He was fiddling with the handle of his coffee cup. No point in further denial.

"Well?" I asked him. "And if you did, why didn't you keep

your big mouth shut? What brings you tittle-tattling up here? What the hell has it got to do with you?"

He looked pained, and patronizing.

"It was my duty," he said. "The honor of this family is at stake."

This was too much.

"The honor of this family?" I looked around the table at each of them in turn.

"And in what ways do you fine gentlemen uphold the honor of this family when it comes to screwing around?"

My father looked at me coldly. Then, there was a bark of laughter from Takis by the window. My father spun around in his chair.

"You," he yelled, "get out! Get out of this house until I say you can come back in it!"

Takis pulled himself out of his chair, indifferent and smiling, and slunk out the door. My father had handled him badly. He would be on his way, even now, to his friends to pass on this juicy tidbit of gossip.

Uncle Louis hadn't finished.

"When I saw you with that woman," he said, "I was not alone. Anna was with me."

No more needed to be said. Anna, his wife. My wife's cousin.

I was suddenly more frightened than embarrassed or angry, afraid of what would happen if word reached Elpida's ears. I was afraid of the tears and the scenes, of the long, wakeful nights with my wife sobbing beside me. I was afraid of the dressing-down from my father-in-law, and the sulky silence of my mother-in-law. I was afraid of the whispers as I passed people in the street. I was afraid of the loss of standing, and of losing face, and of having nowhere to run.

"Has she said anything?" I asked.

"Not yet," said my father.

So I didn't hesitate.

"What do you want me to do?" I asked.

My father had it all planned, had his words—so melodramatic—all thought out.

"Swear," he said, "on the life of your daughter, and on the blood of Christ, that you will not go near that woman again, and we will protect you."

So I swore. It was the easy thing, and an act of pure cowardice. Pappa Philippas moved his attention away from his whisky glass long enough to hold out his hand and I kissed the ring on his finger to seal the oath. They had got me, and nailed me down, in under three minutes.

In those early hours of discovery, my feelings for Irini simply evaporated. I was grateful to be free of them, and of that dreadful lust. Fear is a great antidote to lust. I believed I would easily forget her, and she me. We had, after all, been playing only a harmless game. At that moment, I never wanted to set eyes on her again.

But as I left my mother's, as I walked to the truck on legs that felt like water, someone called out to me. It was Aunt Sofia.

"Theo! Theo, wait!" she called. I was impatient with her. I wanted to speak to no one; I was hoping the earth would open up, and swallow me.

"What is it, Aunt?" I asked. She was clutching at my arm, and looking into my face.

"Theo, listen to me," she said. "You must listen. Think about what you've done, what they've made you do."

My pride made me stick up for myself.

"I've done nothing I didn't choose to do," I answered.

"Theo, look at me," she said. "It's too late for me now. But you can learn from my mistake. Some things are worth fighting for, son. If you love this woman, don't let them make you give her up. Stand up for yourself. Take her away from here. Just go, Theo. Step into the ring, son, and fight for her."

I looked at her. I heard her words, I suppose, but not what she was saying. And then I said a terrible thing. Here's where the lying started in earnest. I patted her on the shoulder and I said, "Don't worry yourself, Aunt. The woman is nothing to me."

I thought then she was going to cry. So I turned her gently around, and said, "Go back inside, Aunt, before you catch your death of cold."

It didn't matter, in the end, what we had decided, or what protection I had been promised as we sat, men of the world, around that table. Word was already out. Too many people knew too much. Takis had been talking, naturally, but the blame may not lie exclusively at his door. Any one of them—my father, my uncles, the priest—might have found the weight of such a gem of gossip too heavy a burden and felt the need to unload it, in confidence, and not to be repeated, to some acquaintance. And Anna, Louis's wife, was likely to have spread the word on their side of the family, in the guise of a selfless act of duty.

It started the next morning. Men I barely knew to wish "good morning" approached me in the street, and, like conspirators, took me by the arm and whispered, "Is it true, friend, you've been with Andreas the Fish's wife? What was she like?"

I'd push them away and laugh. I told them all the same thing: much as I'd like it to be true, it wasn't. If they believed me (and some did), they'd look disappointed and walk away. If they didn't believe me, they'd wink and slap me on the back, call me a randy dog. In their eyes, I'd joined the ranks of the real men, the screw-arounds who used women as they were meant to be used, the serial philanderers who dared, the insatiable adulterers with too much lead in their pencils for one woman to handle.

My life became a misery to me. I wanted to run away from it, but I had nowhere to go. Every time I had to walk in the house, or my mother-in-law's house, I felt sick with dread that the news might have penetrated the citadel, that the real horror and trouble was about to start. I was unable to behave naturally because I couldn't remember what natural, unworried, unguilty behavior was. If Elpida didn't smile at me when I walked in, I would probe and probe to find out why, irritating and annoying her. She became suspicious. As she pointed out, until recently I was totally indifferent as to whether she was smiling or not. I tried, unsubtly, to dissuade her from going out—to her relations, even to church. The churches were the most dangerous places of all. All those wagging tongues, gathered together there in one place. She went, against my wishes, and I paced the house until she returned, asking myself what the chances were that all those sharp, malicious women would be able to resist telling Elpida what they'd heard. Any one of them might have told her, one or two out of misguided friendship, the rest out of spite.

I wouldn't have the TV on; it masked the noise from the street, voices and footsteps of anyone approaching the house. I wanted to intercept any visitors, steer away any bearers of bad news, shoot any messengers. I took up residence in the kitchen, on guard at the kitchen table. It drove Elpida mad. I was in her way as she tried to work. But it was the only time I could relax slightly, the only time I was in control. I could see her, and I could see the door.

I hadn't slept properly for weeks, but where before lust for Irini and pleasurable plotting of sexual liaisons had kept me awake, now it was nightmarish fantasies of confrontation and crisis. Yet when I did sleep, it was often of Irini that I dreamed, but the dreams were no longer a pleasure. I was always hunting for her; I knew where she was and was on my way to her, but I always woke before I found her, and I woke feeling empty. I worked, but couldn't concentrate, making too many stupid mistakes until my father shouted at me to pull myself together or go home. I wouldn't go home, not in working hours. I drove up the mountains and hid there, knowing if anyone saw me they'd assume I'd planned a rendezvous, which could only make matters worse. I went into a church once, St. Lefteris's, lit candles and prayed with all my heart for an easy way out of the mess. Is that what I got?

I ate little, smoked too much, veered from manic good humor to foul temper and melancholy.

Elpida quickly drew the only logical conclusion. She went one day in tears to her mother, and told her I had found another woman.

Sixteen

It seemed to happen in a single day that Theo changed towards me. To everybody else, it was a day like any other; to me, it marked the first hours of a long and bitter end. He walked by me on the street, and there was no hello, no smile or backward glance. He turned his face from me—he turned away!—and passed me by, with no acknowledgement, as if I were a stranger. And I felt a little lurch of fear, and tears pricked my eyes, and I was cross with him; but I forgave him—it didn't take me long—by finding ways to justify his rudeness. I told myself that he was being prudent; the eyes and ears of spies were everywhere.

And then, one morning I was waiting in the post office, and as I stood in line, he came in too. I didn't need to look; I knew his voice as he called out to the postmaster. I knew his voice, because it brought deep blushes to my cheeks, and put a tremble in my fingers.

The queue was long; the new girl they had hired was inefficient, taking too long with every customer, even for the buying of a single stamp. Theo was impatient, and he shouted to the postmaster from the back of the queue. I remember his voice, and I remember his words; I've heard no more words from his mouth, since.

He shouted, "Stellios, give me back that envelope my wife dropped off this morning. She forgot to put the check in it."

And the postmaster broke off from weighing parcels, picked up a stack of stamped mail, and riffled through the envelopes, until he found the one that Theo's wife had brought.

He held it out for Theo.

And Theo, pushing his way forward to the counter, trod on my foot.

He didn't seem to notice—not me, nor that he'd hurt me. He offered no "excuse me," or "I'm sorry," which would have been good manners, even if I'd been a stranger.

And I began to realize that strangers were what he wanted us to be.

Outside, he was there, with friends. He had the envelope still in his hand; he was listening to a joke, and when the punch-line came, I heard him laugh much louder than the others.

It didn't hurt, so much, that he didn't say hello; it wouldn't have been so bad if he only hadn't looked in my direction. But what he did was far, far worse; he saw me there, and turned his back on me.

Days passed, and his remoteness persisted. She, at first, was desperate for contact, for some small sign that he still cared. More time passed, and she would have been grateful for a sign that he knew she existed; to him, it seemed, she had become invisible, and irrelevant. With no word of explanation, without a smile for friendship's sake or the simplest of goodbyes, he had left her.

She could not let him go so easily. She searched for

him in all the places she had been sure to find him, but he was gone. Hour after hour, she waited and watched at the window, but he never passed. In her distress, she became reckless; she walked by his house, brushed her hand against his truck, peered through its window to see again the setting of their magic. It was nothing but ordinary—just the cab of a truck. A blue glass charm against the evil eye hung from the rear-view mirror; an empty carton of strawberry-flavored milk lay on the floor. Of the man she had believed in love with her, she found no trace.

As she walked home, a vehicle slowed behind her. Her heart leapt, believing it was him, but the car which pulled alongside her was gray, and the man behind the wheel was Zafiridis. His hopes were high; he'd heard the whispers of her immorality, and what she'd given one, she'd surely give him too.

"Get in," he said. "I'll give you a ride. I'm going past your house."

His breath was sugary with peppermints, but at the gums, his teeth were thick with plaque.

"I prefer to walk," she said. "Thank you."

"It's no trouble. Get in."

His eyes ran over her body; they scanned her legs, and came to rest on her breasts.

"No," she said. "I prefer to walk."

He watched her go, enjoying how her hips moved, then turned the car and headed back the way he'd come. Her refusal was, to him, quite understandable; with her new reputation, she couldn't afford to be seen with any man. But he could tell by her expression that she wanted him; his timing had been off, nothing more. She wanted romance, and some gentle handling; and the time for romance was the night, when he could come and go, and no one would ever know they'd been together.

It was the hardest thing I ever had to do. At first, I thought it was going to be easy, because I was afraid of discovery and disgrace. I was looking after Number One, trying to believe it had all been a game and I was coming out of it unscathed. If only she doesn't make trouble, I thought. If only she doesn't make things difficult.

She never did.

She changed. I took something from her, without ever meaning to. Every time I cut her in the street, I could see her spirit shrink, though she pulled herself up tall, pretending not to care, because she thought I didn't care. And I didn't care, at first. I thought, she'll get over it. She'll have to. But I could see she wasn't getting over it, and neither, in my heart, was I. In both of us, the cut had gone too deep.

I set my face against her, and with no evidence to feed on, the gossip slowly died. But now came something unexpected: as my fear of exposure diminished, I began to miss her. I missed her more than I can say. My life lacked everything it had lacked before; there was nothing to look forward to except the endless trail of days all the same, the tedious business of life's dull progress. There were no highlights in my days or moments of joy, no liftings of the heart or soarings of the soul at the sight of her smile. As I had witnessed it leave her, the ability to smile left me. Sometimes as I passed her, face averted, in the street, I thought I could feel her reproachful eyes on me; I knew if I looked into her face, what I would see would be the question, Why? Like a dog that's been kicked, she began to cower from me, but, hand on heart, I'd never treat a dog of mine the way I treated her.

I wanted to explain to her; of course I did. I wanted to sit down with her, and tell her why it had to be that way.

But I was afraid to speak to her; I never dared. Not one more word ever passed between us.

What are you thinking, now? Are you asking yourself why I didn't go to her, to be with her instead of with the wife I didn't love? Are you wishing that I still might, and are you hoping against hope there'll be a happy ending? Do you think it would be better for us all, in the long run? Are you saying, Theo, don't be a fool, don't let her slip away, run to her, love conquers all?

Not in this case, my friend. In this case, it doesn't work out like that at all.

I thought about my duty to my wife and child, and to my family. Who would care for Elpida and Panayitsa, provide for them? Would it have been right to put responsibility for them back on her father, to hand that burden to an old man at the end of his working days? What had Elpida done to deserve disgrace, and desertion? She had always done her duty by me; in her own way, she had loved me.

And where would Irini and I have gone? To stay here would have been impossible; in the streets, they'd have spat on her, and shunned her. Maybe we could have gone to Kos, or Athens. We might have gone abroad, to Australia, or America. But I'm from here; this is my place. How could I turn my back on it, on my family and friends, forever? I knew this island would never let me go free; it would haunt me and call me back, always.

And would Irini and I have continued to love each other, after we set up home together, far away; or might we have come to hate each other? That is the question to which there is no answer. Because I was afraid to try.

I chose Conformity over Love.

Do I regret it?

What do you think?

One morning, as she went early to the grocer's, he was sitting, alone, at a café table. Forgetting herself, she stared at him with greedy eyes; he turned his face towards the counter, and called out for his bill. Shaking, anxious, she went on. Service was slow at the grocer's, and, returning, she found him gone. But the cup that he had drunk from was on the table, and the glass ashtray beside it held the dog-end of the cigarette he had smoked.

Dare she sit in his chair? Craving, desperate for contact, she did so, and felt the ecstasy of knowing she touched an object so recently touched by him. She wanted to touch his coffee cup, put it to her lips, learn something of him from it, and furtively she glanced inside it, trying to figure from his dregs how he took his coffee: with milk, or without? With sugar, or not? Such mundane details of his life were unknown to her; the café owner knew more of him than she, for he had had the information to make the coffee.

And the cigarette butt: it had touched his lips a dozen times, and was an object she could treasure, a piece of him to prize. She coveted that worthless, stinking piece of trash as a relic of her saint, as a believer would covet a splinter of the True Cross. But how to take it? At her back, the old men were already at their backgammon; they would miss nothing that she did.

The unsmiling café owner stepped up to her table and, asking for her order, picked up Theo's cup, and swept away his ashtray, and the relic. The old men rattled dice, and cast them on the board, while behind the counter, the café owner dumped the dirty china in the sink, and knocked the cigarette end into the garbage.

She waited for her coffee with tears in her eyes which must not fall. The coffee, when it came, was cold, and bitter; she drank it for appearances' sake, and walked home alone along the road where he always used to pass.

For Andreas, it was hard: hard to watch his wife in her unhappiness, hard only to guess at its source. In the house, she was like a wraith, tearful and remote. He did not ask why; there was no need, because in his heart, he knew. He feared the answer, if he asked; he dared not try and comfort her. He kept his distance, and stayed out of her way.

Then, one morning as he walked down to the harbor, he passed a house whose courtyard door stood open; glancing in, he was amazed. Within the courtyard, a potted Eden flourished. Geraniums flowered in deep reds, pinks and white; miniature roses and slender lilies bloomed amongst squat and spiny cacti; tall grasses rustled against lush ferns. A young lemon tree bore miniature yellow fruit, cream-petaled gardenias grew beside heady-scented jasmine; overhead, a trellis stretched, supporting a canopy of cool greenery and the royal-purple trumpets of exuberant morning glory. Entranced, Andreas stood and admired this work of art, this small, exquisite garden which was someone's labor of love.

In the harbor florist's, he bought seeds, compost and terracotta pots.

"My wife needs a hobby," he told the florist. "Something to stop her brooding. She gets lonely, while I'm away."

The florist watched him go with knowing eyes. He hired a taxi to carry home the makings of a garden, and there he left them beneath the struggling grapevine, to speak to her for themselves, if she would only listen.

Andreas went to sea; he was gone for many days, until one evening, as the swallows dipped and called across the valley, she heard his step behind her. The green shoots of the seedlings were beginning to appear; as she sprinkled water on the pots of sunflowers, he picked one up, and gently touched the new growth with a fingertip.

"They're doing very well," he said.

She turned to him.

"Perhaps you have a talent for it. Green fingers."

"I don't think so."

He rarely touched her, these days, but now he put a hand on her shoulder, and she let it remain.

"I'm glad you're finding an interest, Irini," he said. "I want you to be happy again. I want us to be happy."

She looked down at her own hands, and at the little

pots sprouting blades of leaves, and considered his words. *Happiness*, she thought, *is for other people. What I have is plant pots.*

She turned her face to his, and as her tears began to fall, he folded her within his arms and held her close.

He said, "*I* still want you, Irini." And as her tears flowed into weeping, he was content to be the shoulder that she cried on.

She found a place for her garden beyond the village, near the chapel of St. Fanouris, where the wide-stepped grain terraces still traced the hillside contours. Andreas bought her tools, and went with her to clear the hard-packed ground, cutting back the spreading branches of the fig trees, digging down to uproot the thistles and the long-established weed-grasses.

She made the pilgrimage daily, carrying a bucket to fetch water from the chapel well. As they grew stronger, she planted out her seedlings, working until there was nothing to do but weed amongst the rows, and wait for the blooming of her garden.

Her work stimulated talk; she was a fallen woman, and her motives were in doubt.

"It's not her land," complained the women in the grocer's. "She's after squatters' rights. She'll fence it, and sit tight. Ten years, and it's hers. You'll see."

The grocer, weighing white rice from a sack, asked, "So whose land is it?"

But no one knew. The land was long-deserted, abandoned in the war, and no one was left who could remember who had worked it when wheat was still grown there.

The young men in the bars claimed it was a smokescreen.

"She's meeting someone there," they said. "He puts it to her in the chapel."

But no car was ever seen there to identify a lover (she'd had one; she'd take on anyone, now), and the only man they ever saw her with was her husband.

So, finding no co-conspirator, they questioned her sanity.

"She's touched," they said. "Who in their right mind would walk all that way each day, just to grow a few tomatoes?"

But the old men spoke in her defense.

"You've all gone soft," they said, "with your motorbikes and your supermarkets and your TV. In our day, we walked for miles to scythe the wheat. We worked until our hands bled, in all seasons, in all weathers, tending crops. You walked and worked, or you didn't eat. If the woman's not lazy like you, leave her alone."

Shepherds coming down from the hills detoured to review her progress. In the cafés, they made their reports. She had worked hard, and done well; they confessed themselves impressed.

Word reached Theo that his mistress had turned gardener. There was no need to ask questions; he simply listened, and, learning where, he drove up in the truck to take a look. Too afraid of spying eyes to stop on the road, he slowed to a crawl as he passed the terraces; he saw the hard ground worked into tilth, the seedlings planted out in mounded rows, and in the corners, already blooming, pale-blue flowers he was too far away to identify.

But of the gardener herself, there was no sign.

The forecast for the coming week was good; the breeze had lost at last the undercurrent of winter, the air was light and bright, the alpines were in bloom.

Andreas had stacked the boat high with lobster traps, and, kissing her lightly on the cheek, had left before the sun broke the horizon.

"For certain," he said, untying the oily rope that moored the boat to the jetty, "I'll be back with you by Friday."

She caught hold of his arm, and brushed his cheek with her dry lips; the odor of fish was about him already, even before he cast off.

"Take care," she said. "Good fishing."

Later, when the sun had gained some warmth, she took the new, red watering-can he had bought her, and slowly walked the long road to her garden.

Someone had been there.

The fragile stalks of the tomato plants had all been snapped; the aubergines and sunflowers had been uprooted. Their wilted foliage had already lost its brilliance, bright green slipped into the gray of dying plants. The burgundy-edged lettuces had been trampled; the chick-peas (which had done so well) were strewn across the flowerbeds she had marked out with stones. The pot of spearmint stank, of drying urine.

She sat down on the flat rock where she'd sat for many hours, lately, and surveyed the ruined garden. She gazed beyond the terraces to where the mountains rose in sharp-stoned pinnacles. Behind the chapel, a solitary goat bleated to be free of its pen. Far below, the navy sea seemed still; out there, somewhere, Andreas fished, alone, and here was she, with people close, yet more alone than he.

A single puff of cloud passed overhead, and threw cold shadows as it hid the sun from view. Along the road, not far away, two black-clothed women walked, and talked with heads bowed low.

She sighed, and saw the beauty of this narrow place; just across the bay, the mainland held a million possibilities. There might be a life with Andreas; she tried to force from her mind a man who mattered more. The pills carefully hidden by St. Elizabeth had been thrown away so they could take their chances; maybe Nikos was right, and motherhood was her key to peace of mind.

She picked her way through the garden's desecration, searching for survivors and what might be salvaged. There seemed, at first, to be nothing, but, looking closely, there was much: the root crops were untouched, some herbs still grew, and—unnoticed in a corner—the pale-blue-flowered forget-me-nots still flourished.

She gathered up the broken stalks of chick-peas.

Out on the road, the black-clothed women drew close.

Seventeen

The fat man found Theo where his informant had suggested.

For a short while, the fat man watched him working from across the courtyard. The builders had finished their part of the renovation, but had left behind their litter—a pile of drying sand flattened with boot prints, oddments of broken bricks and breeze-blocks, empty packs of cigarettes and the damp dog-ends of many smokes. Theo had removed the rotting, cracked-glass window-frame; the new pine-wood frame he had made leaned against the mottled smoothness of the freshly rendered wall. He held a chisel and a hammer, and was chipping at the rough stones which lined the window opening; the chink-chink of metal hitting stone was soothing in its rhythm. Then Theo paused; his hands went to his sides, and, laying his forehead on the cold plaster, he closed his eyes, as if too weary to work on.

The fat man took a step forward, but a shard of broken glass snapped beneath his foot, and Theo, startled, turned. Seeing the fat man, his shoulders tensed; without speaking, he put the chisel blade to the wall, and knocked it with the hammer.

"And so we meet again." The fat man used a tone of *bonhomie,* of bygones being bygones. "I came to see if you were ready to talk to me, Theo."

In silence, Theo chipped splinters from the stone.

"Are you working alone?"

The sun cast dark shadows on Theo's face.

"How did you know where to find me?" he asked. His back still to the fat man, he spoke into the empty house, where his words echoed off the unpainted ceilings and the bare-boarded staircase.

"Your brother told me," said the fat man. "I found him very anxious to be of help."

Theo gave two sharp hammer blows on the chisel.

"I'm warning you," he said, quite calmly. "You stay away from my family. You've got no right to come here making trouble for me. Whatever your business is here, it's not with me. I'm a happily married man."

Sardonically, the fat man raised an eyebrow.

At the corner of the courtyard grew an olive tree; its pale-leaved branches cast shade where the old well-head had been. Its ancient trunk had been built into the courtyard wall, a vertical corner piece where two stone planes met; year by year, the knotted, slow-growing wood had grown around the stones which touched it, enveloping their hard edges within itself.

The fat man stood beneath the olive tree, and ran a fingertip along the curving furrows of its bark. Amongst the leaves, a few hard, green olives remained; the fat man plucked one, and, holding it before his eyes, turned it to examine its structure and its form.

"This is a fine old tree, wouldn't you say?" he asked, but Theo gave no answer. "Though I always think the olive is the most stupid of trees."

For a moment, Theo paused in his hammering, and the fat man sensed his wish to challenge and deride him for crediting a tree with stupidity. But Theo remained silent, and hit the chisel another blow.

"Consider the orange tree," went on the fat man. "An orange tree understands the need for prettiness, and charm. The perfume of its blossom is a metaphor for sweetness. And the fruit of the orange tree is seductive; it asks the hand to reach up and take it. *Please eat me*, it says. And why does it do that? Because it knows that it needs help to spread its seed." He touched his fingertip to his temple. "Because it's smart. It knows that, sometimes, a helping hand is beneficial. The fruit will fall to the ground in any case, of course. But the clever old orange tree wants its seed to travel far, and it knows how to do it. It asks to have its fruit picked, and so its seed is carried far away. It works the system to its advantage. Give and take. You know what I'm saying, Theo?"

Theo moved the chisel to a stone above his head, and hit it; it brought a shower of powdery mortar down onto the sill, and the backs of his hands.

"You should wear something to protect your eyes when you do that," said the fat man. "Now, this fellow here." He slapped the trunk of the olive tree. "He's a stubborn old fool. In its natural state, there's nothing less attractive than an olive." He held up the olive he had picked. "It's a fruit so sour, even a goat won't touch it. One bite, and your tongue shrivels like a raisin." He pitched the olive over the courtyard wall. "Yet this tree has the same aims in life as the orange tree. It wants to spread its seed. And we want its fruit. You'd think, the fruit being so unpalatable, the tree would make it as easy as it could to give its fruit away. But no. The olive tree makes it hard. To get the fruit we want, how do we have to take it? We beat this poor old man with sticks! Just consider—a venerable old tree, and a cruel beating, every harvest. It's a tree without brains! We need it, it needs us. Why hold on so tight to its seed? Why not yield its harvest with good grace, like the orange tree? And do you know what, Theo? I think you might be one of life's olive trees. Not easy plucking. Shall I have to beat you to get what I want?"

Theo laid his tools down on the sill.

"Tell me about you and Irini."

Theo turned to the fat man, and, drawing the saliva slowly from his cheeks, spat on the ground.

"I've told you already," he said, "and I won't be telling you again. I didn't know the woman. So you can take that, shove it up your aunt's arse, and fuck off."

The fat man plucked a leaf from the olive tree, and let it fall to the ground.

"Have it your way, Theo," he said. "For now. We'll meet again. And when we do . . ." he crossed the courtyard, and stepped into the street, where the olive he had thrown lay at the heart of a pool of rainwater, "maybe I'll begin to understand what it was she saw in you."

Eighteen

It was mid-afternoon, and the businesses in the port were closed up for siesta. Beyond the clock-tower, a young boy dropped a hook-and-line into the oily water; small, shimmering fish rose to nibble his scattered bait, then disappeared back into the shadows between the moored boats. The police car was not there; where it had parked, a rectangle of dry concrete made a pale island on the rain-wet harborside.

Inside the police station, the fat man was pleased to find that the man he sought was alone. The sergeant sat at his almost empty desk, his jacket fastened and tight across his broad chest, the three silver chevrons on his arm angled towards the door. Spread below his capped ballpoint pens, a copy of *Ta Nea* was open at the sports pages. As Chadiarakis read, his dark eyebrows were pulled low in concentration; the stub of his forefinger followed the lines of print, and his wet, red lips mimed the words he read.

As the fat man entered, the sergeant looked up from his newspaper. Seeing the fat man, sly gratification crossed his face.

"The Chief's looking for you," he said. He closed his

newspaper and folded it in half, running his forearm over the crease.

"By coincidence," said the fat man, "I, too, am looking for someone. And I seem to have found my quarry before your Chief has found his, because it's you I'm looking for, Sergeant Chadiarakis."

But the sergeant showed no curiosity in the fat man's business with him.

"The Chief phoned the Met in Athens," he said. "He asked why they're interested in the Asimakopoulos case. He wanted to know why they sent you. And no one in Athens has ever heard of you! Oh, he's gunning for you, my friend." He lounged back in his chair, folding his hands across the swell of his belly.

"How absolutely absurd!" said the fat man. "Of course there are people in Athens who have heard of me. What you mean is, none of those who have heard of me is employed by the Metropolitan Police. Do you mind if I sit?"

Considering the fat man's words, the sergeant drew his dark eyebrows together in puzzlement.

The fat man lay his holdall on the floor, and, lifting the chair from behind the undersized constable's desk, he placed it before the sergeant, and sat down.

The fat man smiled.

"And why, by the way," he asked, "should the Chief of Police be gunning for me simply because I don't work for the Metropolitan Police? Thousands upon thousands of people don't work for the Metropolitan Police. The vast majority of the population, in fact. Is he 'gunning' for them, too?"

"You impersonated a police officer," interrupted the sergeant, sitting up at his desk. He removed the cap from one of his ballpoint pens, and opened the drawer in his desk where he kept the right forms. "That's an offense."

"With respect, I impersonated no one," said the fat man. "Are you saying that the Chief of Police took me to be a police officer? I wonder why? No, Harris—do you mind if I call you Harris?—your chief's mis-assumption that I am a fellow officer must be corrected. Please tell him when you see him that I am employed by a different authority. And by the way, where is the Chief of Police? Will he be back in the office this afternoon? I have a matter to discuss with him. Actually, it concerns you."

"Me?" The sergeant was wary.

"I believe it my duty as a citizen to inform him that you have been using a police vehicle for non-police business."

"What non-police business?"

"And, more interesting still, that you were seen at the cliff where Irini Asimakopoulos was found."

The sergeant's eyes moved slowly to the fat man's face; he lowered his chin to his chest, spreading his jowls over the tight collar of his shirt.

"Naturally I was there," he said, carefully, "as a member of the search party; of course I was there."

"My information is," said the fat man, "that you were ahead of the search party by two whole days."

The sergeant gave a tight-lipped smile, causing a tiny run of saliva from his mouth's corner to his chin. He wiped the wetness away with the back of his hand.

"I don't know what you mean," he said.

"You were up there in a police car, in civilian clothes. Alone. At least I think you were alone."

"You may think what you like."

"I have a witness who saw you there."

Sergeant Chadiarakis gave a small laugh, and spread his hands in feigned exasperation.

"I wasn't there," he said. "Why would I have been?"

"Now that," said the fat man, "is an excellent question."

The instep of his left shoe was smeared with green—a grass stain, or the stain of sheep or goat dung. The fat man drew his shoe-whitener from his bag and, bending below the level of the desk, dabbed at his shoes; in bending, his voice was indistinct, but the sergeant, paying very close attention, caught every word.

"A major search, with the army and a helicopter, is an expensive prospect," said the fat man from below the desk. "Scrambling a helicopter makes a big hole in a small budget. A budget like yours, for example. Money's tight, I'm sure." He applied the whitener to the other shoe. "So I wonder what the Chief of Police would say if he found out that a helicopter was not required? That all the cash he'll pay out for that search could have been saved? I'm sure that cash was earmarked for something. A new desk or two, perhaps? A motorbike with blue flashing lights which would impress the ladies?"

He replaced the cap on the bottle of whitener, and dropped it back inside his holdall. The sergeant was not smiling anymore.

"I wonder, Harris," said the fat man, reaching into his pocket and withdrawing his cigarettes and lighter. "Do you mind if I smoke, by the way?" The sergeant shook his head, and watched the fat man closely as he lit a cigarette and inhaled with obvious pleasure.

The fat man took the cigarette from his mouth and held the smoking tip before his eyes.

"Some things in life," he said, "are so enjoyable, yet so bad for us. I'm getting too old for these things; they slow you down so, don't they? My father's always telling me I should give up. So I suppose I must. One day. But not today."

He put the cigarette back to his lips, and drew in smoke.

"What was I saying?" he asked. "Ah yes. I was just wondering, wasn't I, how *secure* you feel in your job, Harris. It's a good job, I know. A man in your position earns a lot of respect in a place like this. A lot of... 'respect.' A lot of money, potentially. Little gifts here and there—something for the New Year, something at Easter. An excellent pension to look forward to. That uniform is worth a great deal. I'm afraid it would be an awful lot to lose. But if someone told the Chief that you'd misused the police car, what would happen, Harris? Does he have friends just waiting to step into your shoes? Cousins and brothers-in-law in Patmos just waiting for a nice, comfortable posting such as this? A word of your misconduct in his ear—*finito la musica*. You'd be a cop in disgrace, Harris. And life would taste a lot less sweet then, wouldn't it?"

He drew again on his cigarette, and exhaled a stream

of acrid smoke towards the sergeant, who blinked, twice, slowly, to protect his eyes.

The fat man smiled at him.

"So, Harris." For a long moment, he said no more. The sergeant reached uneasily for a ballpoint.

"Speak to me, Harris," went on the fat man, "or I will make your life a misery to you."

"I have nothing to tell you," said the sergeant, sullenly.

"Tell me what you know."

The sergeant lay his pen back in its place.

"I can't," he said.

"Why not? Because you killed her?"

Wearily, the sergeant shook his head.

"I didn't kill her."

"But you know who did, don't you?"

The sergeant glanced anxiously towards the door; the fat man leaned forward, and put his face up to the sergeant's.

"Tell me, Harris," he said. "My threats are never idle."

The sergeant looked into the fat man's eyes, then away through the window to the gray sky and the sea. His expression was of sadness, and regret. The fat man stubbed out his cigarette, and waited for the sergeant to speak.

"I didn't kill her," the sergeant said at last. "I moved the body. That's all."

"Moved it from where, to where?"

"Moved it from where it was to where it was found."

The fat man dropped his head, and pinched the septum of his nose until the urge for sharp retort had passed.

"Are you saying," he asked, "that you threw her over the cliff?"

The sergeant passed a hand over his face, then, eyes closed, rubbed at his forehead.

"What did it matter?" he said. "She was already dead."

"Do you have a daughter, Harris?"

"Two."

"I'm sure they're lovely girls. But if one of them died, unexpectedly..."

"God forbid!" said the sergeant, crossing himself. "God forbid!"

"But what if one of them *did* die? If one of them had an accident like the one we're going to talk about? What would you want for your daughter, Harris? I think you'd want her at home, with you, where you and your wife could take care of her. I think your wife would want to dress her in her best clothes, and have her family there to watch her, and the priest to pray for her. Isn't that what you'd want?"

The sergeant was silent.

"So if it were your daughter—I want you to be perfectly honest with me—would it matter to you if someone—anyone, an officer of the law, say—threw her body over a cliff? It wouldn't matter, I suppose, if she were already dead?" The sergeant shuddered, as if he felt again the coldness of Irini's corpse. "Are you a hard man, Harris, a man without a heart? Or is it simply imagination, and empathy, that you lack? How can you say to me it didn't matter?"

"She was dead! It didn't matter! Not as much as..."

He stopped, and, knowing that he'd said too much, laid his head in his hands.

"As much as what, Harris?" pressed the fat man. "As much as shielding the living guilty? Now you tell me this: why would you, an officer of the law, shield someone guilty of murder?"

Again, the sergeant was silent.

"All right, let me answer my own question. You wouldn't do it for money. Murder is too serious a crime. So what motives remain?" He tapped one forefinger with another, counting. "There's love. Or there's family. Or both."

Still the sergeant didn't speak.

"Tell me who it is you're shielding, Harris," said the fat man, "or I'll pin it on you."

The sergeant raised his head; his eyes were bright with tears.

"You can't do that," he said.

"But I can," smiled the fat man. "I have a witness who saw you at the scene. A witness who doesn't like policemen. Who would be prepared to swear he saw you dumping poor Irini's body. It'll be big news, Harris, a national story. I could write the headlines myself: COP KILLS YOUNG WIFE. Your face will be on every front page in the country. That's something to make your daughters proud, now, isn't it? So tell me."

The sergeant's hesitation was brief.

"It was an accident," he said. "I was assured of that."

The fat man sighed.

"Tell me everything," he said.

And the sergeant did.

On the steps of the police station, on his way out, the fat man met the Chief of Police, on his way in.

"Good afternoon, Chief of Police," said the fat man, politely. "I'm glad I've seen you."

The Chief of Police looked at him with spiteful eyes.

"Then come back inside," he said. The smell of brandy was on his breath. "I believe you and I have a matter still to settle."

"You're quite right," said the fat man. "But I see no reason why it can't be discussed just here. The matter's simple. I want you to return the money you took from Andreas Asimakopoulos for falsifying his wife's death certificate. Taking his money was both immoral, and illegal, as you know. And it was unnecessary, too. As I suggested to you when I first arrived, there was no suicide. Also, if you have not already done so, I want you to release Janis Psaros, and pay his father the money you owe."

The Chief of Police smiled an inscrutable smile.

"Happily," he said, "I was able to release Mr. Psaros this morning. I've dropped all charges, for which Mrs. Psaros has expressed her particular gratitude. But you're hardly in a position to be giving orders to me, are you? I think you should know, we've done some checking up on you, sir, and I know you're not who you claim to be. That's an offense, and I'll personally make sure you do time for it."

The fat man laughed.

"I gather from Sergeant Chadiarakis you've been confused as to my identity," he said. "I can't believe you took me for a policeman. Do I look like a policeman? And I should be ashamed of myself if you thought I *acted* like a policeman. As for who I am, I've made no claims. So choose for yourself. Perhaps I am a mere philanthropist. Or maybe I am a man of means who simply enjoys meddling in the lives of the less fortunate. Perhaps the Police Authority employs me to combat corruption in our remote police forces. Maybe I am all these things. Or none. Maybe I was sent here by a higher authority still. A *supreme* authority. It's hard to know, isn't it, Chief of Police? Perhaps..." the fat man winked, "I am here to investigate *you*."

The smile was long gone from the Chief of Police's lips. He enclosed his left fist in his right hand, and tightened his grip until the bones cracked.

"I think your leaving this island is long overdue," he said, quietly, "*friend*."

"If you're telling me to leave," said the fat man, frowning, "I think you'll find you're on sticky ground. This is, after all, a free country."

"It's only free as long as I say it's free."

"You have an inflated sense of your own powers, Chief of Police. Give back the money. Don't make me tell you again."

The fat man put a foot on the step below him, but the Chief of Police placed a hand on the wall, and moved to block the fat man's way down the stone staircase.

"Mind how you go," he said. "Accidents will happen."

"Indeed they will," said the fat man, "but not to me. Happily, I am very steady on my feet."

"I should have you locked up. For interfering in police business."

"But interference seems to be necessary, doesn't it?" said the fat man, reasonably. "Since the police could hardly be accused of taking care of things themselves. Now, if you'll excuse me, Chief of Police."

He looked expectantly at the policeman, but as Zafiridis stepped unwillingly aside, the fat man put a finger thoughtfully to his lips.

"There was one more thing I meant to ask you," he said. "I was wondering if you were fond of birds."

"Birds?"

"Caged birds, song birds. Canaries. Larks."

The Chief of Police regarded the fat man suspiciously.

"As a matter of fact," he said, "I can't abide them. I have an allergy to feathers. Why do you ask?"

The fat man smiled.

"Just curious," he said, running nimbly away down the steps.

Nineteen

As the sky grew pale at the eastern horizon, a white cockerel stretched its throat and made its startling call. Head tilted, it blinked its vacant eyes, and seemed to listen; until from far away, a crowing answer came, and soon a second, and a third.

The window of the fat man's room stood open, and the grave-cold of the night sea had crept in. Shivering, the fat man dressed as quickly as he could, in clothes infected by an unseen rime of damp. He placed an empty matchbox in his pocket, and made his way light-footed down the staircase, onto the deserted harborside. In the stillness, the sea slapped and gurgled at the harbor wall; out on the water, the red and green lights of a distant fishing boat rocked to its rhythm.

The fat man took the road around the headland, where the barren rocks gave way to more level ground. Here, while the cold-blooded creatures still slept, he searched beneath the likeliest stones until he found what he was seeking; then, with the greatest possible care, he lifted his prey from the darkness of its lair and closed it tight inside his matchbox.

❖

The call to early mass went out; the Sunday bells were ringing around the island, from the tinny clang of those rope-rung to the melodic, alpine tinkling of Ayia Triander's automated peal.

In the doorway of his *kafenion,* once-handsome Jakos smoothed his Brylcreemed hair and gazed out across the sea, as if his heart and thoughts were very far away.

The fat man sat down at a table, and, cupping the flame of his lighter to protect it from the breeze, lit a cigarette; in silence, Jakos moved from the doorway to stand at his side.

"Kali mera," said the fat man. There was, today, no smiling cheerfulness in his greeting, and Jakos did not answer him, but waited, in silence, for the fat man's order.

"Coffee," said the fat man, "and an omelet, if you've eggs. With cheese and ham, but no tomatoes."

"We've eggs," said Jakos, dourly, "but the bread's not fresh. It's Sunday."

"Then toast it," said the fat man. "And no tomatoes, don't forget."

The omelet was good, well-flavored and bright yellow from the yolks of backyard hens. The fat man lit another cigarette, and called to Jakos for a second cup of coffee; Jakos, placing the fresh cup on the table, sat down beside him, and looked out across the sea.

The fat man took a sip of bitter coffee.

"I'm thinking of a spot of fishing this morning," he said, "if someone can tell me where to drop my line."

Jakos turned his eyes from the sea to the fat man.

"You're too late for fish this morning, captain," he said. "The fish have had their breakfast hours ago."

"The fish I have in mind doesn't eat breakfast on a Sunday," said the fat man. "At least, not before it's been to mass. It goes by the name of Eleni Tsavaris."

Jakos scratched behind his ear, and smoothed the clipped line of his moustache with the side of his forefinger.

"That's a big fish, friend," he said. "You'll need a strong line to land that one."

"I have the line," said the fat man. "The question is, where should I fish for such a catch?"

"If I were you," said Jakos, "I'd try a church. And if I were guessing which church, I'd try my luck with Ayias Lefteris."

The fat man took out his wallet, and laid a generous sum beneath the ashtray.

"Many thanks," he said.

"Still on the trail?" asked Jakos, curiously. "Still think there's foul play been involved?"

"Foul play and bad behavior," said the fat man. He stood and, placing his right hand on his heart, spread his left arm in the pose of a classical actor. *"Look now,"* he recited, "*how mortals blame the gods, for they say that evils come from us, but in fact they themselves have woes beyond their share because of their own follies*. Homer. He understood a great deal of human nature."

Jakos stared at him, uncomprehending, and the fat man, realizing he had understood nothing, wished him goodbye.

But Jakos caught his arm.

"So who did it?" he asked. "Have you identified the guilty party?"

"To my own satisfaction," said the fat man, "yes."

"So who is it?"

"I'm sure you realize, Jakos," said the fat man, "that I cannot share that information with you. But rest assured, in due course, all will become clear to those who need to know."

In the light of many candles, the women of the congregation showed their boredom. At the lectern, a man wearing the thick-lensed glasses of the almost-blind sang an archaic chant from a handwritten, leather-bound tome; a robed priest echoed each *Kyrie eleison,* and rattled the chain of a burning censer. The air was dense, with the heady smoke of incense and candles; from the walls, the gold-painted images of St. Lefteris gazed down with sad expressions, as if despairing at the absence of true piety. The children played with lighted candles, and ran laughing up and down the nave, while the women fidgeted, and whispered, and criticized the clothes their neighbors wore.

At the rear of the church, a sandbox held a stand of burning candles, wilting and drooping in their own heat. An offertory plate filled with coins and banknotes lay alongside banks of fresh candles, stacked in scores; an elderly woman with disheveled hair played needlessly with the candles in the sandbox, snuffing some with spittle-wetted fingers and removing them, rearranging those remaining, tallest to the center, those burning low towards the front.

For a while, the fat man listened from the vaulted porch to the rambling liturgy, until the candle-tender, rubbing splashes of hot wax from her fingers, held up a fist of slender, white candles and beckoned to him.

As the liturgy droned on — *For all those who commit injustice against their neighbors, whether by causing sorrow to orphans or spilling innocent blood or by returning hatred for hatred, that God will grant them repentance, enlighten their minds and hearts and illumine their souls with the light of love even towards their enemies, let us pray to the Lord* — the fat man crossed the red-and-black tiled floor, but raised his hand to decline the woman's offered candles; he placed no money in the offertory plate, and he did not kiss the icons, or make the triple cross over his heart. Instead, he took the woman gently by her bony wrist, and, pulling her close, spoke into her ear.

"Fetch me Eleni Tsavaris," he said. "Tell her I'll be waiting in the courtyard."

Outside, the sky was overcast, but even muted daylight was brilliant after the dimness. Beneath a bush of purple-flowered bougainvillea was a stone bench, from which he brushed the fallen petals before sitting down to wait. Soon, in the church porch, a woman — short, and gone to fat in the way of middle age — appeared; she wore a suit of moss-green wool, and black pumps, and carried tucked under her arm an old-fashioned clutch bag. Her hair, severely short, was damp and lined with the marks of a wet comb; her skin was sallow, as if never touched by sunlight.

The fat man stood, and held out his hand to her; she crossed the courtyard to him but, reaching him, did not take his hand.

"Eleni Tsavaris?" he asked.

"You've fetched me from my devotions, from the worship of Our Lord," she said, stridently. "State your business with me and let's be done. People will talk."

He stretched his arm towards the bench, inviting her to take a seat, but she ignored the gesture, lifting her chin, setting her lips, hugging her bag across her body as a barrier, and he inclined his head, politely, in acceptance of her preference to stand.

"My name," he said, "is Hermes Diaktoros. I want to talk to you about the death of Irini Asimakopoulos."

She blinked, and the tip of her tongue ran across her upper lip, where a few dark, masculine hairs grew.

"Why do you want to talk to me?" she asked.

But she sat down on the bench, and placed the clutch bag at her side; as she folded one hand firmly inside the other, the fat man caught the trembling in her fingertips.

He sat beside her, leaning forward on his knees to close them in an intimate half-circle, and she, to emphasize her modesty, brought her knees together, and moved her ankles close. Her feet above the pinching shoes were red, and the scuffs of long use on the shoes' toes and heels poked pale through the disguise of buffed shoe-polish. On her lapel, the pearls set in the little brooch were fake.

"You knew Irini?" he asked.

"No. I didn't know her."

"You knew of her, though? You knew that she was dead?"

She shrugged.

"Of course. This is a small place. Everyone knew it."

"How did she die?"

"Why are you asking me?"

"What have you heard?"

"Accident, some say. Some say suicide."

"You knew your daughter's husband was in love with her?"

"That," she said, angrily, "is an insult to my daughter, and to the honor of my family. You have no right to say such things to me."

She moved to stand, but the fat man touched her on the arm.

"Just a moment, Eleni," he said, "or I will fetch Elpida from the church—I assume that she is in there with you?—and I will tell her everything I have learned since I have been here."

Eleni sniffed, and snatched her arm away. Her hands lay in her lap. The knuckle above her wedding ring was inflamed, and swollen, as if arthritic; around the finger's base, the tight, gold band dug deep into the flesh.

"Tell me about Irini Asimakopoulos."

"I can't tell you anything about her. I don't know why you think I could."

"Perhaps I should mention that I spent some time, yesterday, talking to your brother, Harris."

"My brother is a know-nothing fool. Don't waste your time on what he tells you."

"He has compromised himself greatly as an officer of the law," said the fat man, "but he's not such a fool as you think. He's smart enough to realize there's no place to hide from this. And so should you be."

"I don't know what you mean."

"Perhaps I should be talking to your daughter instead of you. Perhaps your brother, as you say, knows nothing. Elpida is, after all, the one with all the motive. *Was* Elpida the guilty party, Eleni?"

"Elpida wasn't even there!"

"Where, Eleni?" asked the fat man. "Where wasn't she?"

She gave no reply, but pulled a leaf from the bougainvillea and dropped it to the ground.

"Let me make it easier for you," said the fat man. "I am not the police."

"You have no right to ask me these questions, then. No authority. In which case—"

"Let me finish," said the fat man. "I am a private investigator. Whatever you tell me, you won't go to jail for. That assurance I can give you. But I will have the truth. And if you tell me the truth—if you volunteer it—things will go better for you."

"But you have no authority."

"In the written law of this land, no, I don't. But when the law of this land fails to deliver justice—through corruption, or ignorance, or bureaucracy, or fear, whatever the reason for its failure—it is *my* job to see justice is done. It is my job to see the guilty punished."

"Punishing the guilty is the job of Our Lord, Jesus

Christ," she said. She crossed herself, then raised her eyes skywards, as if seeking confirmation for her homily. "Now, if you'll excuse me, I'll return to my devotions."

"Not yet, Eleni," he said. "Because if you won't talk to me, I shall follow you inside that church, and tell the whole congregation exactly what I think happened to Irini Asimakopoulos. I shall tell them how I believe she died, and why, and I shall tell them who was responsible."

She smiled, unpleasantly.

"You have nothing to connect us with that woman's death," she said.

"On the contrary. I have what your brother told me. And don't blame him, Eleni. He was in an impossible position. He felt no inclination to do time for a crime he didn't commit. Now, I believe I know exactly how it was. I shall tell you how I think it went, but if I get anything wrong, I want you to put me right; I want the full story. And understand, if you lie to me, it will be the worse for you; and if you lie to me, believe me, I will know."

She didn't speak, but fiddled with the faux-pearl brooch, straightening and re-pinning it. Outside the church's walls, the excited shouts of children and the sound of running feet were there, and gone.

"Your daughter's marriage wasn't going well, was it?" said the fat man. "Elpida wasn't keeping Theo happy, was she? Maybe she just wasn't enough for him. What do you think?"

He thought she wouldn't respond, but she turned to him, and said, "He's a dreamer, Theo. For some, the grass is always greener."

He waited for her to go on, but she said no more.

"He did what many men do, didn't he?" asked the fat man. "He found himself a bit on the side. It's common enough, not out of the ordinary. Perhaps your own husband did the same thing." Her eyebrows lifted, in tired acknowledgement. "In the end, they all come back to hearth and home."

"Men are all the same," she said. "Always have been, always will be. And there'll always be whores like her." She used the crudest word for "whore," the word used in the barracks and the bar rooms. "Let me tell you about my husband. My *man*. I put up with it for years, his running around with every whore who'd drop their knickers for a wink and a smile. He wasn't fussy. He'd go with anybody who'd have him. He'd still go now, if he could find one willing. He used to get caught, sometimes; he'd take a beating from someone's husband, come home all bloodied and bruised and not walk for a week, with his balls all swelled up where he'd been kicked.... And me?" She bent her head to the brooch, and twisted it out of line, and back again. "I was the one in disgrace! The shame was all mine. 'Eleni Tsavaris doesn't know enough to keep her old man at home.' I knew what was said, behind my back. But I was strong. I showed them I didn't give that"—she snapped her fingers—"for what they said. We struggled on, and I put up with him. There were the kids. And I knew he'd always come back. So I was strong.

"But Elpida. She was different. He was different, Theo. I chose him for her because he wasn't that way. He was a quiet boy. He had never put it about, tom-catted around.

I didn't want Elpida to go through what I went through. I couldn't have borne to see her hurt that way. I wanted to protect her. But in the end, I couldn't. By the time I knew what was going on, that whore had already got her claws in."

She reached up absently, pulled one of the purple blossoms from the tree, and laid it in the palm of her hand; lying there, plucked from the branch, its beauty was diminished, and, in a moment, its perfect form was gone.

"And as for Theo..." She shook her head, and a sigh of exasperation hissed through her teeth.

"So Theo wasn't different after all."

"Oh, Theo was different, all right. Theo couldn't just go for the fuck. With Theo, it had to be love. All or nothing. I went around there once, and there he was, crying at the kitchen table. Crying like a girl. I knew then there was trouble brewing, and I was right. The bitch had already got him, body and soul. Men don't cry for nothing. When I saw him crying like that, I knew he'd leave Elpida."

Holding its stalk between finger and thumb, she twirled the dying flower.

"I couldn't bear it, for her. The shame of it. She's a good girl, a sweet girl. She didn't deserve that. But I didn't know what to do; I just knew I had to do something. Then rumors started to fly. George heard in the cafés that Theo had been seen with her, so then I knew. I knew my enemy. And Elpida knew something was wrong; she just didn't know what. She cared for Theo—she cares still. But he doesn't love her, and I don't suppose he ever has. And that wasn't important, it was just the way things are.

I told her that. But it *was* important when he fell in love with someone else. Who was going to look after my Elpida, my little Panayitsa, if he left them? When I'm gone, who will there be to take care of them? Your kids come first. Your kids always come first. So when I knew who she was, we went to warn her off. We went to find her. To talk to her."

"We?"

"Me. My other daughter, Yorgia. My mother. She's a tough old bird, my mother. Looks as frail as a canary, but don't be taken in. My father was as bad as George, always putting his dick where it shouldn't have been. But she was strong, and she hung on to him. For what it was worth."

She dropped the flower; its petals spread, opaque and wilted, on the cold stones.

"We knew where to find her. She had a bit of a garden, at the top of the village."

"I've seen it," he said.

"Everyone said she was meeting Theo there. We thought we'd catch them together. But the first time we went up, she wasn't there. We waited, but she didn't come. So we just pulled up a few flowers, broke off the tomato plants, a few vegetables. We made our way to the house; we might have had it out with her, but there was no one there either."

"You didn't go into the house?"

Eleni blinked.

"No."

"Are you certain?"

"We went into the courtyard. We called her name, but no one answered."

"And when you were sure there was no one there, what did you do?"

"We left."

"Before you left, did you do nothing else? Did you, for example, notice a bird in a cage?"

She turned her face from him.

"I don't like to see birds caged," she said.

"So did you turn the poor bird free, then?"

She gave a slow and bitter smile.

"In a manner of speaking, yes. I gave it its freedom. There was no more singing for its supper, was there? The bird was a warning to her, that's all. Maybe we would have left it at that. But Mother said we should go back to the garden, really give the whore a scare. I didn't know exactly what she had in mind; perhaps she didn't either. So she and I went again, the next day. And this time, there she was."

In the high branches of a cypress tree, a dove was calling. Eleni raised her eyes to where it perched, then looked down at her hands, spreading and examining her fingers as if they were new to her.

"Tell me everything, Eleni," said the fat man.

"We walked up from the road. She was gathering up the chick-peas we'd snapped off the day before. She watched us as we came along her little footpath. She didn't know us; I suppose she was wondering who we were, what we wanted. She looked quite ordinary—not as pretty as my Elpida used to be. Sometimes you have to wonder why they do it, don't you?"

She put the question as if he might provide an answer,

but when the fat man didn't speak, she went on without prompting.

"She was polite, at first. She wished us *kali mera.* But then Mother started in. She told her to stay away from him, that he wasn't hers, he was our Elpida's and she called her a whore, a bitch, every name she could think of. So she began to get the picture, then. She asked us who we were, all hands on hips and nose in the air. She asked what the hell it had to do with us, and I told her we were family. I said our family didn't appreciate home wreckers like her. She said she hadn't wrecked anybody's home. She said Theo never spoke to her anymore, that he wouldn't even give her the time of day. She said it was finished, over. So I told her she was a liar *and* a whore."

"I think she was probably telling the truth," interrupted the fat man. "At least as she saw it."

"And how would you know? What makes you think it was true? Whores like that, they'd swear on their own kids' lives that black was white. A woman like that knows nothing about truth. Only lies." Her face was red, and ugly with bitterness; as she spoke, droplets of her spittle marked his clothes. "And we told her so. Mother told her she was a lying bitch. She started trampling on the garden. So then the whore started shouting, 'Get out of here, get out!' and she grabbed my mother by the arm. Well, Mother's frail, her bones are brittle. She might have broken something. So I said to her, 'Don't you dare touch my mother,' and I slapped her across the face. Not hard, but she didn't like it, and she turned to go. She started to walk away. Mother was angry at the lack of respect she'd been shown. She picked up a clod of earth. She said, 'Let's show her the old way, let's show her what happens to bitches like her,' and she threw the clod of earth at her. She threw it hard; it hit her in the back, and then the whore was really angry. She came marching back, shouting, 'Who threw that? Who threw that?' And Mother picked up a stone, and said, 'Me,' and threw the stone, and that hit her on the arm. She looked shocked, then, and I thought, *This is the way to let her know we mean it.* So I threw a stone. Only a small one. But Mother had a bigger one, and she caught her with it on the forehead. That made her stagger, and she put her hand up to her forehead and there was a cut, and blood, and she looked at us and said, 'What the hell are you doing?' And Mother threw another stone. So I did too. We didn't throw them hard, but they were hurting her, and I was pleased. We picked them up in twos and threes and pelted her. She was shouting, 'Help me, help me!' but there's no one up there to hear. Then she started screaming, and she tried to run. But she wasn't running fast—we'd caught her on the knees, and she was limping—so I got in front of her. I cut off her retreat. So then she tried appealing. She said, 'For God's sake, no more,' and Mother said, 'Don't call on God, there's no God for the likes of you.'"

She stopped. The breeze caught the tip of the cypress tree, and the dove rose, flying away towards the sea.

"Eleni?"

"She curled up in a ball. She lay down with her arms around her head. She was sobbing—I could see her body shaking—and she was saying, 'Please stop, please stop,' over and over again. She was dirty; there was blood on her clothes. I prodded her with my foot and she yelped like a dog, so I told Mother, 'That's enough, she's learned her lesson.' But Mother wouldn't stop. She was so angry, fierce. The whore was on the ground, and Mother picked up a rock. She lifted it up over the whore's head, and I shouted, 'No!' I took it off her; I lifted the rock out of her hands. I thought, *It's too heavy for her, she'll drop it.* So the rock was in my hands; I remember the weight of it. I was going to put it down, lay it aside, but then I thought maybe we hadn't done enough; a scar or two would be a lasting souvenir, an everyday reminder to stay away from us. Her face was turned towards me, she was looking up at me, and I thought her cheek, or on the chin . . . She saw what I was thinking, and she said, 'No . . .' And I dropped the rock." She met his eyes, defiantly. "How could I know the damage it would do? We meant to frighten her, that was all."

"You stoned her." The fat man's voice was low. "You stoned her to death."

She gave no reply. The fat man stood, and, turning his back on her, lit a cigarette. For some time, he was silent.

"So you solved your problem," he said. "Except there was a body."

"We covered her with the plants we had pulled up, and I went straight to Harris. I knew he'd help. He wouldn't want a scandal; he'd do anything to avoid trouble. We went, he and I, before dawn the next day. She hadn't been reported missing. Her husband was away." He thought of poor Andreas, keeping company with his whisky bottle.

"We sat her in the front of the police car, and Harris took her up the mountain. I told him if she took a fall, the bruises that we'd made wouldn't be noticed."

He inhaled deeply on his cigarette, and turned to face her.

"Eleni," he said. "Look at me. You have committed a cruel murder."

"Not murder," she said, coolly. "We never intended her to die. It was an accident."

"No," he said. "It was no accident. You thought—you and your mother—that the unhappiness of your own lives gave you the right to punish another. Yet you yourself have just said to me that the right to punish is reserved by higher authorities. Your motive was revenge for your own misery."

"I did what had to be done to protect my child. And I'd do it again. I've no regrets."

"You should be tried for your crime in a court of law."

"But you have no proof. And no legal standing." Rising from the bench, she smoothed the creases from the lap of her skirt.

Resignedly, he shook his head.

"No. There's no proof. Only conscience. And if you truly have no conscience, and no remorse, what can I possibly say to you? Here. Go."

He held out her clutch bag, but as she took it from him, he caught the catch, and the bag fell open, spilling what it held onto the courtyard stones. Quickly, he bent and gathered up the fallen objects—a handkerchief, a powder compact, a few coins, a small icon of the Archangel Michael—and replaced them in the bag, snapping the clasp shut.

"Go."

He watched her walk unhurriedly away, through the open doorway of the church, disappearing into its darkness like a landed fish slipping back into accustomed waters. When she was gone, he picked up his holdall and followed her, and stood watching from the porch as the liturgy droned on.

Master, accept the thrice-holy hymn also from the lips of us sinners and visit us in Your goodness.

The candle-tender picked up the offertory plate, and handed a stack of candles to a young girl dressed in pink. Together, they approached the small congregation.

Forgive our voluntary and involuntary transgressions, sanctify our souls and bodies, and grant that we may worship and serve You in holiness all the days of our lives . . .

The women opened their Sunday handbags, and fumbled inside them for coins to pay for candles.

The fat man waited.

There was a scream, and a gasp, and a muttering which grew to exclamations. The droning ceased, and a babble of excited female voices started up. A woman was crying; the young girl who had carried the candles passed him at a run.

The fat man sauntered into the church, down the nave, to where the women were gathered around one who moaned, and clutched her hand.

Across their heads, he called to her, "Are you hurt, Eleni?"

A woman answered him; her eyes were sparkling in delight at the drama.

"A scorpion!" she said. "A scorpion in her handbag! It bit her when she went in it for change!"

"How extraordinary!" said the fat man. "Are you in pain, Eleni?"

But Eleni seemed not to hear or know him, so he spoke again to the woman at his side.

"I gather the bite of a scorpion is agony," he said.

With relish, she agreed.

"My father's cousin died of one," she said. "His arm swelled up like a balloon, and his blood was poisoned. The doctor came too late to save him."

"To some," said the fat man, "it's nothing but a pin-prick, then to others, it can be fatal. One never knows. But then, nothing in life is certain, is it?"

He glanced at his watch.

"Time presses," he said. "I'll leave you to it. Give my best wishes to Mrs. Tsavaris."

Outside, a little sun was breaking through the clouds; beyond the church walls, the breeze carried the scent of early jasmine. From his holdall the fat man took a bar of almond chocolate, and, savoring the first piece, went on his way.

Twenty

At Theo Hatzistratis's house, the fat man found no one at home, so he wrote a note, choosing his words carefully.

Be good enough, he put, *to meet me at St. Savas's jetty, at 10 a.m. tomorrow. We have a great deal to discuss, and my time here is limited.*

He signed it *Hermes Diaktoros, Investigator,* in an ornate hand, and lodged it in the letterbox, where it couldn't be missed.

In the window of the shipping company, the timetable showed a ferry due that evening. From the public phone outside the post office, the fat man made his call to the police station. It was answered by the undersized constable. In the background, a radio was playing.

"Good morning," said the fat man. "May I please speak with Chief Zafiridis?"

"He's not here," said the undersized constable, shortly. "Try tomorrow."

"I wonder if you could give him a message," said the fat man, "from Hermes Diaktoros. The Athenian. Perhaps you remember me."

There was a short silence. On the radio, a woman sang of loneliness.

"I'll take a message," said the constable. "If it's urgent."

"Would you please tell him," said the fat man, "that I am expecting a mutual acquaintance on the ferry this evening—an old friend of his from Patmos with whom I have some business. I mentioned Mr. Zafiridis's name, and his friend is very anxious to see him. Would you ask Mr. Zafiridis if he will join us for dinner, after the boat docks?"

"I'll pass the message on," said the constable.

The fat man made his way on foot to the remote limits of the upper village. The district lay in silence broken only by the small sounds of archaic domesticity heard behind walls and through open windows: the punch of a carpet-beater on a line-draped rug, the splashing of water from an emptied bucket, the snap of a chopping knife on a wooden board, the catching of the bristles of a yard-brush sweeping stone. Weeds sprouted in the steep, cobbled alleyways, and the branches of old trees—almond, pomegranate, medlar—stretched low over the pathways.

He passed a kiosk, half-heartedly open on a Sunday, where a woman sat popping long, green pods of broad beans, flicking the gray, kidney-shaped seeds into a bowl. She gave him directions, but the directions were complex, and, forgetting them, he asked a young boy to show him the way. The boy led him further through the maze, until they reached a cast-iron gate set in a wall.

"Here," said the boy. "This is where she lives."

The fat man tipped him, and watched him disappear, exuberant, down the lanes where the echoes of his running feet grew faint. Lifting the latch, the fat man pushed at the bars of the rusting gate, and stepped into a garden overgrown with flourishing thistles and feathered grasses, brightened by the heads of wild, scarlet poppies. A stone-flagged path led to a house almost a ruin: from eaves to door-lintel, a deep crack ran across the façade, and tendrils of ivy intruded beneath the loose-hanging shutters at the upper windows.

The door was many years unpainted, and the little paint remaining had disintegrated into brittle flakes; between door-frame and wall, the dry corpse of a crane fly fluttered in a broken web, and the delicately molded brass knocker—an elegant and petite gloved hand—was marred by the patina of verdigris. The fat man raised the knocker, and let it fall, then rapped three times with his knuckles.

She was slow, it seemed, in everything—in the slippered shuffling to the door, in the drawing of the stubborn bolts, in the hunting for the key which wasn't in the lock. As she hunted for the key, she called out that she was coming, and then began a murmured monologue, as the slippered feet tracked back and forth behind the door. She announced she'd found the key, but she was talking to herself, and not to him; he heard the ring of metal as she dropped it on the bare tiled floor, and her complaints at her own clumsiness as she bent to pick it up.

The key rattled in the lock, and she opened the door to him. She squinted a little, and blinked, like a nocturnal creature discomfited by daylight; on the back of her head, her graying hair lay flat, as if she had been sleeping. Beneath the uneven hem of a home-sewn skirt, the lace of a white slip showed bright against the faded black serge.

"Yes?"

"Sofia?" asked the fat man. "Sofia Bakas?"

She peered at him, pulling her face into lines.

"Do I know you?" The question was of herself, and not of him; her brows drew close as she began the slow search of memory.

"No," he said, "you don't know me. My name is Hermes Diaktoros. I've come from Athens. I'd like to speak with you, if I may."

"Well, come in anyway," she said, turning from him into the house. "Come in."

He followed her into a kitchen where the smell of nesting mice was unmistakable; that, and the spores of mildew from the dark growth on the ceiling caught in his throat. He gave a little cough, and put his hand up to his sternum.

"Excuse me," he said. "I've been troubled by a chest cold, these past few days."

"Perhaps you'd like some tea, then," she said, tentatively. "Sage tea is always very good for colds."

He smiled.

"Thank you. That's very kind."

She filled a small saucepan at a single, dribbling tap and, setting the water to boil, moved slowly to a cabinet where a set of the cheapest china was displayed. The open cabinet released a breath of fustiness; black pellets of mice droppings lay amongst the tea-cups. She made his tea, not speaking, as though conversation were a skill she had forgotten, and every tiny task—the rinsing of a spoon, the wiping of the table—grew, and swelled beyond its reasonable duration, as she spun out those little occupations in the way of those with endless time, and no diversions.

She served his tea, and offered him a plain biscuit from a torn cellophane wrapper. Smiling, he took one, and bit into it; soft with damp, it had the taste of must.

She sat across from him, and watched him sip his tea.

"I expect you're wondering why I'm here," he said, though it was clear she had no curiosity at all.

"Is your tea sweet enough?" she asked. "I can put more sugar in, if you'd like."

"No, no," he said. "It's fine. Sofia, I have news for you. It's about your husband, Stamatis."

The slack expression left her, and a frown of deep anxiety took its place. Agitated, her lower lip trembled as though a crumpling into tears were very close, and to hide it she placed her hand across her chin.

"News," she said, to herself. "There's news." She moved the hand that covered her chin and, laying it protectively over her heart, asked, "What news?"

"Good news or bad news, I don't know," said the fat man. "Stamatis is dead."

She hesitated before she asked, "Are you sure? There's no mistake it's him?"

From his pocket, he took a battered, royal-blue box embossed in curling script with a goldsmith's name, and pushed it to her across the table. Cautiously, she raised the lid, and, lifting a wedding ring from the white satin lining, held it up to read the inscription on its inner surface: *Stamatis—Sofia* 1966. She spread the fingers of her right hand on the table, and laid the ring that he had brought beside the one she wore on her third finger. Her own was a narrower band, but that the two were a pair could not be doubted.

She closed her eyes, and allowed a smile to spread across her face.

"Thank God," she said. "At last, thanks be to God."

He said, softly, "You're a free woman, Sofia."

And she covered her face, and began to weep.

The fat man crouched beside her chair, and, disregarding the great impropriety he was committing in touching her, put an arm around her stooping shoulders. As she cried, he held her close, until he sensed the worst was past, and pressed his silk handkerchief into her hand.

He returned to his seat while she wiped her nose, and brushed the wetness from her eyes.

"God bless you, sir," she said. "God bless you as the bearer of such welcome news." The pinkness of embarrassment spread across her cheeks. "What a dreadful thing to say," she whispered. "What must you think of me? Poor Stamatis. Poor, poor Stamatis."

But the fat man shook his head.

"No pretense is necessary here, Sofia. I can only guess how wretched your life has been, and how you've suffered."

"Twenty-eight years," she said, "is a long time to wait for something not to happen. To wait for someone not to come back."

"Yes, Sofia. It is."

She took his handkerchief by the corner, and began to fold it into smaller squares.

"Never a day went by I didn't worry he'd be back. That he'd come and make a bigger fool of me than he did when he left. One week we had together. One week with him, and I paid for it with my whole life. No children, no grandchildren, no money. Never a pretty dress, or an evening's dancing. A widow's life; an old woman's life. Seventeen, I was. God strike me dead, but I hated that man. Yet I protected him. Don't ask me why, because I couldn't answer you. He was to blame, not me. He wasn't a ladies' man. He didn't like women, and I repulsed him. They told me I wasn't pretty enough, that I hadn't pleased him. They told me that, and I believed them, because I was a village girl who knew no better. I was an innocent. But we see more, now, don't we? On the television, they show us everything. I saw the news one evening at Maria's, about some scandal, some politician and his boyfriends. And my brother-in-law called him a *poustis*. I asked him, 'What's a *poustis?*' and he said—he laughed at me, because I didn't know—he said, "A man who doesn't like women, a man who only gets it up for other men.' And it was like a revelation, like a light going on in my head. I said, 'That's what Stamatis was.' And they looked at me. They all looked at me, as if they were embarrassed. I said, 'Mother married me to a *poustis*.' And they said, 'Sofia, sshh. If Stamatis's family hear you say that, they'll take us to court.' And Maria said, 'Don't blame your shortcomings on other people.'"

There was silence. The handkerchief was folded small. She laid it at the center of the table.

He said, "I have something else for you."

From his top pocket, he handed her a business card.

She glanced at the card; it gave a name, and an address in Athens.

"You're a lawyer."

"Not I," he said. "I am merely the messenger. The card belongs to Stamatis's lawyer. Legally, you were still Stamatis's wife, and so his next of kin. By law, you should inherit all his estate."

"His estate? Is it much?"

"I can't say, Sofia. There may be nothing."

"No. I don't suppose there's much."

"There may be a fortune. You know, Sofia, your life isn't over yet."

"You're wrong," she said. "My life was over the day he walked out on me. I have lived the life of an old woman, and so I have become one."

He leaned towards her, and laid his hand over hers.

"Listen to me, Sofia. You have lost many years, I agree, but your life need not be over. By no means. Life is full of chances, twists of Fate. It's not time for you to lie down and die. Now, take that card and phone that number, find out what's due to you. That's my advice. I have a feeling that your luck's already changed. And remember this isn't the only place in the world. Your feet are not chained to this island—to this rock. There are cities, and other islands; there are other countries, if you were brave..."

"But I'm not brave," she said, sadly. "I've never been away from here. And I have no one to go travelling with."

"Now there," he said, "you might be wrong. Just bide your time, and you might find a travelling companion comes along. Just wait a while, that's all." He stood and held out his hand; when she gave him, demurely, her fingertips, he raised them to his lips, and kissed them.

"Thank you for taking the trouble to find me," she said. "And don't forget your handkerchief."

"Please, keep it," he said. "And it's been no trouble, but a pleasure."

Together they crossed the yard. At the gate, he turned to her.

"Look to the future, Sofia," he said. "Your future might be bright, if you choose to make it so."

From amongst the weeds, he plucked a scarlet poppy, and held it out to her.

"I'll do my very best," she smiled. "You can rely on it."

As evening fell, the day's warmth dissipated. The fat man was very early at the harborside taverna—the tables were still unlaid, and last night's garbage stood in reeking bags beside the crates of wine and water.

The waiter looked up from his newspaper. The fat man asked for a table for three, on the terrace.

"In this weather?" asked the waiter. "You'll be better off inside. We've got the fire lit."

But the fat man insisted.

"Set it up," he said, "where I can see the ferry dock. I'm expecting an acquaintance, and I don't want to miss him."

The waiter dragged a table to the terrace, and fastened down the tablecloth against the wind. He set places for three, and brought three chairs. The fat man chose the seat with the best view, and, taking a novel from his hold-all, opened it at random, and laid it in front of him. Out on the dark water, the waves broke up the reflected harbor lights; the waiter lit the red glass candle-lamp, and its ruby light made demon shadows dance around the fat man. Beneath his table, a scrawny black cat rubbed at his foot and yowled for food. The rising wind riffled the pages of his book, turning them like a reader demented.

Along the quay, the passengers for the ferry were gathering. A truck laden with empty wooden crates squeezed by, blowing hot, oily exhaust fumes across the table; a taxi carrying three robed priests blasted its horn at a scavenging dog. The fat man watched each new arrival; they came out of the shadows to pass before him, and merged with those already watching the dark horizon, where black sea met night sky and nothing could be seen. A grandmother chivvied a grizzling toddler. Three shaven-headed recruits climbed laughing from an army jeep, and slapped the driver on the back before he drove away.

By the lamplit table, two men—one squat, one elderly and breathless—paused.

"Just stop a minute," said the old man. "You walk too fast for me."

"I'll take you home," the squat man said. "I'll take a boat tomorrow."

The old man laid a hand on his son's shoulder.

"It's for the best, Manolis," he said. "A little time away, and a fresh start."

The squat man shook his head, and stared down at his feet.

"I never thought she was that kind of woman," he said. "I did my best to make her happy. She was a good wife to me, until he came along. But how could she say no, to him?" He clenched a fist; his face grew hard, and angry. "I should have killed the bastard, when I had the chance."

"If you'd laid one finger on him, you'd be staring at a prison wall right now," his father said. "Just do as I tell you, son—a time away, until the dust has settled. Before you know it, it'll all be forgotten, and you'll be back home with your mother and me."

"I'll miss you all."

The old man grasped him by the arm, and pulled him on.

"There's plenty more fish in the sea," he said, as they moved away. "Work hard, make yourself a bit of money. You'll soon be back."

The fat man watched them go; the squat man went reluctantly, as if towards a fate he didn't want. Beneath the fat man's chair the black cat yowled, as from the darkness, a solitary figure emerged. Keeping close to the walls, away from the weak light of the street-lamps, a man moved silently around the harborside, towards the dock.

The fat man held still the pages of his book, and

lowered his head as if absorbed in reading. The man in the shadows caught sight of him, and hesitated; then, face averted, he stepped into the red light cast by the candle-lamp. Discreetly, head down, the fat man watched him take another few quick paces; when the figure was almost past, and close to being absorbed by the assembly, the fat man called out to him.

"Chief of Police! Chief Zafiridis!"

The Chief of Police stopped; after a moment, he slowly turned to face the fat man.

The fat man called again.

"Good evening, Chief of Police! A word, a word if you please!"

The Chief of Police retraced his steps, back into the ruby light which lit the fat man's table. His hair was slick, and gelled in place; on his face there was a smile, which showed his teeth but did not reach his eyes.

"The great detective," he said, with sarcasm. "You're dining very early."

"Not dining yet," said the fat man, cheerfully. "I trust you got my message. There's a place here laid for you. Please, sit."

"I did receive your message. But I'm afraid I'm pressed for time, this evening. Another time."

"Come, come," said the fat man. "Your friend is very keen to see you. He tells me that he's had no news of you for quite some time. Since you took up this posting, in fact."

From far away, the siren of the inbound ferry boomed. The Chief of Police glanced towards the horizon.

"One gets caught up in work," he said, "and social lives suffer, as I'm sure you know. But for an old friend..."

"Sit down, then," said the fat man, pulling the chair beside him from beneath the table. "When the boat docks, we'll go and meet him together."

"I'll join you in a while," said the Chief of Police, "as soon as I can. I've some matters to take care of at the station."

The fat man held out his hand.

"Leave your bag, then. I'll take care of it while you're gone."

The Chief of Police looked down at the flight bag in his hand, as if surprised to see it there.

"Uniform," he said. "A change of shirts, to hang in the closet. I'll see you shortly."

He took a step towards the dock.

"Chief of Police," called the fat man, "you forgot to ask your friend's name!"

But the Chief of Police walked on, as if he hadn't heard; slipping into the crowd, he disappeared from view.

Out in the bay, the three-tiered deck lights of the ferry were growing bright as the vast vessel drew near. Again, the siren blasted its deep, sad note.

The fat man closed his book, and tucked his holdall underneath his chair. Motioning to the waiter that he would be back, he followed the path the Chief of Police had taken.

As the massive, white hull approached the quayside, the crowd moved closer to the water's edge. There were shouts, and shouted responses; crewmen on the lower deck threw down the lines, and the first links of the anchor chains rattled through the winch.

The fat man left the heart of the crowd, and made his way up the stone steps of the police station. Halfway, he stopped, and leaned his back against the wall, concealed by shadows; from there, he watched as the ramp was lowered, and the arriving passengers disembarked. He watched the departing passengers go aboard, and make their way up iron stairs to the saloon; he watched the boisterous young soldiers who had passed him, the three solemn priests, the grandmother hugging the now-silent toddler, the squat man, unwilling and bewildered. He watched the incoming freight unloaded, and the outgoing freight stacked in its place; he watched the waiting vehicles replace the trucks being driven off. He watched, until the boat was ready for departure.

A whistle blew; on the car deck, an alarm bell rang.

And from behind the clock tower, a figure moved speedily towards the ramp—the figure of a man who carried a flight bag and whose slicked hair shone under the deck lights. As the ramp lifted from the quayside, the figure jumped aboard and slipped away inside the ship.

The fat man watched him go, and smiled.

At the taverna, the waiter and the cook were both inside, warming their backsides at the fire.

"I'm afraid I shall be dining alone," announced the fat man. "My companions are unable to join me, after all. And I find you were quite right about the weather. I think I'd much prefer to eat in here, out of the cold."

✥

From the railings of the upper deck, the Chief of Police watched the island's lights retreat, and in the distance shrink to tiny points. The night at sea was bitter cold; the railings were wet with spray, the deck was slippery with seawater. Overhead, a tattered national flag flapped in the rising wind, and as it dipped and rolled, the ship strained, and groaned.

He found himself a narrow, dead end of the deck, close to the prow, where he could be alone and avoid anyone who might know him. On the deck below, the saloon TV blared music, and men's voices shouted in an argument over poker; but here, there was only the fiercely gusting wind, and the hiss of spray, and the eerie creaking of the ship's fabric as it labored through the rising sea.

On the iron stairs, footsteps rang, slow and heavy. The Chief of Police glanced in that direction, where a man appeared, short and squat, gripping the slick, iron stair-rail to keep his footing as the ship rolled. At the stair head, the man hesitated. Discouraged by the high wind and the cold, he turned to retreat to the saloon, but as he turned, the boat's starboard side lifted, tipping the deck to port. As if taking a shove in the back, the squat man, off balance, made three uneven paces to the deck rail, and held himself steady there, a little way from where the Chief of Police was standing.

Unseen, unnoticed, the Chief of Police turned away his face, and fixed his eyes on the constellations he had learned to name in childhood: Orion's Belt, the Great Bear, the Pleiades.

Along the deck, the squat man pulled a flat pint-bottle from his pocket, and took a long drink of spirit. Settling his forearms on the wet railing, sighing, he too raised his eyes to the stars.

At the Chief of Police's feet, a rope ladder was knotted to the railing uprights. Forgotten by some deckhand, its paint-spattered, wooden rungs swung out and back above the rough, black water, ringing hollow and arrhythmic as they struck the body of the ship. The Chief of Police looked beyond the prow for signs of land—for winking lights, for the soft, electric glow which hangs over towns, and villages—but there was nothing. He shivered, and, cupping his hands, blew into them to warm them, then pushed them deep into the pockets of his jacket. His hand fell on his keys, and he took them out to move them to his breast pocket, where he could zip them safely in.

His fingers were chilled, red and stiff. The keys slipped through them, and clattered to the deck.

The squat man turned.

"Kali spera," he said.

The Chief of Police did not reply, but bent to pick up the keys. He heard approaching footsteps ring out along the deck; as he raised his head, the man was there beside him.

In obvious search of company, the squat man smiled, and held out to him the uncapped bottle of spirits.

"Drink?" he said.

The Chief of Police regarded him: flabby at the belly,

flaccid in the jowls. He had a boxer's nose, crooked at the tip, and sad, booze-reddened eyes, whose lids were lined, and drowsy.

The Chief of Police knew him instantly; he remembered him very well. Mandrakis, Manolis Mandrakis. There had been some unpleasantness in a butcher's shop: the woman crying behind a freezer door with her underwear betraying her on the floor; himself helpless and ridiculous with his trousers round his knees. There had been a rack of knives to hand, and a chopper to split bones; only rank and his uniform had stopped Mandrakis cutting him. Mandrakis's rage had frightened him; he knew he had been lucky to walk away unscathed. The woman, though not pretty, had been in awe of him, and did as she was asked. Just for the moment, her name escaped him.

Mandrakis looked at him; the smile left his face, and the drowsy lids lifted over eyes suddenly focused, and alert.

"You," he said. He looked behind him, and behind the Chief of Police; seeing they were alone, the smile spread back across his lips.

"Well, I'll be damned," he said. "I'll be damned all the way to hell and back."

"How are you, Manolis?" asked the Chief of Police, quietly.

"How am I?" asked Mandrakis, incredulously. He took a step towards Zafiridis, and shook a finger at his chest without quite touching him. "I'll tell you how the fuck I am, you prick. You've ruined my fucking life, that's how I am! I'm leaving home because I can't stand it any longer, the ribbing and the snide remarks. Home! It's no home to speak of, now I've got no wife. And we both know why I've got no wife, don't we?" He jabbed again at the Chief of Police's chest; this time, the fingertip made contact, poking the hard bone of his sternum. The Chief of Police stepped backwards, out of range.

"I've got no wife," ranted Mandrakis, "because some prick thought she'd be a good lay! Some prick who thought she was his for the taking. The same prick who thought he'd get away with it, because of who he is. Because he wears a uniform."

He leaned towards Zafiridis, and tugged at his lapel, exposing the buttons of a plain, civilian shirt and the slender, gold chain of a small crucifix. His smile broadened into a grin.

"Where's your uniform tonight, officer?"

He drank deeply from his bottle, and looked into the Chief of Police's eyes.

"I hope she was worth it, you piece of shit," he said. "You fucking piece of shit."

Mandrakis upended the bottle in his hand; spirit splattered on his shoes and on the deck, filling the air with its sweet and potent scent, warm and golden-brown. He grasped the bottle by its short neck, and cracked it sharply on the deck rail. As the bottle smashed, half stayed whole in his hand, jagged-edged and ready.

Zafiridis held up his hands.

"Come on, Manolis," he said. "We can talk about this."

Mandrakis took up a fighter's stance, the half-bottle held out before his face. A trail of mucus ran from his nose. Agitated, he wiped it away with the back of his hand.

"Go ahead, officer," he said. "Talk."

"It wasn't how you think," began Zafiridis. "She..."

Mandrakis lunged, and hit him in the face. The pain was like a punch, and, dazed, Zafiridis thought he had been struck only with a fist; but in one eye, the sight was gone, and warm, wet liquid was trickling down his face. He touched his fingers to the injured eye; his touch, though gentle, added stinging to the pain, and lowering his hand, he saw dark liquid spread across his fingertips. The warm, wet blood ran down his neck, inside his shirt and to his chest, and from his chin, it fell in slow drops to the deck.

"So was she worth it, policeman?" yelled Mandrakis. "There's more coming to you! Here!"

He lunged again, and caught Zafiridis in the shoulder, causing him to stagger. Lowering his head, he crossed his forearms over his skull to shield himself.

Mandrakis laughed.

"You yellow-bellied prick," he shouted. "Fight! Come on, hit me!" He pointed to his jaw, inviting the blow. "Wherever you like! Come on, you bastard—take me on!"

At the Chief of Police's feet, the paint-spattered rope ladder swung out, and back, ringing hollow as it struck the hull. To the deck below—to the saloon bar, to help, and safety—was a dozen rungs, no more.

He ducked between the railings, and, clinging tight, grappled himself onto the ladder's topmost rungs. The sole of his right shoe slid sideways on the spray-drenched wood, then wedged itself against the wet side-rope. With the tip of his left shoe, he felt out the next plank; moving too fast, and recklessly, hands gripped hard on the rungs, he made his way towards the lower deck.

The ladder was unstable, and twisted with his weight; a wave rose up the hull, and spattered him with fine, cold spray. Mandrakis, looking down on him, was shouting threats; close below, the lights of the saloon bar were bright, and above the rushing of the sea and the steady beat of engines, men were laughing.

On the starboard side, the boat lifted.

The ladder, like a pendulum, swung out; given momentum by his weight, it swung Zafiridis two full arm lengths from the hull.

As the boat fell back, the ladder slammed into the side; between ladder-rung and hull, his knuckle joints were crushed. In agony, he cried out, watching his broken fingers slipping from the rung.

For a moment he was flying; the water, when he hit it, was a shocking, icy cold. As he went down, a rushing filled his ears, but as he came back to the surface, the rushing was replaced by a mighty pounding as the blades of the propeller churned thundering towards him.

Mandrakis watched him fall. Close by, at the stair head, a lifebelt with its coil of rope was hanging. He looked down at the water, and considered. The boat was moving fast; already, the Chief of Police was far behind.

He lifted the lifebelt from its hook, and held it for a moment. The night was dark; between boat and the man overboard, the distance grew.

Mandrakis replaced the lifebelt on its hook, and made his way below to the saloon.

Twenty-one

On Monday morning, the fat man took the earliest bus to St. Savas's Bay. The wind which had blown up in the night had dropped, but the sea was still high, and the waves gathered up white foam as they rolled onto the beach.

The fat man followed the path to Nikos's house, combing the pebbled sand for shells as he went. At Nikos's, the terrace was deserted. The chairs were folded, and stacked against the wall; by the closed door, the thin, ginger cat yowled to be let in.

The fat man knocked at the door, and waited. The cat wound in and out of his ankles, and, purring, rubbed its face on his shins. The fat man knocked again, and waited until he was sure there would be no answer; tentatively he turned the handle, and quietly opened the door.

"Nikos!"

His voice echoed back to him, as though from empty rooms, but as silence settled, he caught a rustling, and the sound of stealthy movement, in the room beyond.

He stepped inside.

"Nikos! It's me, Diaktoros!"

The cat ran past him, to a saucer crusted with dried meat scraps, and an empty bowl ringed with sour milk. The fat man sniffed; there was a smell about the place, the beginnings of a stench, like a latrine.

"Nikos!"

"Here."

The fat man pushed open the bedroom door. On the bed, Nikos lay, propped up on pillows without cases, covered with rough blankets. He wore his outdoor jacket, and his sheepskin cap, but hugged himself to slow the shivering which made his dry lips tremble. Beside the bed, a bucket was filled almost to the rim with dark-stained urine; on the nightstand, the water carafe was empty.

The fat man sat down gently on the bed.

"How goes it with you, friend?" he asked.

Nikos forced a smile, but it stayed only a moment, before it changed into a grimace.

"Not good," he said, "as you can see. You have me at a disadvantage."

"On the contrary," said the fat man. "I'm ashamed of myself. I should have come earlier; I knew it, and I didn't come soon enough. Are you in pain?"

"The pain's a bastard," said Nikos, trying to laugh, "but not as bad as what comes after."

The fat man was silent for a moment.

"Do you think you need the doctor?" he asked. "I will fetch him, if you want me to."

Nikos lowered his head, and hid his eyes beneath the peak of his cap.

"There's no need for doctors, now," he said. "I'm

pissing blood, and the swelling's growing bigger by the day. Just to be warm—that's all I want, is to be warm."

"Then it's time for you to come with me," said the fat man.

"Where are we going?" asked Nikos. "Fishing? I'd like to catch another fish, before..."

"Not fishing, no," said the fat man. "I'll take you to your sister's. It's where you need to be."

"She'll not want me," he said, derisively. "Who'd want anyone, in this state? She'll not want me."

Through the bedclothes, the fat man patted the old man's legs.

"Trust me," he said. "She'll take you in with open arms. There'll be clean sheets, a warm house, and something for the pain."

"And how do you plan to get me there?" he asked. "Since I can't even get myself to the privy to take a leak?"

"Transport is not a problem," said the fat man. "You'll go with me, in style. Give me your sister's number, and I'll tell her to expect us."

Nikos lay back on his pillows with a sigh.

"She'll not want me," he said. "It's too much of a burden. Come back tomorrow, and tell them to bring a box to carry me out."

"Nikos," said the fat man, gently. "Listen to me. There's no need for you to go through this alone. Whatever differences you've had, your sister loves you. She's lost Irini. Don't let her lose you too, without a chance to make things right."

The old man pushed the cap up off his eyes.

"It's always been my greatest fear," he said, "dying alone. And now it's here, I find it's not the being alone, but the dying itself that's hard. I keep thinking, just one more fish; just one more drink. One more of everything, so it'll take another lifetime."

"There's still time," said the fat man, "for one more of many things. The drink and the fish are possible. The care of someone who loves you is possible, too. You choose: die alone, in your own piss, or come with me."

"You're leaving us, then," said Nikos.

"I have another assignment I must begin soon," said the fat man. "And a few more hours will see things tidy here. So if you'll be patient for a little while—not long—I'll send the boys to make you ready for the journey."

At the jetty, a sleek, ocean-going cruiser was tying up. Along her slender, white hull, narrow bands of gold and navy blue picked out her subtle curves, and on her prow, her name—*Aphrodite*—was painted in plain gold. Two crewmen in white uniforms were securing her with ropes, fore and aft. They worked together, like a well-practiced team, with one—short, dark and balding, with the lascivious mouth and eyebrows of a satyr—giving quiet orders to the second—a stately, blue-eyed youth, with an air of unspoiled innocence.

"Enrico, Ilias, *kali mera sas!*" Familiarly, the fat man slapped the crewmen on the backs. "You're late, though. I'd given you up for lost."

Short, dark Enrico pulled the rope he held tight, and tied it off.

"We made poor time this morning," he said. "We were running into wind, most of the way. Ilias, make some coffee, son."

Along the road, the church clock chimed the first stroke of ten.

"No time for coffee now," said the fat man. "Our man should be here, any moment."

For a while, they waited. The fat man wandered to the jetty's end, and, peering down into the deep, clear water, watched the minute, glittering fry trawl the water's under-surface for edibles.

The hands of the church clock moved on, and the bay remained quiet. The fat man lit a cigarette, and frowned. Ilias took out a short, steel file and hooked a little engine oil from behind a white-tipped fingernail.

Around the bend, a vehicle was approaching—a red truck. It drove fast to the jetty, and pulled up sharply, sliding on the surface sand and gravel.

Theo jumped out, and slammed the door. His face was tight with anger.

"You!" He was pointing at the fat man.

"You're late, Theo," said the fat man, calmly. "I don't like to be kept waiting. As these gentlemen will tell you."

"You go to hell!" said Theo. "I'm only here at all to tell you to lay off!"

He faced up to the fat man, jabbing a finger towards his chest. The fat man took a small step away from him, and, with an expression of distaste, brushed at his shirt-front, as if peppered by spittle.

But Theo ranted on.

"I've told you before, just stay away from my family! What do you mean by leaving little notes at my house? How am I supposed to explain that to my wife? Just get out of my life, and stay out!"

As if his own outburst had surprised him, Theo stood for a moment, breathing hard.

"Walk with me, Theo," said the fat man.

He laughed. "Walk with you! You go to hell!"

Theo turned to his truck. Enrico leaned, nonchalant, against the door; Ilias, arms folded, rested his buttocks on the fender.

Theo marched back to the fat man.

"What's this, the heavy mob? Mafia? What? Call off your dogs, fatso. Get them out of my way."

"Theo, walk with me." There was an edge to the fat man's voice—annoyance, a little impatience. "You can talk to me now, or I shall come and talk to your wife. It's entirely up to you."

Theo hesitated only briefly.

"All right, fatso. I'll walk with you. But I won't talk."

"A coward to the last," said the fat man. "The merest threat of a domestic squall, and the big man caves in. Come. I know a place we won't be disturbed, or overheard."

He took him by the elbow, and steered him towards the beach path, but Theo snatched his arm away.

"Don't touch me," he said.

"As you wish."

The fat man led the way, along the sea-front path towards the boatyard. Theo walked slowly, growing the distance between him and the fat man, but the crewmen were following behind, and the further he slipped back from the fat man, the closer the crewmen came to him.

Theo called out to the fat man.

"What do the Mafia want?"

"They are my little helpers, in case you prove difficult. But I don't think you will."

Passing the upturned hulls of the winter-beached boats, they reached the boatyard workshop. The workshop doors were closed, and the boat-builders' houses seemed deserted. In the yard, six skinny chickens pecked for scraps; a brazier stood before the workshop doors, alight with pine-wood offcuts, burning low.

The fat man lifted the latch, and opened the workshop doors.

"In here," he said.

"What for?" asked Theo.

"We won't be disturbed here. You do want privacy, don't you, Theo?"

Inside, the workshop was dark, lit only by a window hung with sacking; it smelled of fresh-planed wood, and tar.

"I suggest you sit," said the fat man. "You'll be more comfortable."

There was one chair only, an old-fashioned carver whose leather-upholstered seat was cracked, and split.

"Now," said the fat man, "tell me about you and Irini."

Theo stood up from the chair.

"I've told you until I'm sick of telling you, and I'm not telling you again: I didn't know the woman."

From the roof, a perching rooster crowed. The fat man's eyebrows lifted into Mephistophelean arches, and he smiled.

"A little cosmic symmetry, would you say, Theo?" he asked. "A cock-crow for your third denial."

The crewmen, entering, pulled the doors to and slipped the inside bolts. Enrico stood a storm lantern on the workbench; its weak, yellow light cast deeper shadows on the fat man's face. Ilias held a parcel wrapped in newsprint, and a coil of nylon rope.

"Sit down, Theo," said the fat man. Theo hesitated. Enrico stepped up to him.

"Please sit down, sir," said Enrico, "or I shall be forced to make you."

Theo spat into the sawdust, and sat.

"Tie him down," said the fat man.

From behind, Enrico pinned Theo in the chair, while Ilias efficiently wrapped Theo's forearms with the rope, binding them to the chair arms.

"You bastards!" shouted Theo, wildly. "What the fuck are you doing? Untie me, you pricks, or I'll call the fucking police!"

He kicked out at them, but they were out of range.

"Theo, Theo," said the fat man, soothingly. He laid a hand on Theo's head, and slowly stroked his hair. "Sshh, Theo, sshh. There's no need to call the police. At this moment in time, I *am* the police."

Madly, Theo shook his head to shake off the caress, but

the fat man stroked, and stroked, until Theo became still. And when he was still, the fat man pulled a red silk handkerchief from his pocket, and pushed it into his mouth.

The fat man and the crewmen stood silently together, watching Theo.

Theo was very still.

"Red, Theo," said the fat man, at last. "The color of passion. The color of beating hearts. The color of blood."

At the bench, Ilias began to unwrap the newsprint from his parcel.

"You and I have a bone to pick, friend. Because you have not been telling the truth, have you?" Theo rattled the legs of the chair, and tried to get to his feet; Enrico moved behind him and, pressing on his shoulders, held him down.

"You know," went on the fat man, "if you had said to me, 'I loved Irini, *fatso,* with all my heart and soul. She was my joy, and my world, and everything in life to me'—if you had said that to me, you wouldn't be here now. But you didn't say that, did you? You said you didn't know her. I wonder how poor Irini would have felt about that?"

From behind the handkerchief, Theo tried to shout, but the gag held in his words.

"How do you think she died, Theo? Shall *I* tell *you?* You think you know. You think she killed herself, don't you? You think she killed herself, out of love for you."

Theo shook his head, violently, and his eyes spread wide.

"I'm still not getting through to you, am I, Theo?" The fat man drew out a cigarette, and leaned against the bench to light it. As he exhaled smoke, he said, "I have not the slightest interest in your pathetic attempts to preserve your status quo. It is time now for the truth. Truth, Theo. Not a concept which has figured largely in your world. Until now. Let me tell you how it is. I know she haunts your sleep; I can see your dreams. I know how you hold her in your arms, and how you cry when you wake, and find that it's not real. I know you see her around every street corner, just disappearing from view. I know you look in every woman's face, looking for her, her mouth, her eyes. Her smile, Theo. The one you threw away. And I think you would give your right hand to have one hour with her, wouldn't you? If I could show her to you, manifest her, what would you give me? What would be a fair price? One finger? Your right hand, perhaps..." The fat man ran his fingertips tickling over the back of Theo's bound hand; the red handkerchief muted Theo's protesting shout, and he strained at the binding rope, raising blue veins amongst the stretching bones.

The fat man laughed, and patted Theo's hand.

"No, no. You misunderstand me. Nothing so violent. Not *quite* so violent."

He leaned in close to Theo's ear, and his face took on a look of anger.

"Because it's too late now, isn't it?" he hissed. "What's done is done. I can't bring her back, any more than you can find her. No regrets though, eh? No regrets? Theo?"

To hide the bright tears in his eyes, Theo stared down at his knees, but the fat man put his fist beneath his chin, and roughly raised his head.

"Tears, Theo? Dear me! Who are they for, son—her, or you?"

He let his head drop, and beckoned to the crewmen.

"Shave him."

Ilias peeled back the pages of newsprint, and laid out the contents of his parcel. Scissors. A can of shaving cream. A cutthroat razor.

"I understand your difficulty," went on the fat man. "You have the heart of a great lover, but the soul of a coward. The two together create dilemmas. You're a closet Romeo, Theo, a lover who dares nothing. So I'm going to take pity on you; look at it like that. I'm going to solve your dilemma for you. I'm going to shove you out of the closet. Now, keep very still."

Ilias took the scissors and cut at Theo's hair. He cut close to the scalp, letting the soft, black curls fall amongst the sawdust and the wood-shavings, cutting until there was only stubble, rough and tufted.

On Theo's knee, a tear fell. The fat man dropped the butt of his cigarette, and ground it out beneath his tennis shoe.

"I am doubly ashamed of you," he said, leaning back against the workbench. "You cry for your hair, but where are your tears for Irini?"

Ilias uncapped the shaving cream and, filling his palm with white foam, began to spread it over Theo's scalp.

"If you had shown *one moment* of decency," said the fat man, "if you had gone to Irini, told her you loved her, admitted you were too cowardly to face the fray and be with her, well, you wouldn't be here now."

Ilias opened the razor, and drew the blade across his fingertip. The blade's thin track appeared in blood. He cut the first smooth swathe across Theo's scalp.

"Or, if you had gone to her husband, and told him you loved his wife, that you wanted to take her away, if you had taken the beating he would likely have given you like a man, you wouldn't be here now."

Ilias scraped the foam and stubble from the razor's blade onto the workbench edge. Where he had cut, Theo's scalp showed gray. Ilias cut again.

"If you had stood up to your father's bullying, said you were sticking by the woman you loved, you wouldn't be here now. If you had run away with her secretly and started a new life elsewhere. If you had stood by her, spoken up for her when your friends were calling her a whore. If you had risked everything and gone to make love to her, just once. If you had confessed all to your wife, and tried to build a better marriage. If you had done *any one* of these things, if you had behaved in only *one small detail* as a man of integrity instead of a man looking out for himself—and only himself—you would not be here now.

"You told yourself you were a Man of Honor, deserting your lover so precipitately, without a word. You have a wife and child. But your 'honorable' behavior was only cowardice. Your overriding concern was sparing yourself embarrassment, and trouble at home. There was no honor there. It was pure self-interest. Admit it, Theo."

Theo closed his eyes, and slowly nodded.

"Good."

The shaving was complete. Cautiously, the fat man

pulled the handkerchief from Theo's mouth. The red silk had become purple, dyed with saliva, and tears.

"And you underestimated, didn't you, the power of passion? Passion is a great gift, a gift not given to everyone. For you, it was too much. You were not man enough for its demands. Now it is time for you to redeem yourself, to stand up and face the music. You've acted the part you chose well, very well. But good acting was not what was required. Good acting is the refuge of those who wish to deceive, not only others but themselves. Especially themselves. What was required from you, Theo, was honesty. Perhaps a little kindness."

Theo was silent. Then he said, "Perhaps if I had been kinder, at the end, she wouldn't have killed herself. That was my fault. I killed her."

"No, Theo. You flatter yourself, I fear. She did not kill herself. Not for you, or for any other reason."

"It was an accident, then?"

The fat man considered.

"Let's say that. Yes."

"So it wasn't my fault?"

"Be careful. You cannot absolve yourself of responsibility simply because she did not die by her own hand. If it weren't for you, she would be alive now."

He signaled to the crewmen, who slid back the bolt on the door, and slipped out.

"It's time for you to do your penance. The time for hiding, and acting, and lying, is past. I want you to take your punishment like the Man of Honor you have told yourself you are. Irini suffered the loss of her good name and reputation for you, and bore it. Today starts a new chapter in *your* life. Everything you have feared losing, what you held most precious—your reputation, your good name, your quiet life, maybe even your family—you are about to lose. Because you valued them too highly, I am going to take them from you. All things in life are transient. The trick is, to value what is most important. There are diamonds beyond price, and baubles which are worthless. Both shine, and sparkle. In the past, you have been fooled. There may be no other chances for you now, but if there are, in future, choose more wisely. Now, be brave."

Enrico, in a pair of leather gauntlets, carried in an aluminum bucket half-full of hot, black pitch; it filled the workshop with its clean, antiseptic fumes. Ilias brought in a paintbrush, and a bag he concealed behind his back.

They moved behind Theo, and began to paint his naked head with the hot tar. Wherever it touched, it burned—his scalp, his neck where it dribbled in hardening rivulets—and the fumes stung his eyes, and made them feel as if they were bleeding.

They painted until his head was glossy black. Then Ilias handed his bag to the fat man, and the fat man, holding it high, tipped over Theo a shower of chicken feathers, red-brown and white, and soft as snowflakes.

At the jetty, the fat man gave Enrico the keys to Theo's truck.

"Put him on the back," he said, "where all the good folks can see him, and take him home the longest way you can find. Don't be more than an hour. We have Nikos Velianidis to take care of, and his time is very precious. Then we'll be gone. I don't believe there's anything else here that requires my attention, just at the moment."

Anxious to deliver news of the scandal, George the bus driver pulled a chair up to the table at Jakos's *kafenion*.

Agog, Lukas listened with the rest: Thassis Four-Fingers, Stavros Pleased-to-Meet-You, the bone-fused Adonis twisting in his seat so his ears could catch every detail. Only Jakos showed no interest; he placed George's order amongst the half-filled wineglasses and the empty cups, and, stepping back inside the kitchen, turned up the volume on a cassette of sad duets.

George tasted his coffee and took a knife to a slice of sticky baklava.

"His wife'll be leaving him, of course," he concluded. "She was coming out of the baker's when they drove him by, dripping with tar and head to foot in a pillow's worth of feathers. She dropped her shopping where she stood and went hysterical. They had to fetch the doctor for a sedative."

"But who did it?" asked Lukas. "And why?"

For a moment, all were silent.

"It's that Krisaxos business all over again," said Thassis, shielding his mouth to cover a belch. "Same family. Bad blood."

"The shame of it," said Adonis. "It's perverted. Disgusting. No man should put his family through that."

They all shook their heads in agreement—all except Lukas, who stared thoughtfully at the scuffed toe of his boot.

"And there'll be no coffee to be had in St. Savas's now," complained George, "with Nikos gone, and in no state to hurry back. They've put him aboard the Athenian's boat, the fat guy's. And I'll tell you what..." He put another piece of honeyed pastry in his mouth; his words were blurred with the cloying paste of nuts. "That's some vessel he's got there, an absolute beauty. He must have got some cash to have a boat like that. Where's he get his money from?"

"I'll tell you what I think," said Thassis. He looked around sagely at his companions; his eyes were tired, and red. "He's family. Know what I mean?"

He tapped a finger to the side of his nose, and gave Stavros a wink.

"What family?" asked Stavros.

"He's no idea what family," said Adonis. "Don't listen to him."

"Where's he headed?" asked Lukas.

"I didn't ask him, and he didn't say," said George. "This coffee's not as good as Nikos's." Around the harbor, the clock chimed the first stroke of the hour. "Christ, is that the time? They'll be building a gibbet to string me up if I'm a minute late."

Lukas drained his coffee to its thick dregs.

"I'll take a ride with you," he said. "If Nikos is leaving Thiminos, I want to say goodbye before he goes."

The bus had few passengers. Lukas took the seat the fat

man had favored, at George's back. The bus drove slowly around the harbor road, climbed the mountainside and descended beyond the village. When they passed the Halfway House, Lukas signed a triple cross over his heart.

But the jetty, when they reached it, was deserted. Along the beach, the shutters at Nikos's windows were closed and barred. George parked the bus carelessly and, pulling yesterday's newspaper from beneath his seat, slumped down to read.

Lukas climbed down from the bus, and walked a few paces towards the jetty. The sea was dark, opaque with the reflection of heavy clouds; around the shore, the fishing boats were bobbing in the swell.

Ahead, magnificent *Aphrodite* was sailing from St. Savas's Bay, moving at speed towards the open sea. At the tip of her high mast, the blue-and-white flag of Greece fluttered below a flag of navy and gold that Lukas couldn't identify; on the deck, diminished by distance, stood the fat man.

Lukas ran to the jetty's end, and waved his arms towards the yacht.

"*Yassou,* my friend!" he shouted. "*Yassou,* Nikos! God speed!"

For a moment, he thought he was unheard, but then the fat man touched his forehead in flamboyant salute, and raised his hand to wave goodbye.

Approaching the headland at the bay's end, the yacht began a turn to starboard. The clouds were shifting in the blustery wind, and between their cracks a few rays of weak sunshine fell in spotlights onto *Aphrodite*'s decks. The fat man moved up to the prow, and stood, legs braced, hands at his back, like a commander of the fleet judging the sea.

As Lukas watched, the clouds moved back together, the spotlights were extinguished. *Aphrodite* slipped away around the headland, and she—and the fat man—were lost from view.

Epilogue

I remember that day. Who could ever forget it, the shame of it? But the truth was, I felt a strange relief. Through the jeering and laughing, the screaming and the crying, I felt free. I thought, I don't have to hide now. The hiding's over.

Elpida threw me out, of course. Was I sorry to go? I was sorry for myself, and I was sorry for her, for the awful embarrassment we both believed she'd never live down. When my mother saw me, she wept; my father was so angry, he took a swing at me, swore he'd never allow me back in the house. But my mother stood up to him, in a way I never have. She made him let me stay. Because she loves me.

She called the doctor, and asked him what to do; then she bathed my head with oil, and wrapped it up in bandages. Every day she tended to me, bathing and rewrapping. Gradually, the feathers worked loose, and after a week or two, most of the tar came away. My hair began to grow. I began to look the way I had before.

But I was not the same.

I fished, and thought. I spent many, many days, out there on the water, letting the sea calm me. Often, in the early mornings, when the sun's rays first strike, instead of twisting off the surface they pierce it like slender arrows; white shafts pointing the way to the depths. Sometimes, I was tempted to follow those arrows and dive into that lovely blueness. The idea held no fear for me. It offered the caress of sleep rather than a choking death; it was an offer I thought I would, one day, accept.

Time passed, and my mother wanted me to see Elpida. She wanted us to talk, she said; what she wanted in her heart was the way things used to be. But I had changed too much to fit back inside that empty marriage—what could I say to Elpida that wasn't lies?—so I refused to go. Besides, there's Eleni. Eleni took to praying in the churches—night and day, fasting and not sleeping, on her knees until they bled and she stank from lack of washing. All through Lent, she prayed, and was admired for her piety. But at Easter, she still refused to stop, so they locked her in the house, and called the specialists. The doctor diagnosed dementia, a swelling of the brain, while Pappa Philippas proclaimed it a true calling, and the grace of God. Months later, there's no change; they say the house is like a cathedral, all incense and candles, and every inch of wall covered in icons. Dementia or true piety, it's all the same; my mother-in-law's made a prisoner of herself, striving for the halo of a saint. As for Elpida, she's happy enough; the burden of her crazy mother's care has granted her the status of a martyr.

And I remain alone.

You know, our language overflows with wise little placebos to comfort the distraught and the desperate—and the plain embarrassed, the mortified, like me. One hundred years from now it will all be forgotten, the old folks say. But it isn't so, not on this island; it just isn't so.

The truth is this: that we who have been infamous are destined to remain so, news forever in a land of nothing newsworthy.

On an island not far from home, Andreas's small catch sold well. In the town square, he sat down at a café table shaded by the branches of a plane tree and, pulling the money—a few notes, a great deal of silver—from his pockets, began to count.

"You'll be a rich man, soon."

She stood before him, holding a tray beneath her arm. Her short-cropped hair was streaked with gray, and when she smiled, the lines of her face grew deeper.

He looked up at her, and returned her smile.

"I'll never be rich," he said, "and if I were, it wouldn't make me happy."

"Are you unhappy, then?" she asked. The question wasn't flippant; the woman seemed to care.

"I lost my wife last year," he said. "Life's not the same, alone."

"You'll miss her, I know," she said. "It's been four years for me, and I still wait for my man to walk in through the door. What can I get you?"

Her eyes, he thought, were like Irini's.

"Coffee," he said. "And if I'm not being too forward, can I buy a drink for you? Don't think you'd have to sit with me, if folk would talk."

Her smile grew broad.

"It's not as if we're children," he said, "or me some blushing virgin."

They sat together companionably; the talk flowed easily, until it was time for him to prepare the boat, and leave.

"I'll be here again next week," he said, "if the weather holds."

"You'll always find me here," she said. "Just ask for Zoë."

Walking away towards the quay, he raised a hand goodbye.

By the café door, her aged father watched her watch him go.

"Do you believe in Providence?" she asked, clearing their table.

"You'd be a damn fool not to," he replied. "No matter what life throws at you, my girl, sometimes the gods are kind."

From the cast-iron gate, Theo surveyed the garden he remembered so differently — infested by chest-high weeds, overrun with thistles. Now the weeds lay mown and rotting by the wall, and shoots of new grass showed amongst their sharp, scythed stalks. The path to the house was swept, and marked with pots of flourishing cyclamen.

Theo stepped through the open door into a kitchen bright with sunshine, light with the perfume of cut flowers and wood polished with beeswax.

"Aunt Sofia!"

She answered him at once, and came to kiss him on

the forehead, beneath the line of his short, short hair. She had, it seemed, abandoned widow's black, and wore instead a dress of lime and yellow; her nose was dusted with powder from a compact, and on her cheeks, she'd rubbed a smudge of rouge.

"How are you, Theo?" she asked. She made him sit, and sat beside him. Reaching out to touch his face, she said, "You don't look very good to me, my love. I'll make some tea."

"I don't want tea." A fly settled on his forearm, and for a moment he let it remain there. "I've been thinking I might go away. Just for a while. A change of scene."

"What a good idea," she said. "Why not? Your feet are not chained to this island, to this rock. There are cities, and other islands. There are other countries, if you were brave..."

"It would cost money," he said. He brushed the fly from his sleeve. "It's money that I'm lacking."

A silk handkerchief, laundered and pressed, lay on the dresser shelf, and on the handkerchief lay the business card of a lawyer based in Athens.

"As a matter of fact," she said, "I've come into a small inheritance, and I've been thinking of a little trip myself. So if you thought you'd like some company—the world can be such a lonely place, sometimes—maybe you and I could go together. We could go far away from here, Theo. We could go anywhere."

She placed an arm around him and pulled him close, as she had done to heal his hurts—cuts, bruises, insults—when he was just a boy.

He let his head fall to her shoulder.

"Laugh at me," he said, "but I'm afraid to go. This place is all I know. It made me what I am, and now it's made me, it's saying it has no place for me. It's telling me to leave, but the leaving will be exile, and every day I am away, I know this wretched place will call me home."

Sofia kissed the top of his head.

"Then you and I shall miss the place together," she said, "and when we're really homesick, we'll call your mother, and she'll tell us all the gossip and the scandal. And one day, when time's moved on, maybe we'll come back here, and call it home again. But now—you're right—it's time for us to go. We'll have each other, Theo. And more than that, we'll have some kind of future."

From the port, the horn of a departing ferry blared a single, somber note.

"So go and pack your bag," said Sofia, "and say all your goodbyes. When the next boat leaves, you and I will sail with it. Trust me, *agapi mou*. We'll find somewhere we are welcome, even though we are unknown—somewhere no one knows the lives that we lived, once."

Acknowledgements

For their enthusiasm, advice and careful reading, thanks to Chris and all the team at Christopher Little, and to Arzu Tahsin, Holly Roberts and Emily Sweet.

Thanks to Julie and Ian Kidd for their highly practical support.

And special thanks to my son Will, who put up with a lot.

About the author

Born and raised in the north of England, Anne Zouroudi has spent much of her adult life in less dour climates. Following some years working in the Colorado Rockies and on Wall Street, she abandoned a lucrative career to lead a simpler life in the Greek islands. Her attachment to Greece remains strong, and the country is the inspiration for much of her writing. She now lives in Derbyshire's Peak District with her son.